Attack on Titan
Kuklo Unbound

Created by Hajime Isayama
A Novel by Ryo Suzukaze
Art by THORES Shibamoto

Translated by Ko Ransom

VERTICAL.

Art by Thores Shibamoto.

Originally published in Japanese as *Shingeki no Kyojin: Before the Fall 2* and *3*.

This is a work of fiction.

ISBN: 978-1-939130-87-7

Manufactured in the United States of America

First Edition

Vertical, Inc.
451 Park Avenue South
7th Floor
New York, NY 10016
www.vertical-inc.com

CONTENTS

PROLOGUE

A foul stench filled the air.

It was the thick scent of death that could only come from a mass of corpses numbering in the thousands.

Not a single one of the bodies seemed to be resting in peace. Some had bloodshot eyes frozen wide open, while others had grotesquely twisted faces. The expression on their faces was one of despair, as though every single one had seen hell.

"I'd imagine this isn't too far off from what damnation looks like."

Carlo Piquer's austere face turned grim as he looked out at the smoke-covered town.

Shiganshina, once a proud district of thirty thousand people and the most thriving area of the country, now looked like pure misery. Over a hundred homes had been mostly or completely destroyed, and that number was rising. A recovery team largely consisting of members of the military had been working nonstop, but they were not making the kind of progress they had hoped for. The scattered mountains of rubble made it difficult to find any kind of footing, and to make things worse, flames and smoke kept workers from where they needed to go.

The total extent of the damage was still unknown, but it seemed certain that at the very least, nearly half of the town had been affected in one way or another.

"This is just terrible..."

As hints of displeasure began to color Carlo's chiseled face, he clenched his blistered hands.

Yet the demolished buildings were ultimately of minor importance. Considering what had happened, the number of casualties, reaching only into the thousands, could be seen as the silver lining on a very dark cloud.

A little over thirty years had passed since the nation's founding. While it had faced many challenges like natural disasters, famine, and plague that imperiled its continued existence, this event was significant enough to make history. A bungled response could have even meant the destruction of the human race. Carlo should have been celebrating that the damage had been kept to merely what was before him, but he couldn't. Though a simple soldier, he was still a member of the Survey Corps. He could not help but feel responsible for the gruesome scene before his eyes.

Though things could hardly have turned out better even if I'd busted my ass...

Sighing, Carlo turned his eyes to Wall Maria, the lynchpin of the fortress city.

The giant wall, a tenacious structure called "indestructible" by some, measured over fifty meters in height. It had kept enemy intruders out for all of recorded history, and its presence was still overwhelming.

Yet look at the town now.

Wall Maria was the impregnable barrier it had always been, but even then the unruly destroyers who had delivered a scathing blow to the town had gotten past it.

Straight through its front gates, thanks to humans showing them in.

"Titans..."

That was the generic name given to the humanoid terrors that were mankind's nemesis. They varied in size, but the largest ones to ever be recorded easily surpassed ten meters in height—true monsters. The extent of the utter destruction they unleashed from their gigantic frames was evident from a single glance at Shiganshina District's calamitous state. Mankind had moved to living inside of walled cities out of fear of the Titans.

"The team leader's gonna smack you if he finds you spaced out like that."

Carlo's body stiffened a little when the male voice flew at him from behind, but smiling wryly the next moment, he turned with a relaxed motion to face the speaker.

Standing there was Solm Hume, a fellow Survey Corps soldier who'd joined the military in the same year. Despite Solm's tireless involvement in the recovery effort, there were no signs of fatigue on his face. Only eighteen, bursting with youth, his body no doubt brushed off the days and nights of toil. While he and Carlo were the same age, Solm was on the smaller side for a member of the Survey Corps, whose ranks were full of grand, muscular specimens. If not for the winged emblem sewn into his uniform jacket, few would recognize him as a corpsman.

"Is something on your mind?" Solm asked with a serious look.

Carlo shook his head. "I was just wondering what's in store for us…"

"The royal government will figure that out." Perhaps Solm actually thought otherwise, as his handsome face wore a deeply grim expression.

So he doesn't expect much from them. Indeed, it would be difficult for the royal government's officials to come up with an eye-opening solution. Reducing taxes and squeezing out a recovery budget would most likely be it. *Dealing with the situation on the ground always falls on us.*

Still, it was beyond exceptional for the Survey Corps to be sent to aid a recovery effort. Defense and peacekeeping efforts inside the walls was the Garrison's job, while the Survey Corps was created in order to explore beyond them.

"In any case, let's just worry about getting this place back to normal."

"Right…" Carlo sighed. "I guess that means we should start by clearing this rubble." He shifted his vision to the townscape, which resembled a burnt-out field.

"The bodies will have to be moved quickly..."

"To prevent disease, you mean?"

"We can't deny the possibility that the Titan brought sickness in with it as well," Solm stated dispassionately, pointing forward with his jaw. Carlo followed the gesture with his eyes to arrive at a grim object a few meters ahead—a meat dumpling, if he had to describe it as anything. Made up of the bodies of multiple individuals, it was a Titan's vomit.

"They just spit their victims out, half-digested... They can't rest in peace like this," Carlo made a face and muttered. He approached the mess the Titan had regurgitated. "If you can't keep them down, don't eat them!"

"You can't hope to understand their actions."

"Nor do I want to," Carlo spat.

So long as humanity made no efforts to know them, however, Titans would forever be man's nemesis.

What a fix.

Not only that, any orders to do so would fall on the Survey Corps' shoulders.

Yeah, bring it on...

Carlo and Solm closely examined the warped clump of vomit. It was held together by a jumble of limbs from five bodies, almost like a three-dimensional puzzle.

There was no data on what happened to humans inside of a Titan's stomach after they were devoured. There seemed no greater point to what sat before the two than a hairball spat up by a cat.

"Man... What a way to eat."

The Titan must have captured fleeing humans and swallowed them whole. Limbs were pointed in impossible directions but otherwise appeared completely intact, and the same went for clothes and belongings. There were no signs of digestion.

Since they're vomiting it all out, they can't really have a sense of taste.

Thanks to the Titan's perverse palate, however, they would be able to identify the victims.

Paying special attention to attire, the two determined that the victims included both residents and soldiers.

So they tried to protect the residents, in vain. That wasn't all Carlo noticed. A familiar woman's body was among the remains.

"This…"

The woman in loose black clothes akin to a priest's vestments was the wife of Team Leader Heath Mansell, Carlo and Solm's superior who'd died on an earlier expedition. Her name was Elena. Part of a heretical cult that worshipped Titans, she was guilty of the grave crime of enabling the invasion into Shiganshina District. If Elena and the other Titan cultists had not rioted, it would have been impossible for a Titan to enter.

"So the one responsible for this is dead. It couldn't have turned out any worse…"

Elena's fate had been sealed the moment she sought salvation from the Titans.

Looks like she's already been punished.

Now a part of the clump of meat, Elena's pose suggested a crucifixion.

They'd only gotten married the other day too…

Worse, Elena had been pregnant. He could tell from her large, full abdomen that she'd been nearing childbirth.

The less said about the fate of the child in her stomach, the better.

Such a shame. Dwelling on the misfortune of the Mansell family was unbearable, and Carlo decided to mourn them later. For the time being, he had to focus his energy on the recovery effort as a corpsman and prevent any secondary disasters.

"Let's get started collecting bodies. We can't just leave them here."

"I'll summon the collection team, then." Even as he spoke Solm charged off on the path, nimbly avoiding the scattered rubble.

It was when Carlo focused his attention back on the clump of meat that he heard it: a faint noise, as of cloth being rubbed against cloth.

"Huh?"

He didn't have to search for the source. His eyes turned toward Elena's lower abdomen, which now squirmed unnaturally.

"No way... Is she alive?!"

Elena's face, as white as wax, couldn't possibly draw breath. Yet her lower abdomen was clearly palpitating.

Bugs? But Elena's body had not rotted to the point of attracting carrion beetles. *Then, what...*

As Carlo gazed upon Elena, he noticed that her skirt was moist. Another matter caught his attention, too.

"Something smells." His nose twitched as the stench coming from Elena travelled through his nostrils. A faint fishy smell unlike the odor from before assailed him, either blood or something raw.

A chill ran unexpected down Carlo's spine, perhaps in reaction to the smell. His pulse also began to quicken. His body seemed to be getting ready for a fight, preparing for an enemy attack.

But reacting to something unseen was ridiculous. Monsters didn't really exist.

Aside from Titans.

Carlo roused himself by slapping his cheeks, then focused back on Elena's skirt.

If the Titan had left a spawn hidden inside its vomit, the town would be plunged into terror all over again. Humanity's ignorance of Titan biology meant he could rule out no scenario as too farfetched.

"Let's do this..." Carlo gulped, then reached for the short sword at his hip. He pulled it from its scabbard, held his breath, and grabbed the hem of Elena's skirt gingerly with his left hand.

Come demon, or—

Preparing for the worst, Carlo held his weapon at the ready as he carefully rolled up the skirt. The cloth was heavy, possibly from all the fluid it had absorbed. When he moved it, the raw odor that had built up inside came pouring forth.

As he brought the hem up to Elena's knees with every bit of caution that he could muster, something tumbled forward along with a copious amount of liquid. Carlo immediately took a step back, putting some distance between himself and the object.

"This…" he muttered, dumbfounded, his eyes wide open.

Shaking his head to regain his composure, he quietly returned his sword to its scabbard. He crouched and gazed at the flesh-colored creature that flailed its limbs about like a fish out of water.

It was an infant.

"So it stayed alive, inside her belly?"

A cursory look at the infant showed no signs of injury. Its luck must have been due to the Titan swallowing the mother's body whole; it wouldn't have survived any chewing. Elena's amniotic fluid must also have served as cushioning to protect the child.

A miraculous escape from the maw of death, literally. Many soldiers had managed to return from beyond the walls barely alive after being attacked by a Titan. Yet, surviving a trip into a Titan's stomach was absolutely unprecedented. *It ought to be a cause for celebration…*

Nevertheless, Carlo's flesh was crawling.

The birth of a new life was always a joyous occasion, no matter the time, place, or circumstance. Strangely though, Carlo could not detect even the smallest seed of joy in his heart. The only thing he found there was doubt, and a question: *Why only you?*

The baby let out no first cry, perhaps already knowing despair. With its tiny, toothless mouth, it was desperately trying to chew off the umbilical cord instead. It was as though the infant realized that to survive in this world, it had to stand on its own two feet, and without a second to lose.

"The child of a Titan—" When Carlo heard the words slip unbidden from his mouth, he understood.

Why fear a powerless infant? The answer was simple.

He instinctively feared a baby born of Titan vomitus.

CHAPTER ONE

The sideshow was filled with a bestial odor.

Cages of all sizes were placed around a grimy room measuring thirty square meters. What appeared to be wild animals collected from around the country were locked inside of them. The choking stench seemed to be a mixture of the beasts' body odor and the smell of their excrement. Apparently no one ever cleaned the place, and the word "unsanitary" didn't begin to describe the miserable environment.

Dario Inocencio opened his eyes and looked over at the cage in the very back of the shack.

"So this is the one…" he murmured in a hoarse voice, making his way toward the rusted, two-meter-cubed cage.

He walked with a heavy gait. While his body had grown so fat that it was difficult for him to support his own body, more than anything it was the powerful fear and hatred he felt for the *thing* lying in the cage that was affecting his pace.

So I'm afraid. Fear was something he had not felt in some time.

Dario, who lived inside Wall Sheena, the country's most interior area, was a merchant baron in both his own and others' estimation, with influence even among politicians. Only a few men in the world struck fear in his heart, and he slaughtered without fanfare any who stood against him.

And yet, here I am, fearing this child trapped inside a cage. Indeed, it was a laughable fact, but his reaction was also a reasonable one considering the child's lineage.

Lurking inside a cage so thoroughly filthy as to forbid contact was no ferocious predator but a boy of scant years. Everything about him seemed savage, from his low growl to his glittering eyes that vigilantly surveyed all around him. His arms and legs were in shackles, denying him freedom. Even an imprisoned felon's conditions would seem preferable to his.

He was unclothed, and judging by his skin, darkened by dust and filth, days must have passed since he'd last bathed. His body odor was repellent. The boy looked like nothing but skin and bones, with a total lack of body fat, yet his vitality had not flagged one bit, as evidenced by his blazing eyes.

"Don't be concerned, sir. He won't bite."

With a vulgar smirk, the head of the sideshow accosted Dario. The man's disfigured face looked like a clump of melted wax—a veritable curio that could have served as one of his own sideshow exhibits.

Dario's heart leapt, surprised by the sight. He congratulated himself for not landing on his rear.

Patting his chest and regaining his composure, he turned to face the ghastly owner. "Is that really him in there? He looks like any other boy to me."

"Whatever could you mean, sir?" the owner said jestingly, inviting Dario to stand in front of the cage. "Please, take a very good look. This is Kuklo"—he pronounced the name as in *cu*cumber—"the Titan's son."

"Titan's son…"

The moment he mouthed the words, Dario's hair stood on end.

Everyone, even children, knew how terrifying the Titans were. Roughly half a century had passed since the Titans' sudden entry into the world, and the fear they planted in humans seemed to have become a hereditary trait. Just hearing their name gave people goose flesh. There was nothing strange about Dario's body reacting in this way, as mankind had been driven to the brink of extinction by the Titans. Moreover, the myth that humanity was safe at least inside the walls had crumbled, intensifying the emotions that the monsters elicited in the hearts of men.

It's been thirteen years since that day. I suppose it isn't the kind of thing you forget easily. The shattering incident—Titan-worshipping heretics opening the main gates of Shiganshina District—had shocked Dario too. While personally untouched, the calamitous state of the town that he witnessed on an observational trip amply proved that the Titans were every bit the monsters the rumors had made them out to be.

Well, it did earn me a pretty penny. Sneering, Dario took another look at the boy inside the cage. *A child born from a Titan's filth, eh?*

Normally, a child of his circumstances would have been sheltered in an orphanage. But Kuklo, born from the vomit of a Titan, was detested by people. His mother having been a Titan worshipper couldn't have helped, either. The tale of Kuklo's misfortunes was spelled out at length in a myriad of wounds, both large and small, that stretched across his body.

Such was the story of the "Titan's son" Dario had paid a fortune to take into custody. Of course, it wasn't out of kindness. He had longer-term goals in mind.

Perhaps it's nothing more than a whim...

Dario's eyes happened to meet Kuklo's. While the boy was covered in restraints, unable to so much as wriggle, his eyes were not dead. He seemed ready to seize the slightest opportunity to cast off his shackles and bite into Dario's windpipe.

A feeling of dread swept over Dario, and cold sweat oozed on his forehead. He sniffed, in a false show of bravado, and looked away from Kuklo. Then, facing the owner of the sideshow, he offered the bag made of cloth that he held in his hand. Though small enough to fit in his palm, it was heavy, filled to the brim with coins.

"You've made an excellent deal, sir."

"So have you."

It was a pittance to Dario, but the sum would be more than enough for the sideshow man. Enough to live a life of luxury for some time.

"That reminds me, sir. There was another eccentric who expressed an interest in Kuklo as well."

"Eccentric?"

"Oops! Pardon my language," the owner conceded, cramming the bag into his breast pocket, a vulgar smirk still plastered on his face.

"Who was this eccentric?"

"A most gloomy man, dressed in black rags."

"What did he want with the Titan's son?"

"Who can say? But he had to have the boy, or so he claimed."

"I don't understand."

"Nor did I." The owner shrugged. "Reasons aside, I always planned to give *you* the boy, master."

Cheeky bastard. The man surely tried to ingratiate himself thus to everyone he met. *Either way, the goods are mine.*

Dario always let his money do the talking.

"Well, I'll see to it that he's transported to your mansion."

"Thank you." Dario nodded his head slightly, then looked at the boy known as the Titan's son one more time.

He couldn't tell if this Kuklo was endowed with intellect. Being near him felt much like being near a wild animal. While Kuklo looked like a child, he needed to be handled with caution. No doubt he was wearing restraints because past events necessitated them.

So, he lives up to his name.

Dario shivered and left the sideshow in a hurry.

***

The cold was too much to bear, waking Kuklo. He'd been sleeping in the fetal position. His breath was white, he was chilled to the core, and his body wouldn't stop trembling. His skin looked pallid, and his lips were a cyanotic pale blue. Naked, he was completely defenseless against the cold, but he'd be shaking like a small animal even if he were clothed.

Kuklo was not in a cage, but rather in a storage shed about ten square meters in size. There was nothing else in the empty room. With no heating, the light that trickled in from a small window was his sole source of any sense of warmth. Of course, it was not nearly enough to heat the room, and his body continued to tremble.

Peeling his body off the floor, which might as well have been a bed of ice, Kuklo held his knees to his body and curled up into a ball. It was a survival instinct—his body forced into a position that forfeited the least amount of heat. The shackles on his arms and legs got in the way, but he had that degree of freedom.

He had no idea where he was. All he knew was that his cage had turned into a storage shed and that his proprietor had switched from the sideshow owner to the man known as Dario. Kuklo's proprietor had changed many times, but other than that, he'd experienced few ups and downs in his circumstances.

That wasn't all Kuklo didn't know—he didn't even understand what he was. He recognized a few words, and being called the Titan's son. He had no education and no one to impart knowledge to him. His world consisted entirely of the smattering of information that entered his vision.

Suddenly, Kuklo's stomach began to growl. There was no helping it since he wasn't being properly fed. He searched for food, deftly moving only his eyes, but spotted nothing that fit the description. As he continued to study the floor though, a small spider started crawling across it, the size of his pinky. He smashed the creature with his palm without hesitation and carried its carcass to his mouth. It tasted neither good nor bad, but it was far better than not eating at all. He couldn't afford to be picky, when he was struggling to stay alive, but at the same time, he had nothing in particular to live for.

Just as Kuklo was searching for more food, the shed door creaked open. Moments later, the room was filled with the morning sun.

Kuklo groaned, squinted his eyes, and shaded his face. Though by no means strong, the light was blinding enough for eyes adjusted to the darkness.

Out of the seemingly divine aura emerged Dario, Kuklo's proprietor, and an unfamiliar boy. While he was about the same age as

Kuklo, his skin had a healthy hue and his clothes were of fine quality. His short-cropped golden hair shone bathed in the sun's rays.

"Is he a Titan, father? He's still just a kid."

There were no traces of fear in the boy's eyes as he stared appraisingly at Kuklo. Instead they told of excitement, as though he'd discovered a new toy.

He casually strolled toward Kuklo.

"Be careful, Xavi."

"I'm fine. He's chained up, anyway."

The boy named Xavi wore a slight smile on his lips. The sight sent a tremble through Kuklo, and the countless scars on his body throbbed. Not because of the cold, but because his instincts sounded an alarm in face of the malice Xavi exuded. Kuklo had encountered many humans like this one, and each time he'd come away with another scar on his body. His intuition told him what Xavi was going to do.

"You're going to be head of the military someday, Xavi. Toward that goal—"

"I know, I know! I'll destroy all the Titans myself."

Grinning at Dario, Xavi unleashed a hard kick into Kuklo's face. A force came crashing through Kuklo's head like a blow from a blunt weapon.

"Guhh…" Groaning, Kuklo fell facing the ceiling.

Either his nose had started to bleed or he had cut his mouth; the taste of blood spread on his tongue. He must have been struck in a bad location since his vision became distorted like a ball of smashed clay and his mind grew hazy and dim.

"Huh? He's such a weakling."

Gazing at the dejected Xavi, he faded into unconsciousness.

***

He was awakened by the cold water that had been dumped on him.

The extreme cold stiffened his body and halted his breathing. After a few moments of writhing on the ground and pawing at his throat, he could breathe again, but his pulse continued to ring like an alarm bell.

"For a Titan, you sure sleep a lot."

It was Xavi hurling his verbal abuse. Dousing Kuklo in cold water was his way of saying good morning. In other words, a new day had come.

While Kuklo's sense of time had grown numb, Xavi's regularly spaced visits lent some sense of rhythm to his life.

Like some sort of farm animal, Kuklo crawled on all fours and diligently licked the water splattered on the floor. Getting enough to eat was out of the question, but he even had trouble quenching his thirst every day. He couldn't afford to let any opportunities get away.

"You're so weak, you're not even worth beating."

Xavi dealt a kick to Kuklo's side as he slurped up the water. The bully's toes gouged Kuklo's torso, and he flopped about, coughing.

"Fight back a little, why don't you? This is no fun."

"Fight, back..." Kuklo slurred, rising sluggishly. His hunger caused him to falter, but it wasn't so terrible as to make him collapse.

Fight. Fist in...front of face...

Standing like a stick, Kuklo balled his hands into fists and held them in front of his face. This was the fighting stance taught to him by Xavi. The chains attached to his wrists jangled, grating on the ears.

"Yes, that's much better. See, you can do it after all!"

Xavi nodded with a look of satisfaction, but Kuklo's fighting stance was one in name only, and he looked like a training doll. No one would mistake him for a kid about to get in a fistfight, and indeed that was not his wish. Yet taking the stance was of utmost importance to him.

Fight, back...

His stomach responded to the words with a rumble.

Seeing that Kuklo was ready, Xavi moved with practiced ease to square off against him and threw a quick jab with his fist. The Titan's son stood stone still, and the punch easily caught his face. His head flew back, then his strength left his legs. He fell to the floor, but Xavi, loath to accept such an easy victory, dug his right knee deep into Kuklo's solar plexus.

"Gagh…" Spitting out a mix of puke and fresh blood, Kuklo held his abdomen as he collapsed. Bile rose from his empty stomach, and his face twisted from the intense blow, which could easily have knocked him out.

Xavi's outrageous violence went on. Straddling Kuklo, who writhed in agony, he cocked his right fist, an innocent, boyish smile on his face.

"You Titans eat people, don't you?"

Tilting his head, he smashed his fist into Kuklo's left cheek.

"I saw one from Shiganshina District a little while back. I didn't get to see it eat anyone, of course."

He planted his left fist firmly in Kuklo's face.

"So what do humans taste like, anyway? I bet we're delicious!"

Xavi continued to swing his fists again and again as though the two were engaged in a friendly conversation.

Soon Kuklo's face was swollen and hot. The blood that came flowing out of his nose stained Xavi's fists a deep red.

"I wonder if you can eat Titans, too." Xavi brought his blood-stained fists close to his tongue and licked them clean. "Do you gain a Titan's strength if you eat it?"

Xavi's eyes filled with a strange glint. He bared his teeth and, not so much as hesitating, bit into Kuklo's shoulder. Unable to stand the sharp pain, Kuklo stirred.

"Blegh!" Xavi spat and wiped his mouth, then immediately punched Kuklo's head, irritated.

"Ugh, aghh…" Groans spilled from Kuklo's mouth as his body stretched out helplessly on the ground. He only felt a dull pain, perhaps because he was on the verge of passing out.

"Did I go a little too far?" Xavi sighed and slowly got up. "Oh, well. You're a Titan. You can't break down so easily." He turned his back on Kuklo and began to walk away, but Kuklo wasn't done. There was more to this than simply getting beaten up.

"Fight... Fight..."

Kuklo's shaky, half-delirious words brought Xavi to a halt. His hands began searching his pocket, and from it he produced a lush red apple. He wiped it with his sleeve and took a bite. Almost finishing it, he tossed what remained to Kuklo.

"Eat it all, now," Xavi said smoothly, and left the shed cackling.

Kuklo quickly snatched up the apple's core and indulged in it. Eat it all he indeed did. It disappeared into his stomach in the blink of an eye. For Kuklo, "fighting back" was not a means to resist Xavi, but the way he received food.

Lying on the ground, Kuklo held his stomach and curled into a ball. It was the start of another impossibly long day.

**

Kuklo's days were the very definition of monotony. He spent the majority of each sleeping, and when he was awake, he sat there, his mind at rest. He aimlessly allowed time to pass by.

The only visitors to his shed were Xavi, Dario, and any guests they brought with them. Naturally, they were not visiting him for the conversation. Xavi beat the daylights out of the Titan's son to impress his friends with his prowess, while Dario saw fit to parade his authority. Of course, none of this had altered Kuklo's everyday life. Nothing had changed for him from the time he was in the sideshow, and it seemed as though things never would.

Titan's son...

Kuklo didn't even know what he was. The meaning of those words was a mystery, but he understood they had to do with him since he'd been called that from the time he was born.

He had no interest in the outside world. He gave no thought to what was beyond the shed door, nor did he think about exiting. Yet he wanted to know what "Titan's son" meant.

It was the only thing he felt compelled to do, but the desire meant nothing on its own. There was no way to learn the answer from where he sat, nor did anyone care to teach him.

Kuklo quickly lost interest, returning to his dull, uneventful days. What was important was survival. Using his head wouldn't fill his stomach. Getting on his hands and knees, he reached out to grab a crawling beetle.

***

Sharle Inocencio lay shivering in bed. Her features made her look like a finely crafted bisque doll, but she clutched a sheathed knife to her chest. The girl was fighting crashing waves of despair. Her porcelain, translucent skin was pallid, and dread clouded her well-formed face. She seemed on the verge of tears, and the moist luster of her long strands of golden hair was perhaps due to them.

She breathed a deep sigh, then silently looked around. The room, overcome by darkness, was completely silent. While moonlight peeked through the cracks in her curtains to illuminate her bed, the rest of the room was close to pitch black. If her eyes weren't adjusted to the darkness, she probably couldn't even make out her own figure.

Her twenty-square-meter room was far larger than what a thirteen-year-old girl needed. It contained a full set of furniture—a closet, a desk, a table, and so on—but somehow looked deserted. The chamber was simply too spacious for her.

I'm scared, Sharle whispered in her mind, and her body shrank into itself as if to vanish.

It wasn't that she was scared of the dark, and she was used to sleeping alone, too. One word to the maid waiting in the adjacent room and she would stay by Sharle's side the entire night. But that wouldn't nearly quell the fear that nested in her heart.

Sharle gripped the handle of her blade, a paring knife pilfered from the kitchen when the maids weren't watching. It was the best she could manage in the way of self-defense against the terrible enemy from whom she had to protect herself.

A Titan's son, in our home... The fact was so shocking, it had caused her to feel faint. It was hard to believe at first, but she knew it was true by the way her father and her older bother acted.

Sharle knew quite well how frightening the Titans could be. A look through her home bookshelves was all it took to find a number of volumes on them, and stories about them had been embellished into an endless number of fairy tales. She was so scared of Titans the day she first learned about them that she couldn't sleep. By now, she knew that Titans weren't figments of the imagination but monsters that existed in reality.

You can't allow a monster...a Titan to live... Sharle, who had seen one with her own eyes, knew how dangerous they were.

She had no idea what the Titan's son was like. Perhaps it could be tamed like a baby animal, but if it was a child, it would grow. What would happen then was obvious. Keeping a Titan nearby was like going about your life carrying a bomb.

They should know how dangerous it is. It was clear why Dario had acquired the Titan's son. It served his political ambitions in some way. *But...I just don't think it should be living in our house...*

Even the thought of "using" a Titan's son seemed absurd to Sharle. Grasping her knife, she exhaled heavily, prepared herself, and quietly got out of bed.

Her attire wasn't suited for what she planned to do, but she couldn't be choosy. She needed to complete her mission without delay.

"I have to do it. I'll kill the Titan's son."

***

It was on a family vacation a month ago that Sharle first saw a Titan.

The trip began in the underground markets of Wall Sheena, followed by visits to locations like the factory city and the Forest of Giant Trees. They went everywhere, from popular tourist destinations to highly restricted areas, but the greatest was saved for last: the top of Wall Maria. It was hard to tell whether Dario had planned it from the beginning or if the thought had just come to him, but after his cheerful proposal was met with Xavi's endorsement, they made their way over.

It was, undeniably, a reckless decision. The walls were the lynchpin of the fortress nation, mankind's most important military installations. They were politically important as well and had been used as bargaining chips for one deal or another ever since their construction.

One political uproar in recent memory: a Survey Corps expedition thanks to which further forays had been banned for the last thirteen years. The Corps' unthinkable transgression of military ordinance had ended up empowering the conservatives, who wished for mankind to live modestly inside the walls. The corpsmen were never charged with any crime, however, and their exploits were still recounted among citizens as a tale of heroism. The unofficial expedition led by Jorge Piquer had proven that the Titans could be defeated.

That's why they didn't have to seal the gate.

Sharle's mouth hung open as she looked up at the sturdy portal. "It's huge…"

The ten-meter-tall gate that truly stunned her was but one part of Wall Maria, however. The Wall's overwhelming presence, so high it almost seemed to pierce the sky, even brought to mind notions of divinity.

Weren't there people who worshipped the walls, too? One native faith indeed did, and in the face of Wall Maria, Sharle was able to understand the urge to cling to the walls.

While she admired the edifice, Dario spoke to the soldiers. He seemed to be having trouble getting permission to climb Wall Maria.

So he didn't have any sort of advance promise. Dario coming from

31

nowhere and demanding a tour must have been quite a nuisance to the soldiers. *Of course, I am curious about the outside world.*

Citizens had to adhere to the rules—although most people understood that, the concept seemed to elude Dario. He and a soldier seemed caught in a tense impasse, but another man who appeared to be a team leader arrived to calm them before it could turn into a shouting match.

Dario exchanged words with the team leader, then inched close to him and whispered something in his ear. Moments later, the officer's face was beaming.

Looks like they've come to a business agreement.

Something passed between their hands while the two were near each other, and it wasn't hard to guess what it was.

I can't believe him... Sharle slumped and sighed gently.

"Looks like they'll let us take a tour. Aren't we lucky?" Dario said, smiling.

"Yahoo!"

Xavi pumped his fist, then ran up the wooden spiral staircase that led up to the top of the wall, with Dario and the team leader following behind.

Not surprisingly, the grunt who'd been refusing Dario's request had a bitter look on his face. Garrison soldiers took special pride in their duty as protectors of Wall Maria, which regular citizens weren't permitted to climb. A family being allowed up because of a bribe was particularly outrageous.

"Um... Sorry." Sharle bobbed her head at the soldier, then quickly chased after the others.

Climbing Wall Maria was even more difficult than it looked. The bodies of the soldiers there were honed from doing so daily, and they were able to climb the stairs with ease. For Sharle, who had few to no opportunities to build such stamina, it was an ordeal. Of course, the first to admit defeat was Dario, whose bright idea this was.

A turret, used as a watchtower, stood atop the wall. A number of soldiers stationed there were monitoring the exterior using binoculars.

"Whooah!"

Xavi rushed to the watchtower as soon as he arrived and hung over the railing. Meanwhile, the soldiers were confused by their odd visitors, but after a glance from the team leader they quickly left the tower.

I don't feel good about this… Sharle was interested in the outer regions, but she felt guilty, as though they were doing something wrong. Unable to hold back her curiosity, however, she slowly made her way into the watchtower.

She had searched but could find no books detailing what was beyond the walls. All she knew was that Titans roamed the land, making it uninhabitable for humans.

It means I'm at the very edge of human civilization. So long as expeditions were not taking place, these ramparts were the farthest a human could go. *I wonder what the outside world looks like.*

Her pulse quickened. This was her chance to witness a sight she'd had no choice but to imagine until now. She put a hand to her chest and exhaled. Then she resolutely turned her head.

So this is the outside world. An expanse of desolate earth—the rust-like, brownish-red soil barely supported any vegetation, and clouds of sand danced through the air every time a chilly southern wind blew. The derelict world that stretched as far as the eye could see indeed looked like a no man's land. She grasped just how small the world left to humanity was.

What's beyond what I can see? With nothing to answer her question in any book, anything could exist past the horizon, even an unknown country. It almost seemed likely that one existed and that only distance thwarted them from establishing the fact. *The rest—*

As Sharle stared out, lost in thought, Xavi suddenly let out a cry of delight. "A Titan!"

The moment she looked to where Xavi's finger pointed, she shivered.

An abnormal figure stood listlessly about a hundred meters from the wall. A little over ten meters tall, it was literally titanic, so huge as to dissuade any comparison to a human despite its human form.

Aaah… Sharle let out an unvocalized shriek that naturally went unnoticed.

Everyone in the watchtower was focused on the Titan that stood there towering like a giant tree, ignoring the change in her demeanor. Xavi was yelling happily, and Dario frolicked like a child.

How… Why aren't they scared?! Sharle found it impossible to understand how the two felt, protected by the wall or not. This was a monster. They couldn't allow their attention to waver for a second. A Titan could destroy the wall and surge into town at any moment. *Just because we've been safe until now…*

The Titan sluggishly turned to face the wall, perhaps reacting to the commotion. The monster looked like a man around the age of twenty. It was skinny but covered in lean muscle and appeared in no way weak. Its cheeks were slack as though it had been met by some happy occurrence. A humming seemed poised to issue from its lips.

The Titan quickly began to close in on them with light, prancing steps. Its speed easily surpassed a human's and probably matched that of a horse. Being chased by it meant certain death.

The Titan rapidly neared the wall. Sharle's body trembled, and her pulse grew unnaturally fast.

"See that, Xavi? One day, you're going to be leading soldiers and defeating that."

Paying no mind to the approaching Titan, Dario plopped his hand on Xavi's shoulder. The idea of placing his son at the top of the military clearly occupied his thoughts—not for his son's good, of course, but for the sake of his own ambitions.

He exhibited the same attitude toward Sharle. At some point in the future, she would be married off to some politician she'd never met.

To Dario, they were all nothing but pawns serving his own

ambition. Sharle, Xavi, and even the Titans.

The grinning Titan got even closer, and its gigantic mouth popped open, stretching from ear to ear, as though to swallow the humans on the wall.

The moment she saw this horrendous display, Sharle gasped. Her eyes opening wide, she grew faint. She felt her heart being ground to dust, until suddenly, it all stopped.

***

Sharle snuck out of her room, knife in hand, and slowly and silently made her way down the hall. It was late enough for all the other residents of the mansion to be sound asleep. The maids wouldn't rise until the second cockcrow. The security guards were still on duty, switching off as they patrolled the mansion's environs, but their eyes did not reach inward into the grounds. As long as she didn't create a ruckus, she'd be able to carry out her mission before the rest of her family noticed.

I have to do this. The Titan's son can't be allowed to live... Yet she lacked any confidence. She'd never killed so much as a bug before, let alone an animal. Taking care of a Titan's son set a high bar. *But I have to do it.*

A Titan's son running wild would wreak unprecedented havoc on the country on the order of a cataclysm of nature. It could even trigger humanity's extinction.

Even if I die doing it... Sharle's tragic determination did not come from a strong sense of responsibility. She was just tired of living as her father's tool. *...At least my life will have meaning.*

Murdering the Titan's son would grant her wish. Living for her own sake and no one else's was more valuable than any treasure. That was why she felt ready to sacrifice her life going into this.

Even if I die, my life will be my own.

Sharle continued to tiptoe down the dark hall.

***

A faint sound woke Kuklo, his nerves apparently on edge thanks to his empty stomach and the freezing cold. Opening his eyes, he deftly moved just his eyeballs to survey his surroundings. It was extremely dark, but he could still see to the corners. He cautiously scanned the area but saw neither rat nor bug. Perhaps because he'd thought about food, his stomach rumbled and ached. When he listened closer, the noise seemed to come from outside his shed.

The gradually approaching noise sounded like footsteps. Yet they were not Xavi's or Dario's. He could tell by the difference in rhythm. Nor did he recall the labored breathing that he heard mixed in with the footsteps.

The lock must have been undone; a metallic rattle echoed through the shed. At last, the door began to swing open.

There standing in front of Kuklo was a young girl he hadn't seen before. He could tell by instinct that she meant harm. Her wide-open eyes were unblinking, and her breathing was rough, agitated. Her flushed cheeks were a pale crimson, and her lips were pressed so tightly her mouth seemed sewn together. The girl held a gleaming silver knife in her hands, and its trembling trip was pointed at him.

Kuklo watched the girl's every move. He knew quite well how dangerous blades could be. A number of the marks on his body were from cuts, some of which had brought him close to death.

The girl continued to creep forward and to close in on Kuklo, but he did not budge. It would be a waste of energy, and he'd end up that much hungrier. If the girl demanded that he "fight back" he would gladly respond, but otherwise, staying still was the best option.

"This is the Titan's son?"

The young girl's murmur sounded like the tinkling of a bell. She drew even closer to Kuklo and was now near enough to touch.

Switching to a backhanded grip, she hoisted the knife high in the air. "Please, don't *fight back*."

Kuklo rose off the ground in response to the familiar words, taking the girl by surprise. She leapt with a quiet shriek—*aie!*—and in that moment of shock, her knife dropped from her hand and tumbled by Kuklo's feet.

"Aaah!"

Her eyes widened as she hastily reached for the blade, but Kuklo, one step ahead of her, picked it up first. The girl's face froze. Knife in hand, Kuklo slowly stood up and grabbed tight the girl's wrist. He made her hold the blade, pointing its tip right at his own chest.

"Huh?" The girl stared in wonder, looking back and forth between Kuklo and the knife. "What's going on?"

Then Kuklo tugged the confused girl's wrist toward his own chest, blade and all. The moment the knife's tip touched his torso, it tore his skin open. A sharp pain. The blood that oozed out of the wound turned into drops and trickled down Kuklo's body.

"W-Wait. Do you want to die?!"

With a baffled expression on her face, the girl released the blade and pulled back her wrist. Making no move to retrieve her weapon, she stepped back to put some distance in between them.

She was clearly confused, but so was Kuklo. He wanted a reward in return for a "fight," but for some reason, she wasn't going ahead with it. At this rate, his stomach would stay empty. He lazily picked up the knife, then offered it to the girl. He couldn't let this fine opportunity to sate his hunger get away from under his nose.

"Why would you do that?" The girl's confusion soon turned to self-mockery. "Why would you, heh. You could ask me the same. I came here to kill you…"

"Fight back, fight back."

"Of course, you would fight back…" The girl stared at Kuklo with a shocked expression. "You can talk? But you're a Titan's son!"

Ignoring her puzzlement, Kuklo focused on the girl's face. He wasn't interested in its features, but he felt like he'd seen it before.

"Xavi."

The moment Kuklo said the name, the girl was struck with wonder. "That's my brother…"

Caring little for Sharle's reaction, Kuklo simply pointed at her, repeating, "Xavi, Xavi."

"Xavi is my brother's name… Are you really a Titan's son?" the girl asked, but Kuklo had no idea what she meant.

This seemed to frustrate his stomach, as it began to growl ferociously. In pain—it felt like some hand was twisting him inside—Kuklo grimaced and crouched down.

"Are you hungry?"

Kuklo's face ran the gamut of expressions as he groaned. Eventually, though, she seemed to realize something. She nodded and turned to walk away.

Reaching for the knife on the floor, Kuklo called out to the girl. "Fight back."

Maybe she didn't hear him; without turning around she left the shed.

"Aahh…" Denied what he'd hoped for, Kuklo was crestfallen. But that was nothing out of the ordinary. By the time the room was silent again, he had already given up. Come morning Xavi would dispense food in return for a "fight."

There was never any guarantee that he would be fed, of course.

***

By the time he heard the sound of footsteps approaching the shed again, Kuklo had lost count of how many times his stomach had protested. These footsteps sounded like the girl who'd left.

"Kuklo fight back…"

Crouched on the ground, his knees to his chest, the Titan's son slowly raised his head.

There standing at the entrance was exactly the person he expected to see. Entering the room, the girl timidly approached Kuklo. Something in her seemed to have changed. He could tell that she no longer meant him any harm.

Kuklo twitched his nose and stared at her. More specifically, he stared at what she held. In her hands were bread, jerky, and an apple, and the aroma coming from them was stimulating his stomach like never before. Within seconds, his mouth was coated in saliva, and drool ran down the sides of his mouth.

Stopping out of Kuklo's reach, the girl took back the knife that had fallen on the floor and replaced it with the food, which she then pushed toward him.

"You're just hungry, right?"

Kuklo began to reach for the food but froze. He hadn't been allowed to fill his belly without first engaging in a "fight." His hesitation was due to a fear that eating now might inconvenience him in some way.

He continued to think but found no answer. To begin with, inconveniences were the story of his life, and not being able to sate his hunger was a far more serious problem. He grabbed the bread and tore in, hurriedly swallowing it before his tongue even had the chance to get a taste.

"You're not a Titan, are you?" the girl asked, but Kuklo was too busy with his feast. "The Titans I know about are monsters, but you just look like a person to me..." The girl observed him closely as she continued her monologue. "Plus, I've never read about child Titans in any books."

Lending an ear to the girl's voice, Kuklo shoved the jerky into his mouth. He needed to eat as fast as he possibly could. He was like a wild animal preparing for winter, absorbing nutrients to store in his body.

"Is it true that if a Titan gets hurt, it just gets better right away?" The girl laughed at her own question once she realized how strange it was. "I guess if you're not a Titan, you wouldn't know." After poking her own head, she asked, "Did father bring you here?"

Kuklo ate in silence, unresponsive to her questions. Within a few minutes, he'd consumed all of the food. His stomach jutted out of his emaciated body like a ghoul's. By the time he let out a burp his stomachache was gone.

"What's your name?"

"...Name?"

"You're not a Titan's son, are you?"

"Kuklo." Kuklo knew few words, but he at least knew his own name.

"I'm Sharle," she said, pointing to the tip of her nose. "It's nice to meet you, Kuklo."

Kuklo furrowed his brow and cocked his head in reaction to Sharle's smile. He couldn't figure out what she wanted of him. Her actions were nothing like those of all the other humans he had met, but he could see that she wasn't trying to hurt him.

"Sharle. Nice, meet you," Kuklo said in a clumsy imitation of her words. A faint warmth seemed to come over his chilled body.

***

After that day, Sharle began to make frequent appearances at the shed. The visits were no easy task. She was only able to drop in at night and had to return by sunrise, lest her family find out.

Sharle always bore gifts, namely food. The amounts were small so that her pilfering wouldn't be noticed, but silence an empty stomach they did. It went without saying that her provisions did wonders to allay Kuklo's once-frequent stomachaches.

She brought more fortune to Kuklo than just food, though.

"So you were never a Titan's son in the first place," Sharle fumed, wrapping Kuklo's body in a towel. "You're human. Just like me."

"Just like Sharle..."

Kuklo angled his head, and Sharle grinned and nodded in

satisfaction. "You know, your speaking has gotten better."

The primary benefit Kuklo gained by meeting Sharle was language. He learned naturally just from struggling to communicate his thoughts to her, and it brought about a near-revolutionary change to both his heart and his mind.

"What is Titan?"

"I don't know," Sharle replied with a shake of her head.

Kuklo was surprised by this response. Sharle was like an omnipotent god to him, and he believed she could address any and all queries.

She shrugged. "No one knows what the Titans really are. It's not in any books…" Flipping through the pages of the volume she'd brought with her, she presented it to Kuklo.

In it, he saw a strange picture. "This is?"

"It's an illustrated map."

"Ill-us-trate?"

"It's a drawing that represents the world we live in…I think."

The book depicted three circles as well as a number of people outside them walking toward the rings.

"This is where we are now," Sharle said, pointing near the center of the circles, "and this wall is called 'Wall Sheena.'" Her finger moved to the next ring. "The circle in the middle is 'Wall Rose,' and the one on the outside is 'Wall Maria.' This is as far as humans can live."

"But here… A man."

When Kuklo pointed to the naked humans depicted outside of Wall Maria, Sharle explained with a dour expression, "That's a Titan."

Titan… Kuklo brought his face closer to the book, his eyes fixed on the drawing of the Titans. With gleeful smiles on their faces they pursued small, fleeing creatures underfoot. *Humans…*

He hadn't noticed the humans at first because of how small they were drawn. Some of the Titans had people in their grasp, while others were eating them. This was enough to help Kuklo intuit the relationship between humans and Titans.

Like it's eating bugs. To a bug, Kuklo must seem a coarse predator.

41

He also understood as a matter of course why the walls had been built. *So this is…why they afraid of me.*

He could almost justify all of the shackles that had deprived him of freedom throughout his life. If what Sharle said was true, he was a human who had been labeled a Titan's son. His predicament was inevitable because Titans were to be eschewed. It must have been just in case, since he lacked the might he saw in the pictures…

Kuklo strained his imagination to come up with a mental image of the Titans, but his efforts were futile no matter how hard he tried. The reason was simple: he didn't possess the material necessary for his imagination to do its work. Kuklo's world was still limited to what was inside the shed, and anything beyond the door was foggy and vague. He at least understood that past the door lay a world he couldn't even envision.

Kuklo stared at the shackles on his limbs. The well-worn iron restraints had grown rusty from his blood, sweat, and excrement, but removing them was nigh impossible. Even his strong teeth that could snap a tough jerky in two stood no chance against metal chains. The keyholes had been welded shut, leaving amputation as the only way for Kuklo to regain his freedom.

"I wish I could do something for you…"

Kuklo shook his head as Sharle looked at his shackles, concerned. They had always been with him, and the thought of removing them had stopped occurring to him—until now. He could never go back to not knowing his true identity, nor did he wish to. Yet, although he was curious about what awaited him beyond the door, at the moment his interest converged on a single point.

What is Titan?

They were responsible for ruining his life. He wanted to meet one if he could.

He wanted to confirm for himself that he wasn't a Titan's son.

But to do that, he would need to cast off his shackles and bound into the outside world. It wasn't something he could do immediately, but it wasn't exactly impossible. He just hadn't given it any consideration until now.

Chain can be broken.

If he did what he needed to do in order to break them, of course. The day would come far in the future, but he had to begin working toward it without delay. First, though, there was something else he needed.

"Tell me. About human world."

***

Kuklo had countless things to learn, mostly regarding the world that he and humans lived in, but it was far more than could be learned in a day and a night. Not only that, his only source of information was Sharle, so his learning had to proceed at a snail's pace. Still, his store of knowledge grew slowly but steadily.

The problem was that Sharle herself only knew so much. After half a year of absorbing all he could from her, Kuklo used the knowledge he'd gained to tackle books. He was such a voracious reader that it stunned Sharle, but that impression wasn't Kuklo's own. Nor was he attempting to take back his idle days—it was simply what he needed to do in order to survive.

Kuklo's efforts reached beyond his studies. Alongside them, he also planned his escape from the shed. No matter how broad his knowledge, it was pearls for swine if he remained in the shed.

His method of escape was incredibly simple. All he had to do was break his chains.

That said, he ran the risk of being found out if he used a tool like a jigsaw, so he'd chosen to corrode his chains, a method that required patience.

Fortunately for him, it was easy to obtain the materials he needed. Sweat, blood, and urine could be used without arousing suspicion and could all corrode metal. True, it would take an extraordinary amount of time to sever the chains, but speaking to Xavi or Dario was out of the question.

The thought of them freeing Kuklo was a flat-out absurdity. Dario had bought him in order to let his son Xavi inflict pain on the Titan's son. For someone who hoped to lead the military one day, beating a Titan's son silly was confidence-building. Xavi would surely puff out his chest and boast, "That's right, I've defeated a Titan before!"

It was annoying, but to the extent that brawn meant everything to Xavi, he was relatively easy to deal with. All Kuklo had to do was feed Xavi's self-regard: rolling on the ground when struck, overreacting to the pain.

Kuklo continued to play the part of the Titan's son. It was exactly what Xavi, Dario, and their guests wanted from him, and it kept their guards down.

In the end, it took two years after he first began to stitch his plans together for all of Kuklo's preparations to fall into place.

***

In the center of the spacious dining room, nearly twenty square meters large, sat a wide, imposing table. It could accommodate ten at once, but only Sharle, Xavi, and Dario sat there now. The room was like a physical manifestation of Dario's vanity.

The topic of that evening's meal was Xavi.

"So, you're about to enter training, Xavi. Are you ready for it?"

Dario looked proudly at his son. Despite his question, he was surely contemplating some measure or other that would let Xavi graduate without issue.

Sharle had no idea what training was like for new recruits, but she wouldn't have found it unusual if greased palms did buy preferential treatment.

It wouldn't be as bad if he was just a doting father.

He wasn't actually worried about Xavi's well-being. It was simply that his son stumbling hurt his own ambitions.

The topic of the evening replied confidently with no inkling of his father's scheming. "One day, I'll be running the military. I've been ready my entire life, father."

Of course. Just look at how prepared he is…

But this was only because Dario had placed his son on rails he'd laid down. Every little thing that might have gotten in her brother's way had been shunted out of the way. Naturally, Xavi didn't doubt that he had his own talent to thank.

While it may have owed to misconceptions, Xavi's confidence was very real. During his childhood it had taken the form of being the neighborhood bully, but now it was transforming into a semblance of leadership. His height had soared in the past few years, and his buffed-up body was the image of dauntlessness. While his insolence had also been honed, he would surely do well as a recruit without Dario's meddling.

Sharle wondered, *Is it just the intimacy of family?* Yet, Xavi had also benefited from the rare experience of having subdued a Titan's son. *Or that's what he thinks.*

Xavi would erupt in anger if he were to learn the truth, but the chances for that were slim. He was genuinely daft, but even so, he would have realized by now if it weren't for Kuklo's acting. Having grown bored, or perhaps maturing, Xavi rarely visited Kuklo these days, and barring any extreme circumstances he would never catch on.

"By the way, what will happen after I've left?"

Dario tilted his head at Xavi's question. "Happen to what?"

"To *it*."

Dario seemed to have understood. "Ahh. *It*."

"We don't need it anymore, do we?"

"Indeed."

Xavi and Dario tried to keep the matter vague by saying "it," but Sharle promptly discerned the subject. *When they really mean Kuklo.*

Recruits were forced to live together in barracks. Xavi would be leaving home, so there was no longer any need to have Kuklo around.

Maybe they'll just let him go free.

Sharle had her hopes, but Dario was a natural-born businessman. "Let's sell it off, then. I'm sure the buyers will be lining up."

This was enough to make Sharle despondent. The word "free" didn't seem to be in Dario's dictionary. *But that means everything must happen on a faster schedule.*

Kuklo's escape plan had entered its final stages. All that remained was to wait for a chance, but now that Dario had decided to sell him, they could no longer bide their time. They had to proceed with the plan as soon as possible.

And I'll have to say goodbye to him very soon... Sharle shook her head, driving off the idle lament that had crossed her mind. *Nothing good will come from Kuklo being here.*

It would surely be the same wherever he was sold.

His life is finally beginning. I must see him off with a smile.

It felt lonely, like being left behind, but she had to think about more than that.

"What's the matter? You've gone quiet," Dario asked, noticing Sharle's distant expression. "I know it's hard to say goodbye to Xavi, but it's not like you'll never see him again."

Dario seemed to have misunderstood, but Xavi's departure was actually convenient. If she just played along, she wouldn't be suspected of anything more.

"And there's little time for mourning. You're about to be very busy."

"I am?"

"I've been holding private talks about your engagement, and it looks like it'll work out."

"Engagement?!" Sharle was so surprised her voice cracked. She struggled to process this unexpected turn of events and found her mind suddenly wiped clean. Her pulse quickened, and an unpleasant sweat began to ooze from her entire body.

She was Dario's tool, doomed to someday be married off by him—this was her fate, the reason she'd come into this world. She thought she understood, but it was all too sudden. She could barely get her emotions in line.

"Do you know Bruno Baumeister?"

"Only that he's a politician…" Sharle squeezed out, feigning calm, resisting the urge to scream.

"He stands at the vanguard of the conservative movement. You'll be marrying his boy."

"They say he's quite the prodigal son," Xavi butted in.

"Would he really want to marry someone like me? Wouldn't another woman…"

"Don't worry," Dario rejected Sharle's suggestion out of hand.

So it's already been decided. The engagement didn't "look" like it would work out, it already had. Considering Dario's money-first personality, that much was clear.

Now it's my turn to be trapped in a cell…

Sharle bemoaned the irony of it.

***

Kuklo was brought out of his slumber by the sound of raindrops knocking on the roof. The rain seemed to have just started, irregularly falling from the sky, the drops so few that you could name each one. It sounded as though they might stop at any moment, but it was still enough to awaken Kuklo. His senses had grown keen with time.

The room was dark, and he could hear nothing other than the rain. He didn't know the exact hour, but his stomach told him that it was the middle of the night. It would probably be another four or five hours until dawn.

Kuklo rose and moved his limbs to see how they felt. All the muscles on his body were stiff from the cold, but they would return to normal once his blood started to circulate. There were a number of bruises on his body that resembled brands, but they were on their way to healing, the pain bearable.

Passed so fast…

He'd spent two years as Dario's possession. The knowledge Kuklo gained brought about a dramatic change for his personhood, but he'd transformed in another way. Having grown fifteen centimeters in height, his body was now surprisingly large. There was no excess fat on his body, and at first glance, he looked lanky, like a bean sprout. In truth, he'd built up a reasonable amount of muscle, so he was slender but not frail. He had forged his body over the weeks and months in order to be prepared for anything the day of his escape. Xavi had put on a hefty, armor-like amount of muscle, but Kuklo needed to be agile. Excess muscle would weigh his body down and limit his limbs' range of motion. Bulk would get in his way and be worse than useless when escaping.

Kuklo looked at the restraints attached to his arms and legs. Since he'd grown, his wrist and ankle restraints felt quite tight. Not tight enough to pinch, but enough to compress. He had to act soon.

When I get out…I must take these off. Walking around with manacles strapped to him would get soldiers called on him in no time. He could sever his chains when he wished. All that remained was to gather his courage and to begin executing his plan.

Of course, that would also mean parting with Sharle for good. She'd saved his life, served as his mentor, and been his only sympathizer. To say that she was everything to him would not have been an overstatement.

If not for Sharle, I would still be the Titan's son. Imagining the terrible possibility, he shuddered.

As the rain turned into a drizzle, he heard familiar footsteps. Sharle entered the shed.

"I want to leave this place," he immediately began talking about his plan, but stopped just as soon. Sharle didn't seem her usual self.

It was hard to see her expression in the dark, but her eyes looked bloodshot, and the flesh around them swollen.

She's crying? To be precise, she probably had been. It appeared as though she'd come after taking a bit of time to regain her composure.

He hesitated to ask her why, though. He could guess from her demeanor that it was a touchy matter. Clumsily bringing it up would help nobody, as Kuklo was sensitive enough to realize now.

A few minutes passed in silence.

Sharle let out a deep sigh and opened her sullen mouth. "Father says he's going to sell you off."

"Me?"

"My brother is leaving home."

Kuklo knew that Xavi was joining the Training Corps—and naturally also be leaving home. "They don't need me...anymore."

Therefore, he would be sold. Not only was it obvious, it was somewhat expected. The prospect only helped him make up his mind.

"There's not much time," Sharle said. "I think they'll find you a new owner within a few days."

"Then I must...hurry to escape?"

"Yes. So I'll bring you some things tomorrow night."

"Okay."

"Just some clothes...and money."

"It's enough. Thank you." Grasping the situation, Kuklo waited for Sharle to speak again. He could tell that she wasn't done.

After a moment she said, "I'll have to leave home soon, too."

"Leave home?"

"I'm going to be married away."

"Oh..."

Kuklo understood. Just as it had been decided that Xavi would leave for the Training Corps, Sharle would marry. It wasn't that different from Kuklo being forced to live his life as a Titan's son.

Sharle. She seems bothered. Otherwise she wouldn't say that she was being "married away." She looked as though she'd given up hope for her own future, but it wouldn't be hard for him to rid her of her troubles.

"Sharle, what do you want to do?"

"What do you mean?"

"Say no, if you don't like it."

"If it was really that easy…"

"You can," Kuklo insisted.

But Sharle's reply was firm. "I can't. I don't have any other choice."

"Then…come with me?"

"Huh?!" If her shrill rejoinder were any indication, she hadn't expected such a proposal.

"I will take back…my life. That's why I leave." He couldn't reclaim it any other way.

"Your life…"

"It's bad to be in a cage. You leave too, Sharle."

"But I'm not strong like you, Kuklo."

"Then even more reason to leave."

"What do you mean by that?"

"Very hard to be inside of here."

No one knew better than Kuklo how tough life inside a cage was. He'd been able to stand his hellish existence thanks to having spent most of it as a Titan's son. If he'd entered a cage as a human, his heart would have crumbled sooner or later. He didn't see Sharle as having a weak spirit, but the fate that awaited her after her betrothal was as clear as day.

Kuklo extended his hand toward Sharle. "Let's go together."

It was a riskier proposition than escaping alone, but Kuklo had faith that it would work out. This was not the first time he'd faced adversity, and pulling through again and again had instilled confidence in him. A will harder than steel dwelled in his frame.

Thanks to Xavi. That, of course, did not translate into gratitude, but Kuklo's many days suffering abuse as a Titan's son weren't for naught.

Kuklo's concern for Sharle was not the only reason he thought to bring her with him. He wanted it, too.

Sharle clutched Kuklo's outstretched hand. Hers was trembling, either from the cold or out of fear of the challenges that surely awaited them.

"Leave everything to me."

Kuklo's face wore a smile as he gently returned her grip.

***

The rain had fallen for a day straight and was now reaching its peak. The merciless, sonorous battering spoke of the downpour outside. It was as if a drummer stood above the shed striking the roof with his sticks. Though it was noisy, it provided favorable conditions for their escape. Their forms would be concealed by the pouring rain, while the thrumming would hush their footsteps.

Now I just wait for Sharle. If everything went as planned, she would appear soon. Kuklo glanced at the door, then shifted his eyes to his shackles. The iron chains were long covered in rust. In particular, the rings that linked them to the bands had corroded so severely that he could spot large cracks. Sundering them would be easy.

Thunder roared in the air like an explosion, causing the shed to shake. Just as the fearsome clap rang out, the shed's door suddenly swung open, bringing violent gusts and rain in to ransack the room.

"I have arrived for you."

What swept into the shed together with the night storm was an unfamiliar man's voice.

Who's that?

A man wearing a black cassock stood in the doorway. His cloak was black, too, perhaps in an attempt to blend into the darkness. He wore a hood low over his eyes, making it impossible to read his expression.

Kuklo, his body on guard, stared at the man. Though he had no idea who it was, and despite being unable to see his face, the man's

unfamiliar voice proved that they'd never met before.

The one coming to buy me? But it was hard to imagine Dario's trading partner visiting in the middle of the night, especially in this weather. Even if it were daytime, most people would stay indoors.

Something else about the man bothered Kuklo. He carried a blade though he was no soldier.

Who is he?

If it came down to it, Kuklo was prepared to break his chains and fight, but he wasn't sensing any harmful intent.

"I had hoped to rescue you sooner. Finding your trail took longer than I predicted. Please forgive me."

While the man reverently lowered his head, Kuklo had only one thought: *What's happening?* Unable to process this development, he felt bewildered. The man, though, seemed to be very familiar with Kuklo's circumstances. On top of that, his remarks suggested that he possessed information that Kuklo did not have.

Should I ask? Doing so would incur a large risk. Until now, Kuklo had played the part of the witless Titan's son in order to disarm people and ensure his safety. So long as he did not know the man's identity, carelessly speaking to him wasn't smart. He needed to extract information from the man first. The only problem was that getting it would be difficult unless he risked conversation.

Even without resorting to speech, there was one thing Kuklo could infer. *He was searching for me.* For quite a long time, at that. From at least before Dario bought him. In other words, this man in black had been searching for *the Titan's son.*

That was more than enough cause for distrust, but the man did not seem to fear the Titan's son. In fact, Kuklo could practically feel affection in the man's words. Still, that was no reason to trust him.

"Come, allow me to undo your bonds," the man said, drawing his blade.

Kuklo was wary, but the man did not seem to want to hurt him. His favorable intentions, however, likely didn't extend to those other than Kuklo.

What do I do? Kuklo immediately thought of Sharle since he knew she would be coming to the shed. What the man would do if he encountered Sharle was a foregone conclusion.

The storm clouds must have squat above them. A flash of lightning tore through the sky while thunder roared. A dazzling flash filled the room, revealing the man's figure in detail.

Hey...

Kuklo's eyes popped open. The man's blade was coated in a thick, red liquid. Not only that, he could see what looked like blood spurts on his face.

The worst of all possibilities began to creep into Kuklo's mind. "Who did you kill?" he asked, standing up straight. The time was past for feigning that he couldn't speak. He had to bring himself up to date.

Upon learning that Kuklo could talk, the man began gesturing wildly in surprise. "How wonderful! You are indeed the great Titan!"

A worshipper... So this man was a heretic who deified and worshipped Titans, a member of the cult that Elena, Kuklo's mother, had joined. Most of the devotees were arrested by the Military Police after she caused the incident fifteen years earlier, but some must have escaped and gone underground.

Kuklo could guess why the believers sought him out. They wanted someone to enshrine. A Titan's son was convenient for the weakened organization since rebuilding it would be easier with one as the group's symbol. Kuklo, however, had no interest whatsoever in the restoration of any group. It was the Titans' fault that he'd been treated like a subhuman in the first place, and helping the believers was out of the question.

Kuklo glared at the man. "Who did you kill?!"

"Security guards, that's all... What of it?" Before Kuklo could breathe a sigh of relief the man added, "As we speak, my fellows are giving them their just retribution."

"…Them?"

"The evil, wicked humans who dared to lock a Titan in a place like this, of course."

"Ngh!!"

With a beastly grunt, Kuklo yanked the chains on his hands and feet with all his might. Thanks to his meticulous preparations over two long years, he tore apart his shackles with utmost ease.

Not having the luxury to savor his newfound freedom, Kuklo rushed in and slammed his fist into the man's face without hesitation. Groaning in pain, the worshipper fell to the ground with his eyes rolled to the back of his head. He'd put up absolutely no signs of a fight, hardly expecting to be struck by the Titan's son.

Kuklo tore off the man's clothes, put them on, and leapt outside. As soon as he did, he was struck by a sideways sheet of rain. He was instantly soaked, but he felt nothing resembling discomfort despite the freezing-cold storm. The sensation was almost a pleasant one as the filth was washed from his body. It surprised Kuklo just how overcome with pure darkness the world around him was. His body nearly melded into the shadows. The decision to exploit the dead of night for his escape was a correct one, but his plans had been ruined by the uninvited guest.

Lightning shot through the sky, illuminating his surroundings. He may have only been in a garden, but the spaciousness of the outside world was overwhelming to Kuklo, for whom ten square meters of emptiness had been everything.

Though he was terribly confused by his range of vision suddenly expanding to dozens of times what it was before, he had no time to waste. He set his sights on the two-story mansion that stood on the grounds. It was clear from the building's size that it had a large number of rooms, but that didn't matter. The shouts, screams, and disorderly noises coming from within did, for among them was a familiar female voice.

She's alive… Kuklo was relieved, but Sharle only drew breath for the moment. Her life would come to an end unless he acted soon.

The mansion's rear door had been left open, and like a banner it flapped back and forth in the storm. It must have been used by the worshippers to break in.

Rather than consider his various options, Kuklo went straight for the door. Freed from its restraints, his body felt even lighter than he'd hoped. He found his momentum hard to control due to his lack of experience. A moment of distraction might send him careening, and so he reserved half of his strength. Even then, his body seemed to move with unbelievable swiftness.

He slid through the rear entrance before he could register the power and freedom he'd gained. As soon as he entered the building's halls, he encountered a man wearing black, probably a believer, but Kuklo struck him down and charged ahead.

The floor plan of the building was unknown to him, but his finely honed senses functioned as a scanning device. He could roughly locate the angry shouts and curses that echoed through the mansion. The faint smell of blood lingering in the air served as handy road signs. Armed with this information, Kuklo stormed through the halls.

Every hallway door had been left wide open. Inside the rooms were people, probably servants, who'd been murdered in their beds. They seemed to have been attacked in their sleep since there were no signs of struggle. Perhaps they never even noticed they were being murdered.

One of the rooms was uniquely extravagant, and inside of it was a giant bed that could easily hold a number of people. Across it lay the remains of Dario, the master of the house.

He is dead… Kuklo glanced at the corpse but felt no emotions in particular, neither hatred nor sadness. He simply took note that someone he knew had kicked the bucket. Dario meant that little to him.

Kuklo spotted what he was looking for just ahead of him. Five believers, each armed with a blade, had cornered Xavi and Sharle at the end of a hall.

I'm not too late... Still, the two were clearly in peril. Xavi had been putting up a fight with his own sword, but he was utterly outnumbered. It was only a matter of time before the attackers' weapons were stained red with blood.

Kuklo had no reason to rescue Xavi, but he needed every bit of help he could get if he wanted to keep Sharle out of harm's way—even if that help came from the despot who had tyrannized his life.

Kuklo's ferocious charge surprised everyone, and they all turned to look at him. Unleashing the power he'd so far kept in check, he swept in like an untamed animal, closing the distance between him and his enemies.

Although the heretics worshipped Titans, they hadn't received any sort of special training. They were too busy quaking in their boots to respond in any adequate way to Kuklo's screaming assault. The black clothes he wore, the same as theirs, must have added to their confusion.

Kuklo pressed in on one of the believers, who stood frozen in place, and slammed his balled fist into his abdomen. The man groaned and sank to the floor. If Kuklo felt no reluctance about killing humans, he'd have stolen the man's blade and finished him off then and there. Thoughtless slaughter was the province of the Titans.

"Kuklo?" Sharle cried in surprise, her eyes wide open. She'd recognized this new intruder.

"What?!" Xavi said, astonished at Sharle's words. "Why are you even here..." Though in shock, he didn't waste this valuable opportunity and cut down a couple of the off-guard believers.

While the tables had been turned, they could not relax until all of the cultists were suppressed. Kuklo sprang toward another and launched a front kick into the torso of his enemy, who stumbled back into a comrade before falling.

"Filthy paupers..." Xavi spat at a writhing believer before backhanding his blade and thrusting it into his chest. Sharle looked away at this cruel, merciless act.

"Why did you kill him?" Kuklo asked.

"Why should I hesitate to kill my enemies?" Xavi replied stone-faced. Then he said, "This is quite a surprise. You can speak."

Though he betrayed amazement, he followed up with a bored snort. He drew his sword from the man's chest.

"Did Sharle teach you these things?" he surmised, glaring at his sister. "I don't know what you were thinking—so you're the ones who brought the cultists down upon us?"

Xavi's grip on the sword hilt tightened. The idea that Kuklo and Sharle were somehow involved appeared to come to him, and his shoulders shook. He seemed ready to turn his blade on them next, and as danger filled the air Sharle turned pale and winced.

"Not Sharle's fault," Kuklo declared, moving toward her. He shielded her behind him, putting her beyond the reach of her brother. Xavi was making no effort to conceal his murderous intent.

"I see it now," Xavi said. The sinister light in his eyes hinted at a crooked interpretation of what had happened. Surveying the scene of the calamity slowly, deliberately, he accused, "Well, at any rate, you are responsible for our current plight. I should have killed you ages ago."

As soon as the words left Xavi's mouth, his blade sliced through the air sideways. Kuklo thought of jumping back, but Sharle was there. He could not dodge to the side, either. No matter which way he went, if he tried to circumvent the attack Sharle would fall in his place to the sword's swipe. Yet he would die unless he did. He swayed back to evade the edge that now came toward his throat, but his range of motion was too limited.

I'm going to be killed... The tip was headed toward his eyes. Kuklo reflexively turned away, but it grazed his right eye. A burning sensation assailed his face as though a heated poker had been pressed against it.

Holding the wound in his right hand, he swiftly moved to make a counterattack and found a target in Xavi's legs. He put all the force he could muster into a roundhouse kick against Xavi's undefended right knee.

"Hrrg!" Xavi lost his balance, having taken the full brunt of a strike that snapped into his leg like a whip.

Kuklo continued his assault, sending a knee into Xavi's chin next. The blow seemed to have caused a concussion; Xavi slumped forward and sank to the floor. It would be a while until he regained consciousness.

"Are you okay? Show me!" Sharle circled around to in front of Kuklo. The moment she saw the wound, her expression clouded.

Kuklo didn't need to be told that his right eye was in terrible shape. It radiated a throbbing pain, and blood, not tears, ran from it, staining red the hand he held over his face. He wasn't so injured that he feared for his life, and he could withstand the pain, but he was worried.

My eye... Whether it was the blood or actual damage to his eyeball, a portion of his vision was gone on the right side. The worst possibility presented itself, but it was no time to dally. He just had to make up for the missing segment with his other senses. Right now he had to leave the estate as soon as he could.

"Sharle! What do we do?"

Perhaps not understanding him, she blinked a few times. "Huh?"

"Dario is gone now. You don't have to escape."

"Right, but there's no place for me in this house anymore... Xavi found out about everything, anyway."

"I see..."

Kuklo took her meaning. Dario's death and the raid by the cultists would cast groundless suspicions on Sharle. He was worried how Xavi would treat her, too. It was easy to picture Xavi acting like another Dario. In other words, there was not a single reason for Sharle to stay home.

"Let's go."

"All right."

Recovering the supplies Sharle had prepared, the two left the house with barely more than the clothes they wore.

The raging storm portended the troubles that lay ahead of them, but heading into it would let them shrug off any and all pursuit.

As if to celebrate the pair's departure, a humongous clap of thunder roared through the air.

CHAPTER TWO

A raid by cultists was nowhere in the escape plans Kuklo had spent every day of the last two years devising. He had come up with every hiccup he could think of and considered countermeasures. In the end, he'd been ambushed by a disaster far outclassing any scenarios in his ironclad plan.

Such perhaps was the Titan's son's destiny—or curse...

Still, the intrusion by the believers was the only unexpected element. Everything else was going as planned.

Kuklo and Sharle headed for Wall Sheena's underground city.

Originally an evacuation shelter in the case of a Titan attack—a special location set up for the privileged classes such as the royal family and individuals in the royal government—the city now had a unique identity as the country's pleasure quarters. It was, in essence, a red light district. It was also Kuklo's hometown; "Titan children" tended to be bought or sold in the underground city, and the sideshow Dario had visited was also located there.

The underground city's population was in the hundreds to the thousands, and its size was indistinct. The city's boundaries were constantly spreading out like a net as its population grew. It was likely that no one person had an accurate grasp of the entirety of the underground city's structure. None tried to know or fancied to create a map. The name of anyone who undertook such a project would surely be added to the list of missing persons by the next day.

The place was a hotbed of crime of all stripes. While it would normally be targeted for crackdowns and arrests, its existence was tolerated thanks to the pleasures it offered the wealthy. As the roster of clients and patrons included the keepers of the very laws it broke, the city's character could be said to be as underground as its location. The residents knew more than a few of the visitors' secrets, and a roundup would cause troubles for a host of individuals. All of this led Kuklo and Sharle to choose the underground city as their hiding place. Its inhabitants, who had come there for a multitude of reasons, didn't scrutinize others' pasts in exchange for not revealing their own. So it was that Kuklo and Sharle avoided inviting undue suspicion despite having appeared out of nowhere.

One thing that was essential to living in the underground city was hard currency. Simple coins, these were spheres of metal the size of the tip of a pinky that bore the seal of the factory city and nothing more. While they were made of low-quality steel, a byproduct of the Iron Bamboo refinement process, thanks to their provenance they were undeniably hard and difficult to forge, and thus widely circulated.

Sharle had readied about five hundred of these coins as their war chest. One was enough to feed an average family for a day, meaning they were well funded. Aside, of course, from daily living expenses, the coins also paid for treatment for Kuklo's eye. Ultimately, his right eye was useless and had to be surgically removed. Half of their holdings went to an unlicensed doctor for his services.

***

To Kuklo, life in the underground city was true freedom. No shackles restricted his movements, and no rascal abused him. Now he lived in a world where he made all of his own decisions, and there was no greater joy. Still, this proved confusing to him. Though he had won liberty, he could not figure out what to do with it.

While Kuklo wrestled with his freedom, Sharle, the once-caged princess, naturally struggled with the burden of subsisting in the underground city. All her life she had left maids to perform the most basic of daily tasks, leaving her a well-bred but utterly inexperienced lady in practical matters.

While the two stood in contrast, Sharle was the first to adapt. This was not because her gender made her more adaptable but simply due to her wealth of life experiences. Compared to Kuklo's, that is.

***

The two made a shabby shack of a room their home in the underground city. It was cramped, only half the size of Kuklo's shed. A good half of the room was taken up by the beds, while the other half was occupied by a table and other furniture.

"Hup!" Waking from a shallow sleep, Kuklo raised his body. He moved his limbs, checking how he felt, then put his hand over his now-darkened right eye. "Kuklops, eh…"

It was half a year ago that he'd tumbled into the underground city to have his eye extracted. He suffered from poor health for a long time after the procedure, but he had finally recovered.

However, he was not exactly satisfied with his post-surgery appearance. He was now one-eyed and a Titan's son, or in other words, a Cyclops.

Adjusting his appearance in front of a mirror was not something Kuklo was used to doing, but since Sharle lived with him, they did at least have a hand mirror in the room. He would occasionally see himself while walking the city too. While he couldn't but feel conscious of the Titan's son, only he seemed to care. Word of him was not widespread in society as it turned out.

Sharle was nowhere to be found in the room, and her bed had already grown cold. Perhaps she had gone out shopping.

I need to do something, too…

The idle time Kuklo spent in the underground city was a true luxury to him. He quite liked it. He had also taken a liking to keeping up his personal appearance, and though clothes once felt foreign on his body, he was beginning to get used to them. A soft bed still didn't suit him and he frequently slept on the floor, but he did feel as though he was now able to act in a more human way. His ability to communicate was growing, too, as he began to speak to more people than Sharle.

But I'm still tied down.

Kuklo focused on his wrists. While he had removed his shackles soon after coming to the underground city, he yet felt them vividly, to the point of hearing chains clang. His body was now free, but his mind was still a prisoner to the Titans. His unresolved feelings about them twisted around his body as unseen chains as it were.

I have to meet a Titan.

It was the only way to break the bonds of fate. It was his goal from the time he decided to escape, but his physical condition had held him back. That concern out of the way, he felt that the time had come to face a Titan so he could be truly free.

Fortunately for Kuklo, there were talks of expeditions being resumed. An unconfirmed rumor was lately the talk of the underground city: a newly reformed Survey Corps, commanded by Carlo Piquer, would survey the area beyond the walls.

The source of this rumor was unknown, and its veracity uncertain, but this was the underground city. A rumor probably meant that someone in the military or the royal government had flapped his mouth. There was other evidence suggesting the Survey Corps might be reformed. A plot had brought about the downfall of the conservative faction's vanguard, Bruno Baumeister, and the reformers had made a political comeback.

Sharle was right to leave home.

Even if the raid by the cultists had never happened, Sharle would have ended up unhappy. Dario's choice of the Baumeister family had been off the mark. Then again, perhaps Dario's judgment had been off the mark from the moment he purchased Kuklo.

In any case, an excellent chance to encounter a Titan had offered itself. The only problem was that there were extremely few ways of leaving the walls. Climb over Wall Maria, or slip through the gate— but climbing over was essentially impossible. Even if Kuklo managed to elude the Garrison's watchful gaze to reach the top, its fifty-meter height ruled out a safe descent, and touching down served no purpose if he couldn't make it back.

In other words, sneaking through the gate was his only option.

The Survey Corps' resumption of expeditions after fifteen years was like a godsend to Kuklo. If he could find some way to tag along, he could stroll straight through the main gate—though his way would have to be illegal… Moreover, he might just get eaten by a Titan, but surely the Survey Corps didn't mean to be slaughtered.

One thing that troubled Kuklo was that the Survey Corps had gone so long without actual experience on the battlefield. Even if they did have the know-how, applying it when it mattered was a wholly different issue. Still, they had the confidence to embark on an expedition, so perhaps his worries were misplaced.

The problem is…

As Kuklo scratched his head wildly, Sharle returned to the room holding a large bag. She grinned at him, then briskly began unpacking her purchases. She had grown handy at housework, her spoiled ways gone without a trace.

"I heard something about my brother…" Having tidied up, Sharle sat on the edge of her bed, which doubled as a chair. "It sounds like he joined the Training Corps like he planned."

"Where did you hear that?"

"An information dealer."

Kuklo nodded. "I see. Xavi would make a good soldier."

"I agree."

In light of his callousness—he'd unflinchingly skewered a believer—there were few other paths for him to take. The question was what Xavi would do next. As long as he was in the Training Corps, he was unlikely to meddle with Kuklo's or Sharle's affairs. But having been knocked out by Kuklo, Xavi's pride had to be in tatters. It had done Kuklo good to avenge his months of resentment, but Xavi was no doubt stuck with feelings of rage. The outrages he'd try to perpetrate if they ever met again weren't hard to imagine. Then again, they'd probably never meet...

What worried Kuklo and Sharle more than Xavi's actions were those of the Military Police Brigade. Between the death of Dario, a man close to the royal government, and the raid by Titan-worshipping cultists, there was more than enough reason for the Brigade to claim the case.

"I just hope they give up soon..."

Kuklo felt the same way, but the Military Police would probably not give up easily with the believers involved. Standing above the Survey Corps and the Garrison, the Brigade was comprised of around a thousand members and was responsible for administering and overseeing the military as well as commanding the police and fire duties in each town. There was yet another side to the group. It acted as a secret police that exposed wrongdoing within the military and by antiestablishment organizations. Not only did they have power in military affairs, their authority stretched into internal politics. In other words, the Military Police were the elite among the elite, and they would never allow any entity that threatened the security of the country to run amok.

Fifteen years ago, none other than the Brigade had investigated the breaching incident and driven the believers' organization to near-extinction. That a Titan's son had occasioned the raid on the Inocencio home must have been established before long. It was a thorny situation where Kuklo was liable to be treated as the culprit just for being the Titan's son.

While running from the scene had been the right choice, it only fanned suspicion, especially because he'd left with Sharle.

There was much reason to feel anxious, but the problem Kuklo had to solve for the time being was a separate one.

"I'm thinking of going to Shiganshina District."

As soon as the words left Kuklo's mouth, Sharle froze in place. Then she let out a long sigh. "I was wondering if you'd say that... You want to see a Titan, right?"

"So you'd figured it out."

"It wasn't hard to notice."

"Are you against it, Sharle?"

"Of course I am." She put her hands on her hips and glared at Kuklo. "If I told you not to go, would you give up?"

"Well…"

"Then it doesn't matter if I'm for or against it."

Kuklo scratched his head. "Will you come, too?"

"Would you take no for an answer?"

Kuklo scratched his head again.

That means saying goodbye to this place… While Kuklo had never felt attached to possessions or places, this was the first time he had a space he could call his own. The thought of clearing out gave him pause.

Not only that, staying in the underground city meant his safety was assured. There was no need to defy danger and leave. He could tell, though, that until he saw a Titan for himself, the desire would linger in him. If he wanted to put a quick end to the problem, he had to make contact.

What do I want to do by meeting a Titan? He didn't think that communication was possible with a Titan. His being a "Titan's son" didn't mean they'd see him as one of their own. What he himself might think or do upon encountering a Titan wasn't something he felt he could predict. *I'll find out soon enough.*

The talk of restarting expeditions was just a rumor. It seemed to be a reliable one, whose authenticity would be verified soon, but that did not mean today or tomorrow.

We can leave the room after that, Kuklo persuaded himself. Then, he began to kick around his plan to meet a Titan.

***

A month after Kuklo first heard the whispers of expeditions being resumed, the rumor was proven true, making his timetable clear. In a week, the Survey Corps would leave Shiganshina District's main gate early in the morning, then scout outside the wall for a few hours. The objective of the survey was not made public, but considering the fifteen-year hiatus, it was unlikely that they'd start exploring in earnest from the outset. At most, they would be observing the surrounding area.

After moving out of their room, Kuklo and Sharle hitched a ride on a carriage with a merchant who said he planned to go to Shiganshina on business. Naturally, the ride came at a cost. They could only get on if they handed over steel coins for the fare and for using the title of trader. Without the latter, their stories would not check out during any inspections, and they needed to avoid any conflicts they could.

Fortunately, they gained the merchant's trust easily. All they needed to make his breed a superb, loyal partner was a handful of coins. Of course, that also meant their relationship would last only as long as their tender did.

***

After leaving the underground city, Kuklo and Sharle stayed a night in Trost District, the halfway point to their destination, then arrived in Shiganshina District the next afternoon.

Shiganshina District was the town at the southernmost edge of Wall Maria. With a population a little over forty thousand, it was the largest in the country and important both militarily and politically— factors that conceivably underlay the calamity fifteen years ago. On top of it all, it was the place where Kuklo was born.

While a Titan had been allowed in, that was firmly in the past. No signs of damage could be found around the place, and none of the citizens seemed to live in terror of the Titans who were still a menace to humanity. Since the Survey Corps had proven they could be defeated, fears were toned down to a more rational level.

Shiganshina District was stirring with talk of the first expedition in fifteen years, and the mood was already celebratory. Of course the citizens were excited—there was hope that the Titans might be driven away, and in that event, humanity could finally move into the outside world.

"Wow…"

Kuklo was slack-jawed as he stared at the towering Wall Maria. He knew that it was fifty meters tall, and he'd already seen Wall Sheena and Wall Rose from the carriage, but the difference in impression between seeing them from afar and up close was like day and night. He almost felt like prostrating himself before it.

Scaling the wall would be an absolutely impossible feat. A single glance revealed the hilarity of the wishful scenarios he'd concocted. A human hoping to scale the wall couldn't do so without the Equipment, which allowed for vertical movement. There were records that its creator, Angel Aaltonen, had wielded it to return alive from the other side of the wall.

If Kuklo had the Equipment, he could easily surmount the wall and forget about tagging along on the Survey Corps' expedition. Yet it could be found for sale nowhere, not even the black markets, nor were there any rumors of its continued production. If it had been developed for use on the battlefield, there were no traces of that fact, either. Perhaps it had been put on hold, but there was no reason for its development to be halted.

Kuklo scratched his head, shifted his gaze to the gates, and said, "Even the gate is huge."

"It's over ten meters on its own," concurred Sharle.

"So Mammon came through this gate…"

The Titan that had eaten Kuklo's mother and turned Shiganshina District into a smoldering plain was also ten meters in height, just as tall as the main gate. That was enough to make it clear how ghastly the Titans were.

"They're monsters."

"Yes…" Sharle agreed.

"What are Titans like?"

"Human-shaped beasts. It's like they were plucked straight out of a nightmare…" Perhaps recalling what the Titans looked like, Sharle shivered and said, "Kuklo? Do you really have to go outside the wall?"

Kuklo shifted his eyes away from the main gate to look at Sharle, who stood next to him.

He could tell from the fearful color she'd turned that the experience must have been truly terrifying. Sharle clearly had a strong antipathy for the Titans. After all, she had once come to kill Kuklo, the Titan's son. That they were so abominable it drove her to attempt murder was proof of their monstrosity, but Kuklo still couldn't form a mental image of a Titan. It was as though he was trying to see one through a pane of clouded glass.

"It's okay. I will be back right away." Kuklo smiled as he put his hand on Sharle's shoulder, but it wasn't enough to dispel her anxiety. "Let's move," he changed the topic, but as soon as he spoke, he noticed the sound of distant footfalls.

He stared at Wall Maria with a frown on his face.

"Was that…"

"Is something wrong, Kuklo?"

"I hear footsteps."

They were surrounded by noise, but he could hear the footfalls coming from beyond the wall. Which must mean—

A Titan…

But the sound was so faint that even Kuklo barely registered it. Sharle, whose hearing failed to pick it up, repeatedly angled her head, but it was steadily closing in on the town.

With every step the Titan took, the ground shook slightly. It was clear that the specimen responsible for the footsteps was a gigantic creature.

The moment Sharle made to strain her ears, a thunderous roar tore through the sky overhead. The air shook, and she reflexively cowered. Her legs gave out and she plopped down on the ground.

Kuklo looked up at the sky, but he could not espy any thunderclouds. In fact, the sky was utterly clear, with not a single cloud in sight. No sign of rain, either—the only thing of note was a slightly burnt smell that lingered in the air.

"The cannons...sure are loud. That was my first time hearing them."

When Kuklo heard Sharle's explanation, it made sense to him. It was the smell of gunpowder that had stimulated his nose.

He sighed and reached his hand out toward Sharle, who still sat on the ground.

***

The night before the expedition.

The mood in Shiganshina District was a lively one as though a festival was taking place. The avenue that ran from north to south through the center of town was jammed full of people, and their numbers were only increasing.

The majority of them were not Shiganshina citizens but sightseers from around the country there to get a glimpse of the expedition. In other words, the activity in the city was a representation of people's high hopes for the Survey Corps. It might be said that the fifteen-year freeze had been a Dark Age for humanity.

"This has gotten annoying," Kuklo muttered sternly as he walked through the avenue with Sharle. Soldiers had been stationed at key points in order to keep a watchful eye. The majority of them were members of the Garrison, but some Military Police Brigade personnel could be spotted here and there, the signature unicorn emblems on their back. It was inconvenient for Kuklo.

The wound suffered by his right eye made him stand out, but

going out of the way to hide it would only draw more attention to him. He had to mind the soldiers' movements but couldn't seem so preoccupied as to arouse suspicion.

An unusually large force had been deployed to Shiganshina District because military brass and royal government officials were headed there. In essence, the troops were serving as bodyguards.

"It doesn't seem like they would have anything to do with us," observed Sharle.

"They might remember. I have my scar, too."

"It's dark, you won't stand out."

Sharle took a look at Kuklo and nodded to confirm that nothing was amiss.

Eventually, the Survey Corps barracks appeared in front of them. It seemed as though the preparations for the expedition were already complete. Light filtered through from the windows, but barely any soldiers were walking around. A number of troops, grunts from the look of it, serviced a wagon on the premises, but that was all. It was most likely the carriage to be used by the cargo team the next day during the expedition.

Maybe I can use it. Kuklo reviewed the wagon's specs surreptitiously. A canopy made it impossible to see inside, but he assumed it was full of supplies, food, and medicine. It was an ideal vehicle to stow away on. If he could disappear into the cargo, getting outside the wall would be easy. The expedition might find out when they resupplied, but he could worry about that if and when it happened. Just as long as he could get past the wall.

Given Kuklo's simple goal to come into contact with a Titan, the existence of a cargo team was fortunate. Consisting of non-combat troops and managing a large amount of supplies, such units generally stayed toward the back of formations. It went without saying that they did not participate in battles. Moreover, they were in a position to be protected by other soldiers and were thus relatively safe. Of course, their opponents were Titans so there was no telling until the game was on.

"That might work out," Kuklo said.

"Oh. That's good."

Sharle's anxious, dissatisfied expression betrayed that she wasn't convinced. She let out a deep sigh.

"Tomorrow looks like it's going to be a long day," she lamented.

"Do you want to get dinner, then?"

"A really long day…" Sharle groaned, placing her hand on her forehead.

***

The moon's dim rays lit the inn room. In the dead of night all was enveloped by stillness. It was so quiet the entire town seemed asleep.

Three hours until dawn. Only the soldiers on watch atop Wall Maria or patrolling the town would be awake.

Aside from us, of course.

With a wry smile, Kuklo stepped toward the window and took a careful look outside. Following his lead, Sharle also peeked at the darkened world.

Hardly anyone was out—unsurprising, considering the hour. Soldiers occasionally walked by on patrol, lanterns in hand, but did not seem to be on alert. While more troops than usual were around because of the big event, moving around undetected seemed feasible under the cover of night.

The Military Police Brigade's movements were worrisome, but they were there to protect persons of interest, not to search for Kuklo. Bumping into a member of the Brigade on the street at night would be no laughing matter, but if they were on special guard duty, encountering any was unlikely. The elite would never be assigned a task as menial as patrolling.

"Are you going?"

"Yes." Kuklo nodded and calmly headed toward the exit. He had no gear or supplies to speak of. Only his body.

"Sure you want to go empty-handed?"

"No problem."

Sharle shrugged her shoulders. "Isn't it a bit brash of you to leave all the preparations to the Survey Corps?"

Everything needed for an expedition—weapons, food, medical supplies, and more—would be loaded into the wagon. Since the professionals could be counted on to do their jobs to perfection, Kuklo didn't have to draw on his non-existent expertise.

"Please, at least take this," Sharle said, holding out a small, familiar knife.

"Is this from when you—"

"It's my good luck charm. It might just weigh you down, but…"

"For good luck?"

"That, and I think you'll need it to survive."

"Survive…"

Kuklo took the knife. He promptly drew it an inch out of its sheath to reveal a silvery-white blade. It seemed to have kept well, as he could see no rust on its sharp edge. While not ideal for combat, it would surely come in handy for miscellaneous tasks. Satisfied, Kuklo sheathed the knife and placed it on his waist.

"It's time for me to go."

"I'll be here, waiting."

"I will be back by noon."

Kuklo gently opened the door. As soon as he did, a blast of freezing air surged toward him, but it did nothing to wither his spirit. He braced himself, then went forth into the darkness.

***

Once he left the inn, Kuklo dashed through the dark night like a wild animal. Nothing impeded his movements. While there were street lamps, they were few and far between and gave off little light,

allowing Kuklo to stay hidden. The lamps used gas from Iceburst Stones as fuel, but their count was limited. Gas lanterns, widespread within Wall Sheena, were only implemented on an experimental basis in Shiganshina District.

While Kuklo was concerned about encountering soldiers, all he had to do to avoid them was listen to their footsteps. Even if he ran into one, it would be easy to escape into the shadows.

Like the rest of the sleeping city, the Survey Corps barracks was still quiet. The few zealous corpsmen who'd begun warming up in preparation for the expedition didn't deter him from sneaking in. Even as the soldiers worked up a sweat notwithstanding the intense cold, Kuklo closed in on the covered wagon within the premises. The area around the carriage was deserted, and horses had yet to be attached, making his approach an easy one.

Kuklo peeled back the canopy and examined the wagon's interior. All the cargo he'd expected to see was packed tightly inside, including weapons, explosives, and food. There was only so much space to hide in, but it sufficed for smuggling himself out. Not only would he be protected from the cold, he would have food. On top of that, he was being taken to his destination at no cost, so there was nothing to complain about. The tradeoff was the high risk the plan involved. Naturally, the Survey Corps had not granted him permission to stow away with them. If they found him, he was certain to get jail time. In the worst case, he might even be executed. The walls were the cornerstones of the enclosed cities, and anyone trespassing through them was subject to severe punishment.

As Kuklo pushed his body through the gaps in the cargo, he quickly pulled out some rations. He found a wide variety of chow, from jerky and cheese to snack bars and dried fruit. Kuklo tried a bite of the dried fruit. A concentrated sweetness and aroma spread through his mouth.

Delicious… Kuklo's palate was not so cultivated that he could describe the finer points of flavors, but he could at least tell whether or not something tasted good. Then again, just about anything did compared to insects.

***

Two hours after Kuklo snuck into the carriage, the expedition was ready to go. The cheers would have drowned out any cockcrows, so he couldn't tell whether morning had come from where he hid in the canvas-topped wagon. Still, he could tell from the rumbling in his stomach and the expectant roar of the crowd that the Survey Corps was counting down the minutes and seconds to departure.

So far, everything had gone the way Kuklo had planned. It was not a terribly complicated course of action, and the smooth going could be chalked up to simple good luck. While there was a chance that he'd be discovered before they left, the cargo team only conducted a cursory check of their supplies and failed to spot him. The idea of someone stealing a ride from them must have seemed nearly beyond the realm of possibility.

Kuklo took out the knife that hung on his hip and put its point to the canvas. The blade was surprisingly sharp and pricked the thick cloth with ease. Kuklo used this peephole to take a look outside. The wagon where he hid sat on the avenue on standby. He also glimpsed huge crowds on the roadside.

Where's Sharle... He scrutinized his limited field of vision, but in the end he didn't find her. He knew her, though. She watched over him from somewhere.

I must return as quickly as I can. That was the only way to put Sharle at ease again. The Survey Corps' first expedition in fifteen years would be over in a matter of hours, but her heart would be forlorn until the moment he returned.

Sharle had no one she could depend on, Kuklo had no family, and they needed each other. Their world was a hard one to live in all alone, and he couldn't leave Sharle to fend against it on her own.

Kuklo knew that what he was doing was utterly selfish. Yet, in order to close the book on his life as a Titan's son and start over as a human, he had to feel certain.

For me… The alias of "Titan's son" would continue to haunt him until his death unless he faced the beings responsible for ruining his life head-on and broke free of them.

He was almost there, though. While the Survey Corps' goals were unclear, there was a good chance that a Titan would emerge within the first hour. A no show was quite possible, but Kuklo had faith.

The Titans must be starved, too. Of course a group of humans would be noticed. It was fifteen years since the Titans last feasted on their prey. Were it Kuklo, tempted by the smell of food he would make a beeline to it.

He was biting into jerky, his thoughts meandering, when the crowd's cheers intensified.

It's finally time… Despite the likelihood of coming face to face with a Titan, Kuklo didn't feel particularly nervous, even though he knew quite well that they were man-eating monsters. Perhaps, having been called "Titan's son" for so long, his instincts were lulled by a sense of familiarity.

"Move out!!" a robust male voice cut through the din. Horses neighed in response.

The expedition was on.

***

A roar of excited voices blanketed the avenue, crowds of onlookers, packed onto the sidewalks, attempting to get a look at the valiant Survey Corps. Over a thousand people were gathered. Though they stood in the frigid dawn air, the heat they emitted kept them from feeling cold. In fact, they were working up a sweat from all of their pushing and shoving.

Sharle had slipped into the crowd to watch over the expedition.

To be more exact, she was there to see Kuklo off on his clandestine journey to the world outside the wall. True, it didn't feel like much of a sendoff with him hidden under the canvas.

This is the first time I've seen them, but they really are amazing.

Commander Carlo Piquer led the Survey Corps' double-file formation, the sight of which could only be called spectacular.

Every soldier there was a giant of a man, and their eyes seemed to reflect their powerful wills. While they were about to head to a no man's land crawling with Titans, their faces were free of any signs of fear. It would not have been a stretch to call them humanity's strongest. Compared to them, recruits like her brother in the Training Corps were like children.

He'll be all right…won't he? It was clear on first sight that Survey Corps soldiers were just as tough as rumored. Yet even this failed to erase the anxiety spreading in Sharle's heart. The cargo team was protected by soldiers and had a better chance of returning alive than other troops, but it was merely less risky than standing on the front lines. Going beyond the walls meant never being totally safe.

I can't help but feel he shouldn't have gone, Sharle succumbed to regret as the Survey Corps headed down the avenue, but it was too late. All she could do now was pray for Kuklo's safe return.

While Sharle sighed, the Survey Corps boldly made their way through the front gates. As soon as the maneuver was complete—a busy one, with only a few minutes passing since Carlo's initial order—the gates were summarily shut. Brisk action must have been the standing order since opening them involved great risk. None of the soldiers had made any efforts to respond to the people's cheers.

And now, he won't be back for hours… If things went perfectly, Kuklo would be back in time for lunch. *I doubt it'll go that well, though…*

Now with nothing to watch, the onlookers who had packed the sidewalks quickly dwindled in number. With a few hours until the Survey Corps' return, they seemed to all have their own plans for the time being. Some were staying in order to secure front-row seats for the triumphant return, but among them were also the kin—Sharle could tell by their troubled expressions—of Survey Corps members.

The look on my face now…must be very similar.

Sharle sighed. She felt like speaking to the soldiers' families but thought the better of it and walked away. Making contact with people close to the corps could lead to all sorts of trouble, and staying on the sidewalk was like daring the Military Police Brigade to find her.

***

The world outside the walls was even more desolate than imagined. The soil was completely unworked and truly barren. A dreary landscape that looked like a burnt-out field stretched as far as the eye could see. While some vegetation grew on the rust-colored earth, it could by no means be called fertile, and it would take many years of cultivation to transform it into cropland.

Humans were said to have lived there until the Titans robbed them of their territory, but there was no visual evidence to suggest that. Either the Titans had wreaked havoc on the area, or time had taken its toll—or perhaps, a combination of the two had turned it into a wasteland.

Kuklo looked at the outside world through his peephole, but nothing caught his attention.

We haven't seen any Titans… Three hours after leaving Shiganshina District, he'd seen only small animals and hadn't encountered his all-important foes. No surveys had been conducted on the number of Titans in existence. While it was said they numbered in the hundreds or thousands, perhaps there weren't that many in reality.

Though Kuklo couldn't help but feel disappointed, a gang of Titans pressing in would pose a problem of its own. The soldiers would have a difficult time dealing with them.

To begin with, the Survey Corps didn't seem interested in fighting them. The soldiers' gear hardly suggested any eagerness to take on the

Titans: cloaks and hoods to deal with the cold, and not much else. The only weapons they carried were the swords on their waists and carbines. Kuklo saw no signs of the vital Equipment with them, nor anything resembling it inside the carriage.

They must have not been out to slay a Titan. Maybe the idea was to avoid combat for their first expedition in years. Even then, it was no reason not to carry the Equipment. Considering its capabilities and past result, it should have been standard-issue.

If we can't meet them this time, then…

Kuklo imagined his worst-case scenario as he played with a pistol he'd pilfered from the cargo. It was a possibility he couldn't rule out, but he couldn't return empty-handed after taking on this risk and venturing outside the walls. He doubted that his plan to smuggle himself along would work twice. He had to figure out a way to settle things during the course of this expedition. It was also unlikely that Sharle would permit another foray.

A wagon wheel seemed to hit a rock the moment Kuklo sighed, and the carriage hopped. Its suspension cushioned the impact, but Kuklo's body was hoisted into the air.

It happened as he reacted to keep his posture. He'd had a finger on the gun's trigger, and he now squeezed it. Just as he realized his folly, the muzzle spewed flames and ejected a shot that punched an air hole in the ceiling.

Oops… Regret would do him no good, though. He had to prepare for what was to come. *What do I do?*

The carriage came to a sudden halt, and he could tell the march had been interrupted. It was only a matter of time before soldiers came to examine the cargo.

Should I fight them? Upwards of eighty soldiers were taking part in the expedition. Challenging the burly Survey Corps members and defeating them was an unworkable plan. If he did fight back, he'd be beaten down in a matter of moments.

Do I run? But Kuklo was beyond the walls. Even if he managed to steal a warhorse to flee and shook off the soldiers, it would be extreme-ly difficult to return to Sharle alive. Sure, he'd probably encounter a Titan—but the point wasn't to get captured and eaten.

Under the circumstances, he could only prepare for the worst. If he couldn't fight or run, he had to meekly reveal himself. Steeling his resolve, Kuklo peeled away the canvas and stepped outside before the soldiers could check the cargo.

No amount of strategizing changed the fact that he was going to get caught. In that case, surrendering honorably gave a better impres-sion, and if he was going to be arrested, he wanted to get to see a Titan no matter what.

Maybe I'll ask the commander… All too bold of him, but he could at least try.

As Kuklo exited the carriage, he could hear surprised voices com-ing from the soldiers. The possibility of someone hiding inside the cart must never have entered their minds. A stowaway was unheard of. Other than Kuklo, about the only other people who desired to go outside the walls were the cultists.

The soldiers were only taken aback by the strange interloper for a moment, after which the corps promptly moved to apprehend Kuklo. Four men assigned themselves the task, surrounding him and creep-ing forward. They were going to use brute force to subdue him.

"I wish to see the commander," Kuklo declared, but the soldiers' mouths seemed sewn shut and did not so much as twitch. All the men did was inch closer. Tying up the insolent citizen who'd dare stow away on an expedition seemed to be the only thing on their minds. Understandable, but Kuklo wasn't ready to oblige. That meant he had only one option.

I must find him myself. He bent forward at an extreme angle, kicked the ground, and leapt forward, relying on his animal agility to slip through the soldiers who threw themselves at him.

They must not have expected him to resist. Their log-like arms coming up empty, the soldiers fell forward and lost sight of their target. While no match in terms of physique or brawn, Kuklo's move-ments were explosive enough to draw yelps of surprise from the men.

"I must speak to your leader!" Kuklo cried, dashing off toward the front of the group.

It was a hundred meters or so from the cargo team in the back to the head of the pack. If he kept running, he would eventually find the commander, but the soldiers were not going to sit and watch as he did so. A number of them already blocked his path, while from behind the quartet he'd just sidestepped chased after him.

Slipping through the hands of the corpsmen trying to catch him, he made sport of them, tripping them when he saw an opening. Though he had no chance of winning a fight, the nimble Kuklo had the advantage as long as he stuck to fleeing.

He was, however, up against professional combatants. They wouldn't let an amateur grief them for long. The soldiers were grad-ually closing in on him, and before Kuklo knew, one had raised his horsewhip atop his mount.

No sooner than Kuklo thought *yikes*, a sharp pain ran down his back, but he grit his teeth, braced his legs, and took it. He was only able to bear the faint-inducing blow thanks to having endured worse on a daily basis. That didn't change the fact that it hurt. He halted, and burly soldiers flanked him.

"Shit…" Kuklo cursed, but he had no strength left to fight back.

A towering man spurred his mount and approached. He looked to be in his early thirties and had deeply chiseled features. He cut quite a manly figure, his aura that of a wild beast in human clothing between the sharp glint in his eyes and the vitality his body exuded.

This must be Carlo Piquer…

The commander of the Survey Corps went by that name. His father, Jorge Piquer, was the former commander and the hero who proved that Titans could be defeated.

Taking off his hood, Carlo turned a pinning gaze on Kuklo and questioned him: "Why did you sneak onto the wagon?"

"I wanted to see a Titan," Kuklo answered.

"For what reason?"

"I just wanted to see one."

"Are you a cultist?"

"Don't compare me to them."

"But you must have your reasons." Apparently satisfied, Carlo looked Kuklo over and asked, "What will you do when you see it?"

"Nothing…"

"You'll do nothing?"

Kuklo nodded in reply.

"So your only purpose is to see a Titan."

"That's what I said."

"I am under no obligation to accede to your demand." He was right. The conversation was nothing more than a waste of time for both the Survey Corps and its commander.

"What will happen to me?" Kuklo wanted to know.

"We can figure that out if we return safely. You're going to stay out of our way and not cause any trouble for us until then, though."

"I've kept well out of your way."

"Aren't you a glib one," Carlo snorted. Then he looked upward.

Kuklo found himself doing the same, and his eye met a trail of green smoke signaling across the blue sky. Evidently, what Kuklo had misfired was a flare, the gun having been loaded with a "Green Star."

"Looks like you went ahead and sent the message yourself."

A Green Star, used to indicate an anomaly, accurately described their status.

"Tell me… What is your name?"

"I—"

A moment before Kuklo could speak his name, he detected a faint sound.

Again… A chill shot through his spine. It wasn't the first time he'd heard it. In fact, the memory was still fresh in his mind from when he stood in front of Wall Maria the other day.

It was the sound of footsteps.

They seemed to come from the north, opposite from where the Survey Corps was headed. Kuklo turned to look north, but all he could make out through the clouds of dust was the hazy form of Wall Maria, the fortress city's symbol. Yet the footfalls grew rapidly louder as though to assert their presence.

"A Titan is coming…"

"What?" Carlo had caught Kuklo's muttered words but looked dubious.

"It knows we're here."

The distant roar of the footsteps approached, unwavering.

Was it drawn by the flare I fired? It was not known what the Titans reacted to, but a Green Star exploding overhead could easily command their attention.

In a way, Kuklo was fortunate. He'd risked leaving the walls in order to meet a Titan, so this was exactly what he wanted. On the other hand, the trusted Survey Corps being too preoccupied with him to register the situation didn't do. He needed them to transport him back to town.

Within mere moments, the Titan's footfalls had grown closer. A dim, human-like outline was now visible in the distance.

"A Titan's coming."

"Why do you say that?"

"I hear footsteps. I've heard them before."

"Heard them before?" Carlo sounded suspicious, not seeing how, but he quickly modified his line of questioning. "Which way?"

As Kuklo pointed north with his chin, Carlo, hardly convinced, brought out his binoculars and checked to the north.

Apparently having caught sight of the enemy, Carlo's face grew grimmer by the second. "That looks like—Ogre…"

He was not the only one to react. Kuklo, the first to recognize the Titan's approach, wore a frozen look, his eye wide open. His body shook. The reason was plain and simple. "It's a monster…"

The Titan was still a few kilometers away, its figure blurred like an object in the summer haze, but even then its size was extraordinary, gigantic. That should have gone without saying, but this attacking Titan was far larger than Kuklo had imagined. He realized that all of the information he'd gathered from books had only given him the most basic of understandings. If a picture was ever worth a thousand words, this was when. He couldn't but think that he hadn't asked for *that*.

The Titan charged toward them forcefully, kicking up clouds of dust as it ran. It was a little over ten meters in height. By human standards, it looked like a skinny male around twenty years old. It beamed with joy, perhaps because its first meal in fifteen years had arrived. Despite its gigantic frame, it moved with such nimble steps that it almost seemed ready to take off skipping. It was rushing in at an astonishing speed, fast enough to rival a horse.

It was humanity's dearest wish to drive away the Titans, to regain the world the monsters had stolen. Yet human hands seemed completely powerless against the huge horror that closed in on them. Seeing it, one wondered if the stories of a Titan being defeated weren't some sort of misunderstanding.

We're bugs... Kuklo vividly remembered his days in chains. *I'm the same as a bug in a cage...*

It was only a difference in scale. Humans were like dishes lining a table to the Titans. All that puny humanity could do was wait patiently to be shoveled into a Titan's stomach.

"Don't just stand there! Run!!"

Kuklo's thoughts were snapped off by Carlo's bellowed command. By the time Kuklo noticed, the soldiers flanking him were gone, and the Survey Corps was assuming an arrow formation in preparation for retreat. They seemed to be planning to charge straight through.

That they did not have a moment to spare was clear from the surging form that was almost upon them. The footsteps that had sounded like distant thunder were now like the roaring cracks of a storm, and the Titan looked as imposing as Wall Maria itself. Its wicked pressure threatened to crush Kuklo's spirit and to force him to his knees.

Pounding some life into his chattering knees with his fists, he ran and hopped into the covered wagon at the back of the formation.

"Retreat!!"

At Carlo's order, the corps began to advance with the force of an unleashed arrow. They must have undergone extensive training in preparation for this expedition. Their immaculately ordered movements resembled a single living being's.

"Damn it!" Kuklo spat and inspected a few weapons in the cargo, carbines and explosives. His safety assured so long as he stayed with the cargo team? It was the kind of pipe dream thought up by someone with no real combat experience.

Now that he'd seen a Titan with his own eye, he understood.

I am not a Titan.

The confirmation, that he was not a Titan's son, meant he'd accomplished his goal. But in exchange, his life was now in danger. Mortal danger.

Kuklo sliced through the canvas with his knife and tore it off with all his strength. When he did, gusts came at him from the front. The pressure contorted his face and he found it hard to breathe, so violent was the wind. Kuklo used one arm as a shield and turned a defiant gaze forward. The Titan, about five hundred meters in front of them, maintained its unwavering, nimble sprint.

The soldiers at the tip of the arrow formation drew their short swords. As though sure of their chances, they charged the enemy without a moment's hesitation.

The Titan responded with a swing of its mighty arm, but the soldiers skillfully maneuvered their warhorses around it, swinging their swords as they passed. Due to the size difference, however, their attacks were concentrated below its knees. Its medulla, known to be the Titans' weakness, remained completely untouched.

But the commander didn't seem to be trying to take out their foe. With its legs chopped to pieces, walking looked to have become difficult for the Titan, and its mad rush interrupted, it staggered and fell on one knee. Taking advantage of this opportunity, the troops began to rush past the Titan's side, the wagon and its stowaway bringing up the rear.

Opening his eye, Kuklo imprinted the image of the Titan onto his mind. *It's a monster...* He did not think this only because of its immense size, which defied the laws of nature. Its recuperative abilities were extraordinary, too. Some sort of metabolic reaction seemed to have been triggered, and steam erupted from the sword wounds the soldiers had inflicted, shutting them right away. It might begin to move again at any moment.

There was no doubting that the Titans were absurd monsters. If the soldiers were able to go and fight against one nonetheless, it was not only because they were strong and fearless but because they knew that a Titan could be slain.

While Titan flesh was known to be difficult to so much as scratch, the hard Iron Bamboo-forged blades sliced through it with ease. Without the Equipment they could not mount a direct attack on the Titan's weak spot, but the soldiers must have felt at least something upon striking a Titan.

In an instant, the wagon passed by the Titan's side.

A hundred meters, two hundred meters, three hundred meters—

The Titan's figure was fast fading into the distance, but Kuklo still vividly felt the overwhelming presence, along with the fear, that it had planted in his heart.

He looked ahead. Five kilometers to the gates—an eternity to him, a distance far enough to induce despair. While he did not know the warhorses' limits, it would surely take five minutes to get there no matter how they whipped and urged them on.

Can we actually escape?! The fact that he had this thought was proof of their precarious situation. Everything was now up to what the Titan did next.

Damn it, he nearly cursed, but the Titan's condition came first. A hundred or so horses had galloped at full speed and kicked up dust behind them; visibility was so poor it could have been a foggy day. No matter how Kuklo strained his eye, he couldn't see the Titan.

It may not have been visible, but its presence was painfully clear. Although Kuklo could not glimpse it with his single eye, his hearing rendered its every single movement. He could tell just how the thing rose off the ground to give wild chase to the fleeing column.

"It's coming…"

The Titan was running four or five hundred meters behind the wagon, hot on their trail. Astonishingly, the Titan had the edge in speed, and little by little it was closing the distance.

Kuklo grabbed a carbine and readied it in imitation of the soldiers. Just as he did, a giant silhouette appeared through the cloud of dust. Noticing it, Kuklo pointed the muzzle at his target and took aim using the front sights. Shooting wildly at it would do no good, though. *Aim for its throat…*

Praying for the bullet to pierce its weak point, Kuklo pulled the trigger. A powerful burst of recoil caused the barrel to leap in the air, and the bullet flew off at a sorry angle. The result—to be expected from a first-time shooter—may have been on the better side considering that his shoulder wasn't dislocated.

With no time to be disappointed, Kuklo continued to reload and fire. His approach truly was to spray and pray, but some shots did seem to hit their mark. Whether they had any effect was a different story. The silhouette was growing darker through the dust.

It's catching up. As anxiety crept over him, a giant head loomed out of the cloud. The bullets must not have hurt or even tickled the Titan. It wore the same cheerful smile it had on when they first met.

Perhaps in reaction to the feast it was nearing, its mouth, which stretched from ear to ear, now hung open. Lined with numerous teeth, the titanic maw almost seemed evolved for the specific purpose of eating humans, and the darkness that spread beyond it smacked of a passageway to hell.

And I was born from there… The sight taught Kuklo why he'd been abhorred as a Titan's son. It overwhelmed him. He realized that even if he wasn't related to them by blood, it wasn't quite true that he had nothing at all to do with the Titans. If people considered him unclean, that wasn't mysterious in the least.

Kuklo readied the carbine, this time setting its sights on the Titan's mouth. He pulled the trigger with a firm conviction.

I'm a human being. Not a Titan.

The bullet that flew out of the muzzle shot straight into the gaping mouth. Without so much as altering its expression, the Titan continued its mad pursuit. Nothing short of a cannonball through its stomach seemed able to halt it.

As Kuklo engaged in a futile struggle, the Titan's full form came into view at last. Waving its arms like a swimmer and clearing away the smoke, the Titan picked up speed for a ferocious rush. They were now about a hundred meters apart, and at the current pace the Titan would catch up in less than a minute.

Kuklo looked to the front, but a little under two kilometers remained to Wall Maria. Its safety was too far off. A number of mounted soldiers, led by a team leader, accompanied the cargo team, but there weren't enough of them to deal with the Titan as the arrow formation had done. Besides, the soldiers who were meant to protect the wagon were now, ridiculously, riding ahead of it.

Bastards, Kuklo fumed, but as tempered as their bodies and spirits may have been, these crack troops were but sons of men. It wasn't unthinkable for their souls to shatter in face of a monster.

While they had acquired the know-how to fight a Titan and the armament to bring one down, perhaps the Survey Corps' time away from actual combat had atrophied their mental fortitude to a shadow of its former self.

Albeit gradually, the wagon was starting to slow. The horse was obviously under strain having to pull the wagon and its cargo. In the worst case, they might be left behind.

This is bad… We can't get away… Devastated, Kuklo hung his head. He saw a mess of scattered cargo inside the wagon. With so many swords, guns, bullet cases, and rations, there was no place to stand.

Wait, Kuklo suddenly realized. There were no cannons or cannonballs in the cargo so lodging a shot into the Titan's belly wasn't an option. *But there are a lot of explosives.*

Grabbing a grenade that had rolled onto the floor, Kuklo moved to the driver's seat, where a desperate cargo team soldier was sending his whip into the horse. Though the beast galloped with all of its strength as the soldier demanded, it breathed heavily and was in no condition to perform any better. It seemed like their speed could only dwindle thereafter.

Possibly preoccupied by the incoming Titan, the soldier did not even bother to glance at Kuklo trespassing into the driver's seat. Instead, he swung his whip doggedly as though straight forward was the only path to survival.

"The horse!" Kuklo pointed at the fiercely galloping animal. The soldier looked puzzled that he would. Unfazed, Kuklo yelled, "Get on the horse!"

"What are you saying?"

"I'll use this to blow up the wagon!"

"O-Oh."

Nodding in apparent consent, the soldier jumped from the seat to the horse, and Kuklo followed him. Riding was difficult with no saddle and two on the mount, and the horse's all-out gallop threatened to fling them off. Whether it was thanks to his father's blood—Survey Corps team leader Heath's—or to his sheer animal sense of balance, Kuklo managed it with ease.

He reached for the short sword the soldier carried on his hip and drew it without permission. Then he immediately attempted to cut the horse free of its harness.

Kuklo had no idea what it was made of, but its weaved bundle of wires was surprisingly resilient. He'd tried to sever it with the short sword, but the blade was badly chipped by the time he was half done. He wondered if it had been dull, but inferior supplies would never be issued to the Survey Corps. He'd seen how sharp their swords were earlier, too, when they tore through the Titan's skin. The harness must simply have been that durable. As Kuklo fumbled at his task, the Titan slowly but steadily closed the distance.

Kuklo clicked his tongue in frustration, then looked at the wagon. *What do I do?*

The image of the short swords within flashed through his mind, but there was the risk of the Titan catching up to them while he moved to and fro. He could shoot the harness with the carbine, but if the bullet ricocheted and hit the horse, that would be the end.

He was out of options.

A little less than a kilometer remained to Wall Maria. If he was lucky, they might make it.

That wasn't good enough for Kuklo. He had lived his entire life under the thumb of one stranger after another. A plan failing and costing him his life was one thing, but allowing his survival to depend on luck was not his way.

At the same time, Kuklo had no idea how to get out of this nightmare situation alive.

—*I think you'll need it to survive,* a familiar girl's voice whispered to him...or so he imagined.

Tossing away the now-useless short sword, Kuklo drew the knife he carried and applied it to the harness that yoked the horse to the wagon. Made, perhaps, of Iron Bamboo, the knife was exceptionally sharp and cut through with little trouble.

Got it! With that unvoiced cry, Kuklo immediately tossed the grenade into the wagon. In no time the abandoned vehicle was receding behind them.

Perhaps it was too small even to enter the monster's field of vision, or Titans were only interested in humans. Ogre charged straight ahead, ready to trample the wagon.

Just as its huge foot came down, the wagon exploded with a thunderous roar, and explode it did.

Engulfed in crimson flames that spewed deep black smoke, the Titan looked like a gigantic torch. As the intense heat of the fire scorched it, countless blisters began to appear. Its skin began to fester as though decomposing.

The Titan's gait, once nimble, was noticeably troubled. Its reddened face wore the same smile as ever, so it was unclear if it was suffering. Either way, being robbed of its physical capabilities forced even a Titan to stop.

Wall Maria's front gate came into view ahead of them. The sturdy doors opened with a roar, and one member of the Survey Corps after another passed through it without a backward glance. Kuklo was no exception. He could hear the Titan's footfalls behind him, but he was done. The soldiers on top of the wall were ready to intercept.

"Fire!!"

With that, the cannons spat fire.

CHAPTER THREE

Liberty Bell rang loud as the Survey Corps marched through the avenue on horseback. The roadsides were overflowing with spectators there to celebrate their return, and the cheers gave the event the feel of a victory parade. Some had indeed mistaken the expedition to be some sort of festival, but it truly was the first thing for the people to be happy about in a while. It was no surprise that some would want to enjoy themselves as much as they could, the expedition's results of secondary importance to them.

What should I do? Kuklo rode on a spare horse as though he was a member of the Survey Corps, but he was painfully out of place. Mere happenstance had led to this outcome, and by all rights he should have been bound and led at the end of a rope. Still, things could have been worse. *I need to get away somehow.*

Kuklo saw the crowd of nearly a thousand that had gathered to see the Survey Corps. They might aid his escape. The problem was timing. While the scene looked like a victory parade, the Survey Corps couldn't have shared the mood. Unresponsive to the cheering throngs, every soldier, without exception, wore a sullen face. As far as the troops were concerned, they were just riding back to their barracks. And of course, as soon as they got there, Kuklo would be tied up. He needed to find an opening for his escape before then.

As he kept an eye on the movements of the soldiers and the spectators, planning his escape route, he suddenly heard a voice ask, "Did you fulfill your purpose?"

It caught Kuklo off guard and he almost screamed.

The voice belonged to Carlo. He rode alongside Kuklo, possibly as a measure to prevent his escape. "You said you wanted to see a Titan.

Did you get anything from it?"

"I did," Kuklo managed, but his response was anything but crisp. He was now certain that he was not a Titan's son, and in that sense, he'd fulfilled his long-standing wish. Yet, there was no decisive change in how he felt. *What could it be? I feel so gloomy...*

Perhaps he had expected a dramatic metamorphosis on the order of a caterpillar turning into a butterfly. He wasn't disappointed, but he felt like something was missing. After all, despite having narrowly escaped a Titan's clutches, he'd confirmed nothing beyond the self-evident fact that he was a child of men. It was not meaningless, but perhaps the cost he'd paid along the way had been too great.

"Using the wagon to stop the Titan was a brilliant idea."

"Thank you," Kuklo replied curtly. He had absolutely no interest in talking to Carlo about the expedition. *I just need to get away...*

He'd thought the spectators would aid his escape, but the turnout was actually inconveniently large. He'd meant to hide among them to shake off pursuit, but there were no gaps to slip through. The crowd was a barrier that cut off potential routes, and taking advantage of the turnout seemed impossible.

"You are very nimble on your feet, boy. A burglar, perhaps?"

"No."

"Did someone teach you to fight?"

My chance to escape is slipping away. At this rate, they might reach the barracks before their little chat was over. "Don't mind me. You should wave to the crowds," he urged the commander.

"It is an expedition, not an exhibition."

"Then why did you go beyond the wall?"

"For observation and experience. Of course, we could've surveyed better, but a certain someone prevented that."

"So it's my fault?"

"Our poor job is to blame, too," Carlo casually admitted.

If Kuklo was able to sneak along, that proved there were holes in the expedition's planning. It seemed like a foolish oversight, but they hadn't shirked their preparations. Kuklo knew firsthand, though, that the unexpected could occur despite the most careful planning.

"By the way, I haven't heard your name yet," Carlo asked for a second time.

"Oh," Kuklo replied evasively. There was no reason to be an honest fool. "I am…" he began, considering what to say. That was when the parade suddenly came to a halt.

For a moment, everything fell silent, as though time stood still. Then the spectators began to stir. The Military Police Brigade, lined up in front of the troops, prevented their progress.

"Looks like something happened," Carlo said, wary.

Kuklo's face turned grim. He could guess why the Military Police had stopped them. Their gazes, directed at him atop the horse, only seemed to prove him right. This couldn't be about him going past Wall Maria without permission. In that case, Carlo would have been expecting them.

Kuklo didn't know how the Military Police had found him, but all eyes were on the expedition. It wasn't hard to imagine him catching someone's attention. Perhaps the Green Star he'd mistakenly fired had put the soldiers on alert.

The Military Police gave orders to the soldiers guarding the sidewalks, who began closing in on Kuklo from all sides.

"Did you do something that would make people keep an eye out for you?" Carlo asked.

"*I* didn't do anything." While Kuklo was at the scene of the crime, he couldn't think of anything he'd done that was against the law. In fact, to the extent that his rights as a human had been so flagrantly ignored, he might be considered a victim.

I have to explain. He had no choice but to meekly cooperate with the investigation. He was guilty of nothing, so simply offering his account ought to do—assuming, of course, that they'd bother to heed the words of a Titan's son.

Meanwhile, the soldiers continued to inch closer as if to encircle

Kuklo. To judge from the tight, unbroken ring that they formed, their orders must have been to apprehend him without fail.

Kuklo let out a deep sigh. *So they're treating me like a criminal...*

Just as he made up his mind and began to dismount, he met eyes with a girl pushing through the crowd toward him.

Sharle, he nearly called out to her reflexively, but stopped himself in time. He couldn't let the Military Police Brigade know she was there. Sharle seemed to see the fix he was in. Her face was noticeably pale, and she looked ready to faint at any moment.

I can't get her involved... Staring at Sharle, he shook his head slightly so only she would notice. That sufficed to convey his thinking to her, and she stood frozen, her eyes wide open.

Good. Kuklo scouted the area unobtrusively. It seemed as though no soldiers had noticed Sharle. The only person who followed his gaze was Carlo, who nevertheless showed no signs of taking action.

"You should have no problems as long as you have a clear conscience," noted the Survey Corps' commander.

"I hope so." Kuklo laughed drily and took the knife on his waist, presenting it to Carlo.

"What's that?"

"I'll leave it with you. It wasn't mine in the first place..."

"This isn't one of our weapons."

"But if not for this knife, I would be in that Titan's belly by now."

"I see." Carlo took it with no further questions.

"You're kind of different," Kuklo remarked.

"Not as much as yourself."

With another dry laugh, Kuklo hopped off his horse and walked to where the soldiers stood.

***

Sharle watched dumbfounded as the soldiers arrested Kuklo and took him away. She couldn't tell exactly what he was suspected of. If he was wanted for going outside the wall without permission, then that certainly counted as a crime, but interrupting the parade to capture him seemed unnecessary. For that, he had to be facing different charges, and she knew all too well what they might be.

What should I do… She could not act thoughtlessly, Kuklo having stayed her. It was unlikely to improve the situation and could even put her in danger, and he'd motioned her not to come out of concern for her. Yet, it was pure agony for Sharle to be left with no clue as to how many days he'd be detained and where she should wait in the meantime. It was like a bad dream.

Still, she did have some hope. She turned to look at the Survey Corps, still halted in their tracks. Among the rows of stalwarts, the one that held her particular interest was the commander, Carlo.

Kuklo gave him something. Wasn't that…

She recalled the odd exchange between the two. She had no way of making out the words, but Kuklo had passed Carlo her charm. Of that she was certain. Perhaps he'd been forced to disarm himself before surrendering, but the circumstances suggested that he concealed some other intention.

Or maybe I'm just hoping he did. Sharle saw it as a good luck charm, but to a soldier, a knife was a deadly tool. *But…*

As Sharle struggled with her thoughts, her eyes met Carlo's. By the time she tried to look away he was already facing in a different direction, but she was certain she'd been subjected to his razor-sharp gaze. Her goose bumps said as much.

Maybe he noticed, she wondered, regarding her and Kuklo's eye contact. Eavesdropping on their silent understanding seemed like an impossible feat, but then again, Carlo was the sort of man who'd been chosen to command the Survey Corps. Perhaps a couple of amateurs' tricks didn't stand a chance of getting past him. *Which means…*

The soldiers began to move forward once again, Kuklo apparently handed over to the Military Police Brigade. As the brave troops pulled away, Sharle considered her next move.

***

Carlo Piquer sat in his cramped executive office in the barracks thinking back on the expedition. If he had to summarize it, the first in fifteen years, in one word, "deplorable" fit the bill. The only silver lining was that everyone had returned alive, but the decline in troop quality was obvious. While they were equal if not superior to their predecessors physically, as a result of their lack of combat experience they didn't begin to stack up mentally. In fact, a number of soldiers felt so crushed they were applying for transfers to the Garrison.

"Boy, oh boy…" Carlo lamented theatrically, eyeing the documents that sat on his wide desk. It was an application for transfer and dismissal he'd just received from a subordinate. He hadn't read through it, but he made a point of accepting all of these. Useless even if dissuaded from leaving, such personnel would only drag down morale.

Carlo did not boast ample combat experience, either. Yes, he had participated in Survey Corps expeditions under his father Jorge Piquer's command, and he had nearly died in a fight with a Titan. He even witnessed the historic moment when a Titan was felled. He had no remarkable achievements of his own, however, and graded himself an average soldier. He'd viewed his promotion to commander as some sort of mistake.

My father was more suited to the role… Jorge was now bringing up the next generation as a Training Corps instructor. Though as virile as ever, considering his age there was no way he could reassume command of the Survey Corps.

The ranks who had joined the same year as Carlo were also out of the picture. They all tread their own paths, and not a single one of them had ended up with the reformed Survey Corps.

If only Solm were alive… If either he or Heath, their team leader, were alive, perhaps they could give him some advice. But that was a vain wish.

I have no right to complain about my men. Just as Carlo grimaced, a knock announcing a visitor echoed through the room.

The girl who opened the door and entered the office looked nervous and out of place in the barracks. Her expression was stiff, and she had the creaky movements of an unoiled machine. Of course, this was a natural reaction given her identity and the dilemma she faced.

So she mustered up some courage to come here. She doesn't seem like some aristocratic family's little princess, either.

Carlo had foreseen that Sharle Inocencio would come to visit him in order to save Kuklo. She'd been able to reach his office without ado only because he'd instructed his men to that end. It was not something Carlo had done thoughtlessly. He had made his decision after getting information on both her and Kuklo from the Military Police Brigade. Since they'd interrupted his procession, the commander had a right to know why and he had exercised it.

I would have never guessed he was the Titan's son, though... The Military Police's explanation had made Carlo doubt his ears, but their encounter somehow also made sense. *It is destiny...*

Nodding to himself, Carlo offered Sharle a chair and said, "Don't get too nervous, you won't be able to tell me what you're here to say."

She took the chair, but her eyes wandered around the room even after she sat.

Yet Sharle was the first to break the silence. "Um... I've come here to ask for your guidance about something."

"About *him*? Or about something personal, Miss Sharle Inocencio?"

Having only phrased herself in a hackneyed way, Sharle looked shocked. She realized that Carlo already knew everything. This only strengthened her resolve, and her hesitation vanished. "What is he... Kuklo doing now?"

I see. So she's more worried about the boy than about herself. Her words could be considered proof of her determination. "He is on his way to Wall Sheena in a convoy carriage right about now."

"To Wall Sheena…" Sharle murmured with a ponderous expression. Perhaps she was already trying to figure out how to get there.

"And I have a question for you."

"Yes?"

"Is he a criminal?"

"No, he's not!" she denied without missing a beat.

His reaction was the same. When he'd probed Kuklo about it, his denial had been just as immediate, as if any such accusation misconstrued him. It indicated a clear conscience, but unfortunately the Military Police did not see things the same way. If they were to be believed, Kuklo was a vile criminal with few precedents in the annals of history. *But—*

Carlo tilted his head, wondering if he really was that. They hadn't spoken at length, but he understood Kuklo's character all too well. Beyond the walls, proximity to death laid bare one's temperament. Masks fell off within moments. Troops tasked to protect the cargo team taking flight to save themselves was a case in point.

"He is accused of several crimes. For the murder of your father, Dario Inocencio, of servants of the Inocencio family, as well as the murders of several devout believers. As well as your abduction, I expect. Of course, the abductee herself is now safe and sound in my office."

There was also the matter of going past Wall Maria without permission, but adding the charge wouldn't worsen Kuklo's plight—not unless a punishment worse than the death penalty existed.

Carlo had spelled out the gravity of the situation, and Sharle looked even grimmer than before. "Kuklo…didn't do anything wrong," she objected.

"However, there was a witness."

"A witness?!"

Carlo presented her with the exact information he'd received from the Military Police. "Your brother, Xavi Inocencio, has testified that

Kuklo committed the crimes."

"My brother…"

"Is he wrong?"

"He is!" Sharle cried. "I'm also a witness! I was there! Kuklo did nothing at all!"

"Then who did it?"

"The cultists. They snuck into the mansion that night and unleashed that horror…"

"He did not command them to do it?"

"He couldn't possibly have."

"Why not?"

"He was locked up at our home. There was no way for him to send any orders…"

"So he was held prisoner…"

Sharle nodded in reply.

A life befitting the son of a Titan. It would seem that he is yoked to a cruel fate, Carlo mused as though it wasn't his business. In truth, he had played a part, if only incidentally. Either way, his face did not betray any of his thinking. His first priority was to draw out whatever information Sharle had to offer.

"Is it possible that he met with the believers in secret, without your knowledge?"

"I don't think so! He was chained up. And besides…"

"And?"

"He only just recently learned to speak…"

Sharle explained how, bought and sold in black markets, Kuklo had gone without any education.

So the boy has lived not as a human being, but as a "Titan's son." The toughness and nimbleness Kuklo exhibited owed to years of abuse, then. There was another reason, too. *Like father, like son, I suppose.* The boy's father was Heath. No surprise if his nerves were made of steel.

"Kuklo's life was ruined because of the Titans. There's no way he would ever join the cultists' side."

"And what is the reason he snuck outside of the wall?"

"He needed to know that he wasn't the son of a Titan."

This lined up with what Kuklo had said about his goal being to see a Titan.

So he went out there to become confident he was a human. The deed was incredibly risky, near suicidal, and foolish, but it made sense given Kuklo's background. It must have been like a ritual he had no choice but to undergo. He'd wanted to exorcise the label of "Titan's son" that haunted him.

"Was there a reason for the abduction?"

"I had reasons…for not wanting to be at home anymore. So when Kuklo plotted to escape, I decided to join him." Sharle explained how her own circumstances matched up with the plan Kuklo had been forming—in other words, the fact of her marriage of convenience.

So just as they were off to their fresh start, something huge got in their way. Carlo felt as though he had gotten to the truth of the situation, but one large question still weighed on his mind.

"So why did your brother provide false testimony?" Things would be quite different had Xavi not lied.

"He was knocked off his feet by Kuklo as we escaped. Perhaps he is holding a grudge over his defeat…"

"I see," Carlo said, satisfied. He took out the knife he'd stored in his table's drawer and presented it to Sharle. "I don't think he wanted the Military Police to confiscate the weapon, so he slipped it to me first. It's yours, isn't it?"

"Yes." Sharle took the knife and held it close to her chest. "This is my good luck charm."

"A rather deadly good luck charm, if you ask me. He said that the knife saved his life."

"Is that so?"

Carlo had no idea how she came to regard it as a charm, but he could tell it was like a treasure to her.

"Actually, I was planning to use this to kill Kuklo."

"Well, that's very brave of you." He had no way of knowing what had happened between the two, but Sharle neither spoke nor acted like the stereotypical aristocratic girl.

"Um, so… What's going to happen to Kuklo?"

"If nothing changes, he won't be able to avoid punishment. Of course, if you were willing to testify, he might have a chance." But that, Carlo realized, wasn't to be taken for granted considering Sharle's position. It meant not only giving up the freedom she'd finally earned but also cornering her brother, Xavi, who'd given false testimony. When he saw the look of determination on her face, however, he realized she was up for it. *On the other hand, Kuklo might not be happy to be freed in such a way…*

He even seemed liable to take the blame if it meant saving Sharle. In other words, there was no point in a plan that only saved one of them. Carlo saw that solving this problem involved overcoming a host of challenges, but there was nothing but to tackle them. If he made good use of his place as commander, freeing Kuklo wasn't impossible.

"It may take time," he warned, "but I might be able to use my connections to make something happen."

"Really?!" Sharle leapt out of her chair with a smile.

"I want to talk to him as much as you do. And there's someone else I want him to meet as well."

That man was his father, who now trained recruits. *If I can give him Kuklo, he might make the boy into an even greater soldier than Team Leader Heath.* Whether Kuklo would agree was another question, but it was worth trying to convince him. He would surely be a major addition to the Survey Corps, as freshly reformed and short on talent as it was. *Plus, I suspect he might be able to master* that *thing.*

"I want to ask you a question," Sharle said looking straight at Carlo, who was lost in thought. "Why are you helping us? We're total strangers to you."

"Strangers? That's not quite true."

"Have you met either of us before?"

"Well, you see, I was there the moment he was born."

Sharle blinked. "Huh?"

"You could say it was me who burdened him with the fate of being the 'Titan's son.'"

With a solemn look, Carlo closed his eyes.

***

Kuklo woke up alone in a cell. A dreary gloom surrounded him; the only illumination leaked in from a candlelit corridor. The cell was located underground, so there were no windows for lighting. If the candles were extinguished, pitch darkness would come over the cramped space.

He had been given no privacy. His cell was completely visible from the corridor, with only its bars obstructing the view. True, with nothing but a crudely made iron bed and toilet adorning the cell, being seen posed no particular problems. Degrading environments were familiar habitats to Kuklo. He was not shivering from the cold, nor was he suffering from starvation, so it was downright pleasant compared to his old shed.

Still, the cell amounted to a cage for a beast of prey. The other ones confined various offenders, from jaw-droppingly fiendish criminals to political prisoners who aimed to overthrow the government. Everyone placed in the dungeon was there because of serious crimes, and many could barely be called human. Any inmates with a chance of being released were held in shared cells aboveground.

Will I ever get out of this prison alive?

Kuklo wasn't sure how many nights he'd spent locked up. With no way of keeping time, it felt in turn like a few days or a few months.

Breaking out would be extremely difficult. Unlike his escape from the shed, this facility wasn't one that he could overcome given time. Jailers patrolled the corridor, making it hard to tamper with the iron bars. Made of Iron Bamboo at that, they admitted nary a scratch no matter how hard he tried.

Still, Kuklo wasn't the type to give up. He rose from his bed and carefully observed his cell. Severing the bars was a nearly impossible task, but the walls, floor, and ceiling were made of stone and could be bored through. Of course, not only would that take an enormous amount of time, he also had no tools, so it was hardly practical.

"Hey, kitty-corner. You looking to escape? Very bold of you," the prisoner in the cell opposite the corridor, an airy fellow in his late teens, called out casually.

Despite his time in prison, his skin looked healthy, and while he was thin, he was not emaciated. He looked like some well-bred beau, but he must have been deemed guilty of an appropriate crime to be imprisoned underground. Kuklo had no interest in learning what it was, though.

"If the guards catch you trying any funny business, they're going to beat you black and blue again," the guy snickered. He seemed more interested in watching Kuklo's next confrontation with the guards than his wellbeing.

Kuklo didn't care to oblige him, but the run-ins with the guards would persist as long as he kept trying to escape. Kuklo ignored the fellow and continued his work.

"Give it up. You're underground, you can't get out to the surface by digging."

That much was obvious, but Kuklo ignored him again and kept at his investigation. He might give up on his hopes of escaping if he were only looking out for himself, but he knew Sharle was waiting for him. He had to get out before she took desperate measures.

"What's your name? You look real young. What're you in for? Theft? Murder? Could you be a revolutionary?" The words came at a machine-gun pace to no reply. "Is your scarred eye a badge of honor?" The guy seemed to be a born talker, and he prattled on. "It's a waste of your time trying to escape this place. You'll only wind up hurting yourself, like just now. Give it up."

Indeed, Kuklo had already earned a number of beatings. The guards kept an eye on him due to his clear determination to escape.

"If you're going to try this, you need to be smart about it. I mean, the patrols come at the same time every day."

What is this guy's deal? Kuklo furrowed his brow, annoyance writ large on his face, but he chose to pretend not to hear. It was vexing to find himself in agreement now and then. Yet, silencing the fellow would be difficult thanks to the iron bars between them. He scrubbed the fellow's existence from his mind, resigned to letting his statements pass through one ear and go out the other.

"It's actually quite easy to get out of here."

"Really?" Kuklo's voice cracked with surprise, and he turned to the speaker.

The youth chortled, having managed to ensnare Kuklo. "Oh, so you *can* hear me."

"You tricked me…"

"No way. Would I really be that wicked?"

"Well, why else would you be in here?"

"Not all people in prison are criminals."

"You're saying that describes you?" When the guy responded with a smile, Kuklo followed up with another question. "Is it true that you can escape this place?"

"Of course."

You lie. The guy's presence in the cell was proof. If escape was easy, then he would be celebrating his freedom by now.

"You don't believe me? But it's true."

"How, then?"

"Just sleep and wait."

"That's not funny!" Kuklo spat. If not for their bars, he'd have gone over to punch the guy.

"What I'm telling you is true, but I admit it sounds like a lie," the inmate continued in his casual tone. "In two weeks, we'll all be banished out, right through the main gate of Shiganshina."

"What do you mean?"

"I mean nothing. That's just what we've been sentenced to. The fact that we're here means that is the fate that awaits us," he said jestingly, perhaps not understanding what banishment signified.

As he said, they would be freed in time. But exile meant *being thrown outside the walls*, in other words, a death sentence—no, something even more vicious.

There the prisoners would find their starved executioners waiting for them with bated breath. Humans could die by way of accident, disease, and a host of other causes that also happened to include capital punishment, but having one's life end in despair in a Titan's jaws was the worst fate imaginable. Familiar with the irrationality that was the Titans, Kuklo understood the cruelty of banishment more than he cared to.

But at least I'll be free. It seemed like the only way to overcome his present difficulties. The eventuality probably allowed for far more constructive plans than plotting a jailbreak in his current cell.

"I suppose I haven't introduced myself yet. I'm Cardina Baumeister. And you?"

"…Kuklo."

"Hmm? Where have I heard that name?" wondered Cardina, staring without reserve.

"It is common," came Kuklo's blunt reply. While he didn't know what kind of information was out there about a Titan's son, he was sure the facts had been embellished into a bunch of worthless stories he had no interest in hearing. "I think I've heard your name before, too," he countered.

"Well, it's a pretty famous name." Cardina shrugged. "So, why did you get thrown in here?"

"I didn't do anything!!"

"No need to stare daggers at me…"

While Kuklo had no defense for his unauthorized trip past Wall Maria, he was in prison for "leading the cultists in an attack on the

Inocencio family." It was a ridiculous charge, but the victim's testimony provided by Xavi had ruled the day, and unable to mount a proper rebuttal, Kuklo had ended up incarcerated. The alias of "Titan's son" may have worked against him as well.

Shit... While he knew Xavi bore a grudge, he hadn't expected to be smeared with a crime. If either of them was a murderer, it was Xavi, who had killed the cultists. Yet, between the remonstrations of the Titan's son who had fled the scene and the testimony of the victim of a cultist assault lay a large gap in credibility.

"It's a pretty common story down in these cells. People caught in political warfare, and so on," Cardina remarked with a shrug. "That would be me, as it happens."

Kuklo suddenly remembered. *Oh... He was Sharle's...*

Of course he remembered hearing Cardina's last name. Sharle was going to be married into the Baumeister family. In other words, Cardina's father was Bruno Baumeister, who'd fallen to a plot. Known as a conservative vanguard, he'd been made the reformers' prime target. It wasn't shocking in any kind of political struggle.

Kuklo now knew Cardina's background, but there was something he still couldn't understand: his level of composure. Being banished to the outside world meant certain death.

Finding Cardina's demeanor unnatural, Kuklo demanded, "What happens once we're outside? Eaten by a Titan, and that's it?!"

"Yes, I suppose so."

"I don't want to be eaten by one of those things."

"Well, neither do I."

"So..."

"Have you ever heard of a town named Naraka?"

Kuklo shook his head.

"It's a town outside the walls. Supposedly, it was built by criminals who were no longer allowed in the country. Oh, and Naraka means Hell. Seems like an unimaginative name, but that's just my opinion."

"Supposedly?"

"No one knows if Naraka really exists or not. It's only a rumor," Cardina said matter-of-factly. "But it makes sense. It's a hiding place for criminals, so they don't want anyone knowing where it is."

"What if it's not real?"

"Then we can build Naraka for ourselves." Cardina hardly seemed hopeful about its existence and apparently intended to create the place.

But things wouldn't go that smoothly. With Titans roaming around, even the most cunning plans were meaningless. Kuklo knew down to his bones how ruthless the outside world was; he could see that creating a town there was just wishful thinking. The unreasonably powerful Titans wielded such destructive force they could turn all to dust, and Cardina's plan would be crushed with the flick of a wrist.

"I understand why you'd be worried, though."

"Because it's impossible."

"But that's not quite true," Cardina said, oddly confident. "Are you aware that the Titans supposedly come from the south?"

"South?"

"I don't know the full details, myself. But all of the soldiers stationed in Shiganshina District are proof that there are a lot of Titans down there, right? The royal government also softens taxes and whatnot to make life easier for the residents there."

"Because they're using humans as bait."

"It's a convenient way to draw them in."

"So?"

"The Titans come from the south, lured by the smell of their food, and get stuck around Shiganshina District. Which means…"

"What?"

"Oh, don't be thick. It means, if you get banished, go north."

"I see…" In other words, they could find the town of criminals Cardina spoke of there. "But why? Why would you tell me this?"

"Nobody else around here is going to believe a story like that."

"But I will?"

"Well, you have to admit, you're pretty stupid," Cardina said, not mincing words. "Even after all you've been through, you keep on trying to escape. Only an idiot would fail to take the hint."

"I can't tell…if you're insulting or praising me."

"Why, it's a compliment, of course. Regardless of your motive, it's a sign of your strength of will. That's why I decided to tell you about it."

Kuklo nodded in understanding, then began considering Cardina's plan. He already knew in his heart what he would do, though.

I cannot escape from this prison. My only hope is that his story is true. With no prospects for escape, exile was unavoidable. It was a gamble, and a long shot at that, but his only option was to accept Cardina's proposal. Kuklo had no desire to lend a hand to a criminal, nor did he intend to live in Naraka, but there was no telling what could happen outside the walls. He needed to search for any way back even if it meant working with outlaws.

"I'll help you. It's hell out there…" Kuklo muttered with a grave look. "But I have business on the inside."

"I see. And that's why you want to escape. Keeping someone waiting?"

"…You might say that."

"It's a girl, isn't it?" Cardina teased, but Kuklo didn't answer.

If Cardina learned it was Sharle waiting for him, he'd surely be surprised, but Kuklo wanted to stay out of any further trouble. Fortunately, Cardina didn't press the issue, but there couldn't have been a worse place to run into him.

Kuklo scratched his head and snorted at his luck. Soon, though, his expression clouded over, and his thoughts began to take him outside the walls.

***

Kuklo's course of action in preparation for his exile was to rest his

116

spirits. By replenishing both his body and his mind, he'd be ready to take on the outside world in peak condition. In practice, though, that wasn't how it felt. Resting his spirits sounded good, but sitting there and doing nothing until the day of his release was a passive measure. All it did was irritate him, but he knew that there was not much to be done in a cell.

A punishment worse than the death penalty... For humanitarian reasons, executions were carried out in ways that inflicted minimal, if lethal, suffering. Meanwhile, exile brought with it the highest degree of mental and physical agony, eclipsing the death penalty to make it the ultimate punishment. Kuklo couldn't help but think that it was an outrageous sentence.

The Titans seemed to live only to eat humans. They were undeniably monsters. But that was all they were.

They're just hungry... Their stomachs were empty, so they ate. Their bodies were large, but it was a normal thing to do. Humans were no strangers to the act.

Humans are scarier. Seeking the cruelest way to kill their own kind was nothing but demonic.

In any case, Kuklo had no choice but to do anything he could to survive. It was hard to imagine any worse circumstances, with neither weapons to fight with nor a mount upon which to flee. His only option was to pray to the heavens that he didn't encounter a Titan as he pushed northward with all his strength. He couldn't rely on the mirage that was Naraka, but the bit about the Titans coming from the south was persuasive enough. If Cardina was right, the farther north they went, the lower their chances would be of meeting a Titan.

"My life has always been like this..." Kuklo sighed deeply.

"Hey, chaos can be fun," Cardina pointed out in a carefree tone.

"Speak for yourself..."

"Well, all that desperation makes you feel alive, right?"

It also meant living on the brink of death. Perhaps it was the perfect way to describe Kuklo's life.

The prisoners' sentence was being carried out in a hush before day-break. The early hour seemed to be chosen out of the royal government's desire to conceal the existence of exile as a punishment. All it entailed was banishing criminals to the land outside the country, but any citizen could imagine the outcome that lurked beyond the walls. Letting Titans deal with the guilty was an inhuman, unconscionable act, which was why the punishment was carried out while citizens slept.

About twenty criminals, including Kuklo, were to be exiled. They had been split into groups and sat waiting in covered wagons by the main gates of Shiganshina District.

The gates would open before long, and the wagons were ready to head straight into the depths of hell. There were, of course, no drivers, nor did any of the damned take the reins. The wagons would be left to run freely with no guidance at all.

This is bad… It was impossible for Kuklo to stay calm.

Cardina, who rode in the same wagon, had a solemn look on his face. Everyone there had their hands tied behind their back in order to prevent escape, and they had been gagged in order to keep them quiet. They were in no shape to search for Naraka. For all they knew, they were headed straight into the Titans' embrace.

Kuklo tried wriggling his arms to loosen the ropes, but they seemed expertly tied, not budging an inch. The same went for the gag. In his state, he could not so much as confirm his intentions with Cardina. In the worst case, he would have to leap out of the wagon and accept whatever injuries came as a result. Even if things went well for them, restrained thus, surviving the impossibly dangerous lands outside was hardly guaranteed.

The first thing I need to do is get these ropes off. Kuklo continued to try to wrest his wrists free, but all he sensed was his skin being worn down. As he struggled, an aging soldier, seemingly with the Garrison, flipped back the wagon's canvas and inspected the interior. He seemed to want to be extra sure. He began to check the prisoners' ropes and gags one by one.

Shit! A string of curses would have spewed from Kuklo's mouth had it not been shut for him. Coming to Kuklo, the soldier stared at him for a while and nodded some sort of understanding. *That I'm a Titan's son, probably.*

His piercing gaze seemed to bore into Kuklo's darkened right eye. Being the target of an inquisitive stare hardly bothered Kuklo at this late date, but the intensity of the soldier's gaze gave him pause. Few men's eyes could make him shrink into himself, and Kuklo had only met one.

Pretending to inspect Kuklo, the soldier handed him something resembling a wooden stick.

This is... The item felt familiar in his hands. It was not the first time he'd held it. *The charm? Why did he have it?!*

Kuklo wanted to ask the soldier, but the gag forbade him. Instead, he pled with his eye to extract some sort of information, but the soldier got off the carriage without a single look back at Kuklo.

What does this mean? He was unable to digest the situation, but one thing seemed clear. *Am I supposed to use it to escape?*

Carlo must have instructed the soldier. The commander was using the knife to inform Kuklo that he was pulling strings behind the scenes.

What is he thinking? Even the head of the Survey Corps had no right to interfere with the execution of a criminal's sentence. Kuklo could not think of any benefit to be reaped from taking this risk to save him. But reasons did not matter to him at the moment, only ways out of his bind. If he wanted to know why, he could meet Carlo later and ask him.

The gates seemed ready to open, and the wagon began to storm off.

It's starting...

Kuklo tried to calm himself as he wiggled the knife back and forth. It was difficult to use due to the ropes binding his hands, but the blade's sharpness made up for that. As soon as they passed the wall, the worn-out carriage began to bounce violently up and down. It had no suspension.

Kuklo had to move as quickly as possible and get off right away. They were being pulled by a slow draft horse, but it was a horse nonetheless. Every moment he wasted put him that much farther away from the town and hurt his chances.

Kuklo slowly cut through the rope—it felt like one thread at a time. When he was nearly through, he put all of his strength in his arms to snap free. He immediately removed his gag and proceeded to undo the other prisoners' bonds with the knife.

Once he completed his chain of actions, Kuklo looked down at the knife in his hands.

Her charm... He was sure of what it was from the moment he felt it, but now he knew he was right. *It saved me again.*

Kuklo thought of how much he owed it and smiled in spite of himself.

"When did you get that thing?!" Cardina asked, but he soon lost interest and peeled back the canvas.

It was too dark to judge distance, but the light from what appeared to be a watch fire atop Wall Maria hinted that they were already four or five hundred meters from Shiganshina District.

"All right, let's hurry and jump off," invited Cardina.

"Jump off? What about the wagon?!"

"We need it to keep running off. They're probably watching it."

"So what?"

"They might do something if they realize we escaped."

"Oh, that's what you're worried about..."

"I mean, they probably won't send anyone after us, but I suppose they might shoot their cannons." Perhaps picturing this, Cardina's body shivered. Then he casually raised his hand and said, "Well, so long!" And just like that, he jumped out of the wagon with a der-ring-do that belied appearances.

Kuklo was taken aback for a moment, but he quickly regained his composure and followed suit. He tried to absorb the shock of the impact as he hit the ground, but his momentum made it hard to come to a stop. He rolled, banging one part of his body after the other before he finally lay unmoving.

"Kuklo! You still alive?"

"Yeah…" He rose slowly, checking to make sure his body was still functional. As dramatic as his tumble had been, he seemed to have gotten away with just a few scrapes, along with whatever bruises that might show up. He breathed a sigh of relief, but soon gasped and tensed himself. This was no time to be celebrating merely getting off the wagon.

We're now outside the walls… A chill shot down his spine, and a desperate scene played in his mind all too vividly. Nightmarish images of being chased down by preposterously gigantic monsters—just remembering the Titans dealt a fierce, electric jolt.

While fear had been driven deep into Kuklo's heart, he rarely thought of the Titans inside the walls, thanks perhaps to the sense of security they afforded. But as soon as it sank in that he'd stepped outside them, the image of a Titan came back to him, broad smile and all.

Keeping calm was a tall order outside of the walls, but if he allowed himself to despair or panic, he'd be done for even before encountering a Titan. Maintaining composure had to be his first priority.

Calm down… Calm down… Kuklo put his hand to his chest and exhaled deeply, repeating the words over and over as if to hypnotize himself. Yet, while it might muster some makeshift bravado, mere chanting didn't dispel his gnawing fears. He had to overcome his terror if he wanted to return alive. In other words, an unyielding will, certain of survival at any cost, was vital.

Kuklo looked at his knife, nodded, and slapped his cheeks to gather his focus. He opened his left eye wide and listened closely for any signs.

The darkness was covered in a thin haze that made it hard to see, and all he could hear was the wagon running off into the distance and the blowing wind. Luckily, he didn't detect any signs of the Titans he so feared.

Kuklo sighed again, this time in more honest relief. He turned to Cardina and asked, "Where are the others?"

"It seems we're the only ones who jumped off."

"Huh?!" Kuklo looked toward where the wagon had gone off, but he could make out nothing.

"Perhaps they'd already given up long ago."

"Give up on what?"

"On life."

"Oh…"

They must have lost hope as soon as their punishment had been decided. Thinking back, Kuklo realized that none of the other prisoners in the carriage had made any attempts to escape. They'd all worn lifeless expressions like they were no more than breathing corpses. Resignation was a reasonable reaction to being tossed out of the walls.

Meanwhile, Cardina did not seem that tense, thanks either to his positivity or to a sense of daring sustained by ignorance. After all, if not for the Titans, the outside world was simply an uncivilized expanse. It would still be a spooky place, but not one that froze one into a stupor.

The noise made by the wagon faded away as Kuklo and Cardina chatted. The fate of the prisoners on it was sure to be as dark as the world that spread before the two. Kuklo felt bad for the others, but there was nothing he could do now.

"Perhaps we ought to be off before we're set upon by Titans," Cardina suggested.

"Yes."

They nodded at each other, and in unspoken agreement, began

retracing their path. They'd been thrown into an empty wasteland, but by no means were they at a loss as to which way to head. The watch fire was to their north, and the gate leading into Shiganshina District would be nearby. Since they wouldn't be able to pass through, the gate only acted as a landmark, but it helped. Dawn would come soon.

"Do you mind if I ask a question?" Cardina said as he ran panting next to Kuklo. "Where did you get that thing from?" he asked, referring to the knife.

"This…" Kuklo struggled for words and scratched his head.

He couldn't rightly tell him that the Survey Corps commander had helped out. Kuklo still questioned whether such a thing was really possible. Since Carlo's intentions were unclear, Kuklo was reluctant to offer any false hope.

"Don't tell me you're gonna save us?"

"I don't know." Kuklo indeed did not. The Survey Corps wasn't about to ride in gallantly to their rescue. That was why he'd been handed the knife.

We can only proceed north.

Even if Carlo was pulling strings behind the scenes, they hadn't hashed things out together, and Kuklo had no way of knowing what was in store. God knew, indeed, while he had to believe in his instincts and act on them to find a way not to die.

But aimlessly wandering a wasteland that offered neither food nor water promised physical and mental hardship. If they at least knew Naraka's location, he'd force his body to its limits. With its very existence in doubt, the town might not do much to spur him on. At the same time, Kuklo was accustomed to crude environments. He was confident he could adapt as long as he wasn't attacked by any Titans.

"Wait a second!" Somehow Cardina had gone from running next to Kuklo to falling ten meters behind. He seemed to lack endurance and was heaving.

"You're slow."

"You're just abnormally fast," Cardina complained, but Kuklo did not feel the same way. He'd simply been moving forward at his own pace. Having had few opportunities to compare his physical abilities to anyone else's, he honestly had no idea how they rated. He now knew he had more stamina than Cardina, at least. Kuklo was in fact constantly conserving some of his strength because he lost control of his body when he pushed it as hard as he could.

It was about five hundred meters to Shiganshina District's main gate. While their ultimate goal was to the north, at the moment they had to choose between east and west.

"Now, do we take the eastern or western route?"

"I don't care which," Kuklo said. The choice wouldn't affect their fate. Still, he balked at the idea of picking at random, so he studied both routes. All he could make out were watch fires placed at regular intervals on the wall, nothing that helped decide one way or the other.

East...or west? He trained his eye to the east but only saw a vast darkness. For the most part, the west route offered more of the same. A weak source of light somewhat away from Shiganshina District caught his eye—it looked like a torch—but that was all.

Why there? As he focused on the irregular, unnatural illumination, Kuklo's hearing seized on a faint sound. He stopped, turned around, and sought it out, his hands to his ears.

This... The south wind was blowing, and it bore the sound of *those* footsteps on the ground.

Not one. Two, three, four—he could distinguish differing scales.

"Titans..." Kuklo gulped. Nothing else made footsteps outside the walls.

"I don't hear anything, but could it mean the sentence was executed with due haste?"

"I suppose so."

The footsteps could be explained by a Titan attacking the prisoners' wagons. What worried Kuklo was that he could hear other steps, too. Something seemed to have roused and attracted wandering Titans, whether it was the sound or the smell of the prisoners' blood being spilled. It was only a matter of time before they noticed Kuklo and Cardina. In fact, some of the footsteps were already heading their way.

Cardina began to run off to the northeast, apparently hearing the Titans' footsteps now. "Let's go!"

"This way!" Kuklo called to him, taking off toward the northwest.

"Is there a reason for this?"

"I see a light."

He was referring to the torchlight that he'd made out earlier and that still glowed like a will o' the wisp atop Wall Maria. Floating at a spot a few kilometers from Shiganshina District, the faint illumination looked awfully out of place.

"Does this have something to do with that thing?" Cardina said, pointing to the knife.

Kuklo only replied, "Maybe." But in his heart, he headed to the west with similar hopes. They were better than nothing at all.

Nearing dawn, the sky began to brighten. The sun would soon appear out of the horizon, its rays assisting their progress but also increasing their likelihood of being discovered by the Titans. If the creatures acted based on their vision, of course.

Kuklo turned back to look, but it was still too dark to see around him. He couldn't make out so much as a Titan's shadow. While he didn't know exactly how far from them the Titans were, considering their ability to run at a horse's pace, he knew the situation was dire. It was about two kilometers to their destination, but even a full dash meant several minutes on human feet. There was a very real danger of a Titan catching up to them.

Kuklo and Cardina ran across the wasteland with all their strength, but their athletic abilities were no match for the Titans. The footsteps that had been distant just moments ago were now keenly audible.

"Hurry!"

There was no longer any doubt that Kuklo and Cardina were being chased by a Titan. If they wanted to stay alive, they had to tear through the wasteland like madmen and somehow work their way back in.

But how?! It would be another story if the wall contained hidden passages, but overcoming its fifty-meter height was impossible without help. *What if there's nothing there?*

Kuklo had a bad feeling, but he put aside idle thoughts and rushed ahead.

The sun appeared from across the plain when only five hundred meters remained to the spot on Wall Maria. In an instant, the darkness was wiped out and the world rapidly regained its hues. The sky was a beautiful, cloudless blue, and it would have been a refreshing new day had they not been outside the walls.

Kuklo set his sights on the area above the wall and rushed toward it at full speed.

That's... Up on Wall Maria, he saw a familiar soldier waiting for him. It was the same aging man who had given him the knife. He seemed to have noticed Kuklo and was eagerly beckoning him on.

About a hundred meters to the soldier. While their likelihood of survival had increased, the footfalls of the Titan, advancing with the wind on its back, swooped closer. Kuklo didn't have the time to turn back and see how close, nor did he have the courage. Whether he lived or died still seemed like a coin flip.

"Make haste! Titan approaching!!" the soldier on the wall yelled out as Kuklo came within fifty meters. The rescue method was a simple one. One look at the rope dangling down from the top indicated what he had to do. Additional fugitives seemed not to have been expected, as only one length of rope offered itself.

Can it support us?! They didn't have the luxury of climbing up one at a time. Both of them would have to use the rope at once.

The problem was the order: Kuklo first, or Cardina first?

Kuklo tried to catch Cardina's eyes, unaware that his partner had lagged behind. Clicking his tongue, he looked back to find Cardina about fifty meters away, still running but out of breath. Right behind him was a giant male figure roaring forward with the sun on its back.

The Titan closing in on Cardina was about three meters tall. That placed it among the smallest of the Titans, but even then, it was large enough to pry open one's eyes with awe. If it were a human, its appearance could be described as elderly; its wrinkled face wore a sad expression as if to bemoan old age. While its cruelly bent back gave the impression that it was about to stumble and fall, it maintained its forward rush with a steady gait. At this rate, Cardina would soon be Titan food.

The wall was right in front of Kuklo. At least he should be able to get away. But—

"Damn it!" Kuklo braced his legs to come to a sudden stop. He turned around and headed back toward the Titan.

"Forget about him! You cannot save him!" the soldier yelled from the wall, but Kuklo ignored him and continued to run.

Kuklo would have abandoned a criminal, but Cardina was nothing less than a victim caught in the crossfire of political strife. Just like Kuklo, his life had been jostled by events beyond his control, and Kuklo couldn't see him as a total stranger. Saving him seemed like a right and human act.

I have to do it.

Thankfully, the Titan was a smaller one, so buying time seemed like a possibility if he played his cards right. The Survey Corps had taught him how, and he had the weapon he needed. Titans possessed bodies that were impervious to average arms, but he knew the knife he possessed could slice through their skin. It was just as sharp, if not sharper than the Survey Corps' standard-issue short swords, which meant that it had to be made of Iron Bamboo.

The Titan's skinny arms resembled dead branches, but they went for Cardina, who was running with all his might to escape its wicked clutches. Yet, outpacing a Titan's untiring legs was an unlikely proposition. When the Titan swiped with its rod-like arm, one of its fingers grazed Cardina, and that was all it took to send him flying. His body rolled wildly across the ground amidst clouds of dust.

"Cardina!"

He stirred in response to Kuklo's scream. While he groaned and his face twisted in pain, his injuries did not look fatal. In no time he would be back on his feet, but they could not afford the wait. If Cardina didn't want to be eaten by a Titan, he had to move any way he could, even if it meant crawling.

"Get away from it!!" Kuklo hollered, and Cardina grit his teeth and stood. Watching this out of the corner of his eye, Kuklo closed the distance between himself and the Titan. Its clouded eyes settled on him.

Kuklo was now closer to the Titan than Cardina, and both were food alike to it. The monster switched targets and charged at Kuklo. While small for a Titan, a creature with a three-meter-tall frame was now advancing on him with malice aforethought. The oppressive force of this was like a raging gust of wind. It should have caused Kuklo to cower in fear, but he was running toward it at full speed, and it was too late to retreat.

The Titan held out its arms as though to receive a beloved baby grandchild. Kuklo ran with his body bent low to avoid it. Still in the same posture, and aiming at the Titan's left ankle where a human's Achilles tendon would be, he swung his knife. He didn't need to kill the Titan. All he had to do was buy a little time.

It was the same technique used by the Survey Corps during their expedition. Practically immortal, Titans were intimidating monsters that kept coming back to life unless their weak point was destroyed. Their movements, however, could be curtailed. That was where their legs came in. In other words, no matter how absurd a monster the Titan was, when you took away some of its physical abilities, it found itself unable to move. Kuklo had even seen a Titan fall to one knee with its ankle sliced. If he hadn't witnessed the Survey Corps' tactics in action, he probably would have mounted a frontal assault—a form of suicide.

Dealing his first blow to a Titan bolstered Kuklo's confidence.

Cutting through its exposed right Achilles tendon next, he ran off without confirming the result. It was a once-in-a-lifetime chance to slay himself a Titan, but his goal was to return inside the walls alive. The soldiers could take care of eliminating the monsters, and in any case, there were other Titans behind the current one. Escape was his only option.

"Hurry! Over here!"

Guided by the familiar voice, Kuklo looked up to the top of the wall. For some reason, Cardina was up there waving his hand. The life-or-death situation must have provided him with the strength needed to climb up the rope.

"Hurry! It's coming!!"

The rough, sonorous voice belonged to the soldier on the wall. Though the Titan should have been immobilized, Kuklo looked back to find it rising to its feet with a spring. The deep wounds would have kept a human from ever walking again, but they were like insignificant scratches to the Titan.

You damned monster…

Kuklo arrived at the wall and reached for the lowered rope. When he took a closer look, he realized it was not a rope at all, but a wire. There were no knots to hold onto, and the wire itself was thin and unsuited for climbing. Kuklo doubted he had the last-ditch strength, but if Cardina could do it, he ought to as well.

The Titan had recommenced its charge, and Kuklo heard its footsteps behind him. An earth-shaking rumble alerted him to the incoming attack. *It's over…*

"Grab the handle at the end! I'll pull you up!!"

Kuklo looked at the wire. Something resembling a handle had been placed on its tip.

"Hold on tight. Don't throw out your shoulders!"

Kuklo grabbed on with both hands, unsure of what the words meant, and immediately found himself flying into the air. Intense pressure came over his body, and his face contorted as though he was having a convulsion. The seemingly impossible vertical movement put a strain on his body. The slightest lapse in concentration would make him pass out.

He flew away from the ground in an instant, and the Titan, arriving too late, yet unable to stop, crashed into the wall.

"Serves you right!!" Kuklo spat, traversing the wall's fifty meters in the blink of an eye. He'd gotten a taste of what it was like to be a fish on a pole.

INTERMISSION

Having made a miraculous return from beyond the walls, Kuklo and Cardina found themselves on a gently rocking carriage. The same soldier was driving it north on an artery road along the main route connecting Shiganshina District and Trost District. Kuklo and Cardina hadn't been told their destination, though. If they kept going north, they'd eventually reach Wall Sheena, but it seemed unlikely that they'd be taken back to the underground prison considering what had transpired.

—At least, that's what I hope. The ride was comfortable. Kuklo, sprawled out, wondered what came next. *I can't complain, though.*

The soldier had saved his life. Even if Kuklo was headed back to prison, he would have no choice but to accept his fate.

But why did he save me? Not only that, the man was in a special position in the military. That much was clear from the unicorn emblem sewn into the back of his jacket.

"So how do you know him?" Cardina, sitting upright next to Kuklo, whispered with a stiff expression.

"Don't ask me."

"So you two aren't acquainted with one another?"

Kuklo shook his head. "Of course not."

The same Military Police Brigade had captured and tossed him into prison without any solid evidence. Had Kuklo known anyone in it, he would never have waited patiently until his exile was meted.

"I see," relented Cardina, but he did not look convinced.

"I'm Jorge Piquer, instructor for the Training Corps," the soldier spoke in what seemed like a reply to their chatter.

Jorge Piquer?! The hero... Even Kuklo knew the name of the previous commander of the Survey Corps, Carlo's father.

The story behind the dramatic rescue dimly came into view, but there was still no reason for Jorge to brave the risk and save Kuklo.

"Did he ask you to do this?" Kuklo said rising up, his eye on Jorge.

"I heard about an interesting talent on our hands. So I took it upon myself to come and see."

"If that is so, why didn't you do something before…"

"I would have, if it were possible. I did not have the time to prove your innocence, or pacify the prison guards. So I waited for them to carry out your sentence."

"On purpose? We nearly died out there!"

While Kuklo criticized Jorge, Cardina nodded. "And that was the point."

"Huh?"

"He's saying he took advantage of the special qualities of the 'exile' sentence."

"That is correct." Jorge nodded, then elaborated in a dry tone, "The sentence of 'exile' does not exist on paper. If such a punishment were made public knowledge, it would cause great mistrust of the royal government." No imaginable punishment was worse than allowing Titans to end the lives of prisoners. "You were dead the moment your sentence was carried out. That's what it means to be exiled. Furthermore, no dead person could be living inside the country. And even if they were, they would not be tracked down for crimes after having received a sentence that doesn't exist."

"Meaning you needed me to be exiled beyond the Wall…"

It was a fairly reckless plan, but the payoff was fittingly large. Now Kuklo would be able to operate in broad daylight, freed of the need to slink away into the dark depths of the underground city in fear of his pursuers.

Yet it was only a miracle that had carried him to safety. Given his itinerary, he could have easily met a bitter end.

"What if I'd died?"

"Then that was what fate had in store, nothing more." In other words, Jorge would have given up. "But because of that, I was able to save another life that I didn't expect."

"I'm sorry," Cardina apologized, nervous for some reason. There were no signs of his usual big mouth, and he was visibly tense.

"Do you two know each other?"

Cardina ducked his head with a start when Kuklo asked this. The answer seemed clear.

"He's my pupil."

"You're in the military?" Kuklo's eyes widened in surprise.

"Well, I was. I dropped out while in training. I don't strike you as soldier material, do I?"

It was nothing to brag about, but in fact, Kuklo didn't see a soldier's uniform suiting him well.

"My parents insisted I become an MP, though," Cardina shrugged.

The Military Police Brigade exercised political influence. It was natural for his father to want him to serve as a channel. Dario had persuaded Xavi to strive to that end, but perhaps Cardina hadn't liked the idea.

"You could have been in the top ten," Jorge said with disappointment in his voice.

"Top ten?" asked Kuklo.

"Depending on your marks," Cardina explained, "you're free to choose the Military Police Brigade as your assignment after you graduate. It's the only chance for a recruit to join the Brigade. It's like getting yourself on the fast track."

"But...you? An MP?" Kuklo looked attentively at Cardina but couldn't even imagine him in a Brigade uniform.

"I know, right? That reaction tells you all you need to know about how out of place I was." Cardina sighed and added, "I suppose you'd make a much better soldier."

"And my son had the same idea. I believe that his assessment was correct."

"You're trying to turn me into a soldier?"

"This is incredible. You have both the former commander and the active commander's personal recommendation."

"I'm sure it's very entertaining to you…" Kuklo objected.

"But think about it. It's like you really are the Titan's son."

Cardina let the name slip from his mouth casually, but Kuklo's eyes opened wide. "You knew?!"

"Well, of course I noticed."

"How?"

"He always bragged about cutting out your right eye."

"Xavi did…"

"Our families knew each other well, and we were in the same class in the Training Corps. He talked about you quite a lot. I got bored of hearing the same stories so many times."

It was easy for Kuklo to imagine Xavi triumphantly reciting tales, filled with lies and exaggerations, of his heroics.

"Xavi has excellent marks," Jorge noted. "If he continues to train, he should be able to apply to the Military Police Brigade as he wishes to do."

"Him? You have to be kidding!" If that were to happen, the country would crumble from the inside before the Titans ever destroyed the walls.

"In that case, why don't you get in his way?" encouraged Cardina.

"Get in his way?!"

"If you join and work your way to the top of the class, you may be able to take his spot."

"That sounds interesting."

Not only had Xavi taken his right eye from him, he had sent him to prison with his false testimony. Beating him up wouldn't make Kuklo feel any better, but smashing his ambitions would be quite satisfying. It was an impure motive, but a perfect way to teach Xavi a lesson.

But… Kuklo quickly shook his head. He didn't have a moment to waste on Xavi. "There's something I need to do first," he said.

His top priority was to be reunited with Sharle. For the time being, everything else was trivial.

Sharle has had to go through so much because of my selfishness... He couldn't go off to start something new quite yet.

"Once you tie things up, will you consider the Training Corps?" Jorge insisted.

"I don't know when that will be." Kuklo sighed and scratched his head.

"If you're talking about meeting that young lady again, that should be happening tonight."

"What?!" Kuklo shouted in spite of himself.

"She was the one who begged Carlo to save your life. You ought to be grateful."

"Sharle did that?"

Sharle meeting Carlo seemed improbable, but when he thought about it, both of them had been at the parade. He'd handed over her charm to Carlo. It wasn't surprising if she'd seen that.

"Oh, her. The one you kidnapped, who was supposed to be my betrothed?"

"I didn't kidnap her," Kuklo retorted and pouted. Then he asked Jorge, "Where are you taking us?"

"The factory city. The young lady is there, too."

"Why is she there?"

"I can't abandon a girl with no family to go home to, can I? My friend works in the city, so I thought it would be the perfect place to have her stay. There's also this machinery I need to return."

Jorge pointed at the strange device he wore on his hips. It was the same mysterious contraption that had yanked Kuklo to safety from the outside world. Without it, he never would have been able to scale Wall Maria.

"What is that contraption?"

"This is the Equipment."

"The Equipment? The one used when a Titan was killed?"

"It was originally a machine used in order to travel to high-up places, but I guess it can be used as an elevator, too. We put the handle on it specially for this plan of ours. Quite a brilliant idea, wouldn't you say?"

As someone who owed his life to the Equipment, Kuklo agreed wholeheartedly, but it also gave rise to a question. The Equipment had even managed to defeat a Titan, so it could have been made standard-issue for Survey Corps members. Not seeing why it hadn't been, Kuklo asked Jorge as much. "Why don't you use it?"

"The Equipment had a fatal flaw."

Jorge explained how the defect had led Angel Aaltonen, the Equipment's creator and user, to halt development. It didn't allow for sideways movement. The prototype Equipment, which served so long as a Titan stood completely still, ran into difficulties against moving targets. That was why the Survey Corps had not been equipped with it.

"So he gave up on defeating Titans…"

"No, he's already completed an anti-Titan model that overcomes the problems of the original Equipment."

Kuklo's voice cracked. "What?"

"It's called the Vertical Maneuvering Equipment."

"The Vertical…what?"

"The Vertical Maneuvering Equipment. It's a version of the Equipment that allows for a full range of maneuvers in all directions." According to Jorge, it was a unique armament they could employ to take on the Titans.

"We can kill Titans by using it?!"

"Without a doubt."

Kuklo had no idea how the device worked in reality, nor could he picture a Titan going down—by human hands, no less—but Jorge's words gave him hope.

In the near future, the Survey Corps would surely go on another expedition beyond the walls, there to slay Titans with the help of the Vertical Maneuvering Equipment.

But the words Jorge spoke next utterly derailed Kuklo's train of thought.

"Kuklo. You're going to use it to defeat them."

CHAPTER FOUR

The monster, a super-dreadnought of a creature surpassing ten meters in height, came storming forward. It took the appearance of a tall, thin youth. Its ferocious charge trampled homes and bowled over humans attempting to flee.

A Titan.

That was the name given to these monsters who acted with such impunity. The sworn enemies of humanity.

While, as one would expect, they were shaped like titanic humans, they bore nothing like compassion in their hearts. Their temperaments were demonically savage, and in face of them humans were no more than crawling insects. The town was overrun with flames and smoke and transformed into a living hell.

Not a single man or woman with the courage to stand against the Titan was anywhere to be found. That was only natural. It meant taking on an absurd mountain of an opponent. Going up against it sword in hand amounted to throwing one's life away. Screaming in terror and scrambling for safety was all that humans could do—except for one boy, one-eyed, known as the Titan's son...

"Damned monster." Kuklo twisted his face in displeasure and fixed his glare on his abhorrent enemy.

Devouring humans with the ease of a glutton stuffing his cheeks with nuts, the giant avatar of the absurd brought total destruction to the town. Could it be enjoying itself? A full smile graced its face.

The Titan then turned to face Kuklo, perhaps noticing his intense stare, and broke into a delighted grin as if it'd been reunited with a best friend.

Exposed to the wickedly overpowering presence, a groan spilled from Kuklo's lips. All it did was look at him; already he was cowering and ready to crumple, having forgotten to breathe. How could a frail human ever hope to withstand the pressure exuded by a Titan?

Just as Kuklo faltered and shrank away, the Titan began its assault on him.

Though it was ten meters tall, it descended on him with the agility of a winged creature. Barely weighted down by its gigantic frame, it was a natural disaster on legs, a living tornado. All that remained in its wake was rubble and corpses.

Kuklo took a step back, then another, subdued by the attacking Titan as it made the ground rumble. The Titan was the one predator that regularly fed on humans. The mind could not but picture death, and the body withered as a natural response. If Kuklo's will failed for the slightest moment, his legs might buckle. Yet he grit his teeth and stood his ground.

It will be the same no matter where I run. Once a Titan had its eye on you, it was nearly impossible to escape from its demonic grasp. The thing would chase Kuklo to the end of the world, lusting to devour his body. *I have to do it. I have to kill it…*

It was a reckless course of action and the only way to come out of this alive.

He drew the sword that hung from his waist and stared at the Titan as it approached with a bizarre cry.

***

"Aaaaahhhh!!"

Kuklo snapped awake, surprised by his own scream. His clothes were drenched with night sweat after his utterly realistic, vivid nightmare. As though he'd been running at a full sprint, his breathing was wild and out of control. His heart rang like an alarm bell to the point of pain.

A dream…

While Kuklo let out a sigh of relief, a hand to his aching chest, the monster he saw in his nightmare did exist in reality. His body had overreacted to a mere dream, a sign that his fear had worked its way to his very core. If he closed his eyes, he could recall the image of a savage Titan in detail.

Not only did the Titans have size on their side, they defied common sense by reviving any number of times unless their single weakness was destroyed. Kuklo had nearly been eaten by one of these ghouls not once but twice, so forgetting them was something he'd never be able to do even if he wished. They had left an immeasurable impact on him and pressed their figures deep into his psyche as with a brand.

"Did you have a scary dream?" a young man in prison clothes asked casually.

Cardina Baumeister. Though a patrician's scion, luck had not been on his side, and he'd been imprisoned after getting wrapped up in political strife. He had been Kuklo's comrade-in-chains, and they'd been banished from the country together as well.

Kuklo finally began to find his bearings. *That's right. We came back from out there…*

His foolish choice to face a Titan, if only in a dream, owed to his earlier escape from the outer lands, which crawled with the monsters. He'd challenged a Titan in order to save Cardina and just barely survived. No wonder he dreamt about it. It didn't take much thought to realize how insane an act it had been—and what a miracle it was that he'd returned alive.

I never want to do that again. Kuklo had been forced to relive his terror. Yet, he might confront a Titan again in the same situation. His temperament did him no good, but he didn't need a reason to save someone's life. *My facing off against those things is like fate, anyway.*

He'd been slapped with the dishonorable name of "Titan's son" at birth and been treated as though his life meant nothing. He was prepared to challenge the Titans because it was his destiny.

As his breathing settled, Kuklo looked around him. Instead of a bed, he was spread out in a horse-drawn carriage with nothing but the clothes on his back, next to Cardina.

I feel like I've slept for a while...

His miraculous return from outside the walls courtesy of Jorge Piquer had only taken place earlier that morning. Since the sun was almost perfectly overhead, he'd slept for a few hours. The carriage was headed north along an artery road that connected various towns, but it would be some time before they reached Wall Rose, let alone their destination, the factory city.

"Want me to guess what you were dreaming about?" Cardina asked in a humming tone. He cheerfully continued before Kuklo had the chance to answer. "I won't beat around the bush. You dreamt that Titans were chasing you."

Cardina's white teeth were visible as he beamed, and Kuklo could only shrug his shoulders in resignation.

"Hm? Was I off?"

"I was being chased by Titans. What else would I dream about?"

"You said it." Considering his own frivolous bent, though, it was hard to imagine Cardina dreaming of Titans.

"To begin with, I had that dream because we had a weird discussion before going to sleep."

"Weird?"

"Something about having me use the Vertical Maneuvering Equipment."

Cardina seemed to take his point. "Ah…"

The Vertical Maneuvering Equipment was an anti-Titan piece of gear based on the "Equipment," the machine used to defeat a Titan for the first time. The original Equipment, however, had the fatal flaw of *only allowing for movement along a single axis*. Improvement after improvement had been made in order to remove this flaw, and the completed Vertical Maneuvering Equipment enabled free movement in all directions. According to Jorge, it was the definitive anti-Titan armament.

Yet it, too, faced a significant issue.

"No one has ever been able to master it, right?" Kuklo recalled. In other words, the Vertical Maneuvering Equipment lacked competent users.

"If it's just the Equipment, I can handle it... It only goes in one direction, after all," Cardina said. Indeed, the original limited movement to a single axis. Since the wielder entrusted his or her body to the machine, which did the rest, Kuklo could easily learn how to pilot it, too. "Unlike the Equipment," Cardina went on, "the Vertical Maneuvering Equipment lets you move in all directions. You need superhuman balance and reflexes to maneuver freely in space like that. One little mistake and you're sure to come crashing down to the ground."

"Have you used it before?"

"Yeah, and I fell out of the sky every time..." Cardina trembled a bit as he spoke. The experience must have been terrifying.

"I'm convinced that you'd be able to master it," broke in the driver of the carriage, a soldier in his early fifties.

This was Jorge Piquer, who cut a dashing figure in his unicorn-emblazoned jacket. Now a soldier belonging to the Military Police Brigade, he had once commanded the Survey Corps and was moreover the national hero who'd proven that Titans could be defeated. Having ceded the post of commander to Carlo Piquer, his son, Jorge now trained soldiers of the next generation as a member of the Military Police Brigade. Cardina had been a student, but he'd withdrawn from the Training Corps before he could be assigned to duty.

"We have to master the Vertical Maneuvering Equipment if we want to get rid of the Titans," Jorge declared with some passion. "No matter how high its quality, the Vertical Maneuvering Equipment is nothing more than junk if no one can use it."

"Speaking of which, it had no development budget, right?" Cardina said. Then he whispered into Kuklo's ear, "Rumor's that the instructor paid for it out of his own pocket."

"Vertical Maneuvering Equipment training is not a part of the

Training Corps curriculum. That's why the Survey Corps uses the same primitive tactics against the Titans that it always has." As the former Survey Corps commander, and as a Training Corps instructor, Jorge didn't seem to be content with the current state of the military. His voice was tinged with irritation.

"I would be able to master that thing?"

"I can't say for sure, but the possibility is there."

"I get the feeling you can do it, too," Cardina chimed in.

"Based on what?"

"Well, you've never even been trained, but look at how you're able to move."

"My son wouldn't have recommended you if you didn't have the potential," Jorge concurred.

Cardina and Jorge had great expectations for his physical acumen, but Kuklo was doubtful. It was true that his years of abuse had endowed him with perseverance. He was confident that he could put up with hell and not give up.

But what good is that against a Titan? A single blow from a Titan's fist would be enough to send Kuklo to the afterlife. Feral quickness and keen senses might help one run away but were clearly insignificant pitted against a Titan's powerful frame.

"Just the fact you stood against a Titan is worthy of praise. Do you know how many soldiers' spirits got crushed in the last expedition?"

The first Survey Corps mission in fifteen years had exposed the troops' mental unpreparedness. As for the personnel who'd deserted the cargo team they'd been ordered to guard, they seemed unlikely to venture outside the walls with the Survey Corps again. The fear that Titans planted in people wasn't easy to wipe away.

"You may have gotten your courage from Heath."

"You mean my father?"

"Heath Mansell served under me, and he trained and served alongside Carlo. He was a daring, fearless exemplar of a soldier."

"Hmph…" Kuklo's uninterested reaction owed to never having

known his father.

"And maybe it was fate that Ogre attacked you."

"Ogre?"

"The name of the Titan you encountered during the expedition."

"That big one…" Kuklo did not have to think back to it. He'd just met the Titan in a dream. The image of its monstrous body, over ten meters tall, clung to his mind like a scab.

"Ogre was the one who got Heath. One might say that you and it are linked by fate."

"So that's what you meant…" But Kuklo didn't feel the bond implied by Jorge. By the time Kuklo was dropped into this world, both of his parents had already left it. A cage had been his cradle, and derision his only lullaby. He felt no particular emotions sprouting in him for Heath, his father.

"Heath wasn't the only one who fell victim to the Titans. Elena's life, too, spiraled out of control when she lost him."

A heretic who worshipped the Titans and wished for the things to enter the city, Elena was the perpetrator of a grave, unprecedented crime. She was also Kuklo's mother. She died after being eaten by the Titan she allowed in, and Kuklo was born from its vomit, earning him the name of "Titan's son."

So both of my parents had their lives ruined by Titans. He seemed bound by a string of fate to the Titans, just as Jorge had pointed out. It was an accursed string, red from the pools of fresh blood it had been soaked in.

That wasn't enough to make him want to avenge his parents. Vengeance for himself was another thing entirely. He'd been forced to live his life as a Titan's son thanks to the Titans, and he was dead set on destroying them.

I hadn't cut my link to the Titans. He'd hoped coming face to face with a Titan outside the walls and learning for sure that he was not a Titan's son might set him off on a fresh new life as a human. Unfortunately, the odd bond seemed to persist.

"Can I take them on if I use the Vertical Maneuvering Equipment?"

"The machine can make that a reality. If you master it, you can fell them," Jorge assured.

And it might let me sever my ties to those monsters. But to do that, Kuklo would have to head outside of the walls and face the Titans once again. *Do I have it in me?*

He'd be up against monsters that he feared so deeply they appeared even in his dreams. He'd rather not encounter them again. No one did.

But I have to do it. Until he severed his ties of fate to the Titans, he'd have to live in perpetual fear of their shadow. That was something he had absolutely no interest in, and he was being offered a perfect opportunity to rid himself of the moniker of "Titan's son." He had no choice but to gather his courage and fight.

That was not all Kuklo had to worry about, though. His thoughts next turned to a precarious young girl who looked like a bisque doll— Sharle Inocencio. Kuklo's savior, she'd bestowed him with knowledge and led him to the world. Without Sharle, Kuklo would undoubtedly still be on display somewhere as a Titan's son.

I'm sure she'll be angry...

It was Kuklo's selfish wish to meet a Titan that had ended up getting him exiled in the first place. He'd reaped what he'd sown. The entire affair must have been unbearable for Sharle, who'd been swept into it. After fleeing her home empty-handed following an unforeseen attack on her family by cultists, she and Kuklo had survived by relying on each other and no one else. It wasn't hard for him to imagine her anxiety. It was only thanks to Sharle's wits and tact that Kuklo had returned safely from beyond Wall Maria.

And I'm going back out there anyway? The mere thought was enough to dampen his mood, but now that he'd learned more about his relationship to the Titans, Kuklo couldn't go on living pretending that he hadn't. He would have to convince Sharle.

"Well, do your best. I'll be cheering for you from the curtains." Cardina spoke like it wasn't his business.

"Hah?" Kuklo's voice cracked. Patting Cardina on the shoulder, he said, "You're coming with me."

"Wha?!" It was Cardina's voice's turn to crack.

"If not for me, you wouldn't have been able to come back. You should join me."

"I've already withdrawn from training, and I'm not talented like you…"

"Jorge said you could make it into the top ten with some work."

"Ugh… I feel like I've dug my own grave."

"You've saved me the hassle of roping him in," Jorge thanked, still looking straight ahead and muffling a chuckle. "Both of you have what it takes. I guarantee you that much."

"So he says."

Cardina grimaced and scratched his head. "Oh, fine. I do owe you."

By the time their conversation had come to a close, a gigantic wall that seemed to scrape the heavens came into view ahead of them. The sheer cliff was Wall Rose, a distillation of the human intellect. The solemn structure boasted a height of fifty meters, the same as Wall Maria, and its presence was overwhelming. While less prominent due to its central placement, it would be humanity's new defense line if Wall Maria were ever to be breached. It went without saying that it played an important role both politically and militarily.

"We're at the halfway point. Why don't we get a little food and rest in Trost District," Jorge proposed.

Kuklo's stomach grumbled his reply for him.

***

The workshop chief's office was shockingly messy. The floor looked like a child had overturned a box of toys onto it, and scattered about were documents, parts, and junk inventions with unknown uses. If a visitor were told that this was a dumping site, it would have rung true. So unseemly was the room—and truth be told, the majority of the items there were, in fact, trash.

It was not easy, but a path could be discerned. However, going off it would be a mighty challenge. Bookshelves, a work desk, and furniture used to receive visitors were all present and visible, but the piles of junk extended even to those, leaving them unusable. Among it all, a single shelf that presented a mysterious apparatus beamed like a store's showcase. The room seemed not to have been cleaned in years. It was full of dust and stank slightly of mold.

"Ack." Having arrived at the workshop chief's office with a broom in one hand and a dustpan in another, Sharle Inocencio stared blankly at the scene before her. *How does a room even turn out like this?*

For Sharle, the high-bred daughter of the famed merchant baron Dario Inocencio, the sight of the office was like something out of a nightmare. It wouldn't be a surprise if some bizarre verminous bug lived under the sheaves of paper.

The old Sharle would have gotten cold feet and left, but her heart had grown stouter, especially after her brush with death. A dirty room still surprised her, but it wasn't enough to stop her in her tracks. When she thought back to the days she'd spent in the darkness of the underground city living in fear of pursuit, the office she faced seemed like a trifling hazard.

"All right, why don't we get started."

The room wouldn't get any tidier if she just stood around. She needed to work her hands, not her mouth, and get to cleaning the room like it was nothing. She'd gone to the trouble of borrowing a set of working clothes, so she could leap into this battle against messiness without having to worry about getting her own dress dirty. Compared to other clashes the one she faced was less stressful, but this was a mission, and she had tasked herself with it.

"Okay!" Sharle fired up her spirit and waded into the room,

pushing trash on the floor aside with her feet.

It was now a month since Sharle first came to the factory town. Her life here was utterly peaceful. These, perhaps, were the first days in her fifteen years spent entirely carefree. Strictly speaking, she did worry about something, but it'd surely be resolved soon.

I'm happy. She'd been made to live as her father's tool, but that was now in the past. Dario, who'd put her life under his thumb, had succumbed to the daggers of murderous heretics that worshipped Titans. She was finally free from the Inocencio family's spell and lived as she wanted—even if her freedom had come in the unwanted form of her father's demise…

Sharle now lived in the workshop that acted as the factory city's core. Its chief was Xenophon Harkimo. Under his command, it was singlehandedly responsible for weapons and gear sold to the military and handled everything from development to manufacture. In essence, it was an armory. As many as a thousand craftsmen toiled from day to night, and Sharle rented a room there.

She had no complaints about life in the workshop. While it was impossible to keep from being annoyed by the noises and vibrations that came ringing, it was a minor issue compared to all that she'd faced before. They seemed to treat her like a guest, and she wasn't put to work, but she didn't feel comfortable about simply accepting their generosity. So she'd volunteered to clean. The state of disorder of the workshop chief's room seemed like an accurate reflection of its occupant.

Sharle began by reaching for the reams of paper piled on the floor like confetti. Fortunately for her, no poisonous vermin came flying out at her, but she was surprised nonetheless at what she found written on the documents.

"Blueprints? Contracts? Aren't these important?" Even Sharle, with her sheltered upbringing, could tell at a glance that these were precious documents. Perhaps Xenophon had been made workshop chief by some sort of mistake, but surely his talents were so great that they compensated for his weaknesses. At least, that was the favorable way Sharle decided to interpret it as she continued to clean the room.

Just as she'd finally cleaned the floor to the point of walkability and moved on to the bookshelves, a man who looked to be in his fifties popped in wearing a dirty, chemical-soaked set of work clothes.

"Ah, seeing a girl toil away like that reminds me of the old days."

The distinctive man with an unkempt head of salt-and-pepper hair, a face full of stubble, and thick, rimless glasses was none other than Xenophon, the workshop chief. His appearance suggested that he was perhaps better at hands-on work than reigning as the master of his own castle. Few in his position would ever emit the same chemical stench.

He's a good man, but... The suspicions Xenophon inspired in others overpowered his virtues.

"Yes, and she cleaned the rooms just as you're doing now." He seemed moved as he stroked his beard.

"Does she still work here?"

"No, she passed away fifteen years ago."

That means... The deceased craftswoman must have been attacked by the Titan that had invaded Shiganshina District. Xenophon would not have specified the number of years otherwise.

Fifteen years ago, the workshop city wasn't functional yet, and workshops were scattered among different towns. Xenophon and the woman in question must have worked together in the Shiganshina District workshop.

"She may be gone now, but her spirit is alive and well," the chief said. Trekking down the trail blazed by Sharle, he headed to the shelf that held the mysterious apparatus. It seemed to be something he was proud of, and his eyes glimmered like an innocent child's.

"What is that?"

"It's the Vertical Maneuvering Equipment."

"The Vertical Maneuvering Equipment?"

"I guess you could call it the only machine capable of matching the Titans."

"Is that some sort of successor to the Equipment?"

"That's about right."

Satisfied with the explanation, Sharle looked closely at the machine that sat on the shelf, but she had no idea whatsoever of how it worked. Considering what the Equipment had been able to do though, it was easy to imagine that the Vertical Maneuvering Equipment was an astonishing breakthrough.

The Equipment was the invention used to defeat a Titan for the first time. That would mean the Vertical Maneuvering Equipment was capable of even more. As she observed its parts, she noticed an inscription that appeared to refer to a celestial spirit.

"ANGEL?"

"It's pronounced 'an-hel.' The man who developed the Vertical Maneuvering Equipment."

"And the one who created the Equipment, right?"

"And also my rival. *He* should have been made workshop chief, but he decided to retire, of all things. Yes, he was having trouble with his eyes, but still, how unfortunate." Xenophon slumped his shoulders, either lamenting the absence of his rival or exhausted by the burdens of being workshop chief. Possibly both. "But it was surely the right decision. It wouldn't have been easy to outdo himself after inventing the Vertical Maneuvering Equipment."

"So he went out on top?"

"Well, he left one hell of a parting gift."

"Is that so?"

"There's such a thing as a machine's controls being too responsive. What good is a steed that no one can master?" Xenophon sighed as he pushed his glasses back up with his index finger. "You think this guy you're waiting for can tame it?" he threw out, watching for Sharle's reaction.

I'm happy they're saving Kuklo, but... Carlo and Jorge were planning to recruit Kuklo. They weren't so stingy as to stipulate any conditions in exchange for their help, but considering his debt to the two, Kuklo seemed likely to go along with them. In fact, he might do so quite eagerly.

Of course, that worry could wait until his safe return.

"Oh, it's nothing to get worked up about. If Carlo and Jorge, two generations of commanders, see something in him, he'll surely make it back fine."

"If you say so…" Sharle, who knew quite well how dangerous it was outside the walls, couldn't bring herself to trust Xenophon's reasoning. How could she stay calm? If he came across a Titan, it would be over.

The daring plan to pluck Kuklo up from outside the walls had already been set into motion. If everything had gone smoothly, they would be reunited in a matter of hours. She only wished she had some way of knowing.

"For now, we just have to wait," advised Xenophon. "You don't have to agree with me, but you do believe he'll return alive, don't you?"

"Yes."

"Then I shall wait and believe, too. For our ultimate challenger to return." Xenophon grinned. "I can't wait to see the path he draws across the sky," he said, taking the Vertical Maneuvering Equipment from the shelf.

"Challenger"?! There was something disquieting about the word, but Sharle willed herself not to mind. After all, she couldn't imagine any misfortune worse than his latest ordeal visiting Kuklo.

Forcing herself to feel satisfied, Sharle wielded her broom and got back to cleaning the office.

***

After taking an hour-long food break in Trost District, Kuklo's party split from the artery to enter a side road. Passing through multiple checkpoints, they continued to head north. The security seemed almost too rigorous, perhaps because they were headed to the factory city. Kuklo saw no regular citizens, only soldiers and the men and women they guarded.

Glancing at the patrolling soldiers, Kuklo noticed their gear and muttered, "High alert…"

Unlike the soldiers stationed in Trost District, these troops seemed on edge, ready to strike the moment an enemy appeared. They carried short swords on their waist that must have been made of Iron Bamboo, and even shouldered carbines. Ammunition surely filled the horses' saddlebags. Even the Garrison troops in Shiganshina District on watch for Titans didn't appear as tense as these soldiers.

"Speaking of strict, how about those checkpoints?"

As Cardina pointed out, the soldiers manning the checkpoints were so heavily armed they seemed ready to start a war. While the town gates were like sieves despite being guarded, the personnel here were scrupulous in their inspections. Once, Kuklo and Sharle had purchased false identification from a merchant to escape from Wall Sheena; it was doubtful that the same trick would work along this route. It went without saying that any attempts to grease a soldier's palms were likewise bound to fail. Merely approaching a checkpoint would be out of bounds if Jorge weren't with them.

"The factory city is practically an armory. Its loss could imperil the nation's very existence," the instructor explained. Judging by the airtight, heavy security, they'd already faced an incident along those lines.

"It's singlehandedly responsible for everything from the development to the manufacturing of arms," agreed Cardina. "This is the only place where Iron Bamboo and Iceburst Stone can be processed."

On top of that, a mint was located in the city. Cultists or anti-establishment groups occupying it would be a grand debacle.

Humans are scarier than Titans…

While the Titans were absolutely ridiculous monsters, their lack of intelligence made them easy to manage. It certainly helped Wall

Maria maintain its proud reputation of being indestructible. Meanwhile, humanity's intellect made up for its powerlessness. A good example was Elena, the cultist who let a Titan into town without needing to destroy the wall. It explained the military's excessive defense measures for the factory city.

But thanks to that, Sharle can live there safely.

Letting out a sigh of relief, Kuklo stared ahead of him. The road went gradually uphill, and he was starting to feel cold from the slightly increased altitude. He did not know the factory city's location, but taking convenience and secrecy into account, it was most likely in the outskirts of Wall Sheena. The chilly and clear air reminded Kuklo of the harsh days he spent living in a shed.

Not that they'll ever turn into fond memories… Still, Kuklo wouldn't be who he was without the experience. If a stroke of luck had freed him from the shed, he surely would have ended up dying on some nameless street. In that sense, even his days of abuse at the hands of Xavi Inocencio, Sharle's older brother, seemed meaningful to him.

"Eh, another checkpoint? How many more are there?"

Cardina looked fed up, but Kuklo was unperturbed. Though certainly irritating, the body searches were as noninvasive as possible thanks to Jorge's presence. The increased number of checkpoints also proved that they were nearing their destination.

I can meet her soon.

Kuklo felt a slight quickening in his chest.

***

By the time the factory city was in sight, the sun had long set.

It was still as bright as dusk thanks to the city's many gas-powered street lamps. You didn't need a lantern to walk the streets. With an Iceburst Stone extraction site nearby, the city was prone to reaping the mineral's benefits. Even Shiganshina District, with its full array of facilities, was shuttered at night by darkness. The difference was stark.

The city's scale was also far beyond what Kuklo had imagined. He'd pictured small, compact factories, but the place's size put it on par with Shiganshina District. Not only were there businesses to address workers' daily necessities, the area was even home to amusement facilities. The city appeared to be its own independent country, the result of having gathered the gamut of resources, human and otherwise, needed to let it stand on its own. Of course, security was strict. While not fifty meters tall, there was a defensive wall, and countless guards kept watchful eyes on the factory city. No run-of-the-mill attack would ever bring it down.

A large blast furnace loomed like a landmark in the center. The giant furnace, which *was* fifty meters tall, clearly generated copious amounts of heat. Refining Iron Bamboo demanded as much, and it was no wonder that weapons made of the material were astoundingly sharp and durable.

The workshop, the trio's destination, stood at the foot of the furnace. Even now, countless craftsmen seemed to be toiling away, and the shrill, intermittent sounds of metal being forged rang from within it.

Kuklo, Cardina, and Jorge left the carriage and headed straight to the workshop chief's room. The chief seemed to be a well-organized man, as his room was neat and tidy. What appeared to be weapons and gear developed by the workshop lined the walls. It was practically a showroom. In particular, a mannequin stood out. A machine resembling the Equipment was attached to it.

Is that the Vertical Maneuvering Equipment? At first glance, it seemed no different from the Equipment.

Be that as it may, it wasn't the prized invention that compelled their attention, but rather a craftsman type who lay sound asleep and snoring on a sofa.

Is he Xenophon, the workshop chief?! Compared to the elegant room, the slumbering man gave a vastly different impression. His disheveled hair seemed to have not once met a comb, and his mouth hung open.

His aloofness was evident from his filthy work clothes, stained as they were by some mysterious liquid. He certainly didn't look like someone who oversaw all the craftsmen. A sleepwalking underling accidentally napping in the chief's room was more like it.

When Kuklo looked at Jorge questioningly, the instructor replied with a nod and a wry smile.

So he is the workshop chief. Looks could certainly be misleading, but it was still baffling to Kuklo. "So—" he began, hoping to bring up an important topic.

That was when Xenophon, apparently sensing that he had visitors, opened his eyes.

"You've finally decided to arrive," the workshop chief greeted, quickly sitting up. He took a deep yawn and stretched. "I was worried you might have been eaten by Titans."

"So worried you fell asleep."

"I hope you'll excuse me, but all the waiting tired me out. I was asleep before I knew it," Xenophon confessed without a trace of guilt, turning towards Kuklo. "Allow me, then: Welcome, my challenger!"

"Challenger?" Kuklo parroted.

Xenophon grinned. "You're the daredevil who's going to try to learn how to master the thing. I believe challenger is an appropriate title."

Kuklo sighed. "It wasn't my idea."

"Controlling the Vertical Maneuvering Equipment will be a truly difficult task, but I would love to see you dancing in the skies like an angel."

"An angel?"

"You'll understand soon enough. More than you might care to." Smiling like a mischievous child, the workshop chief ran an assessing pair of eyes over Kuklo.

I'm getting a bad feeling about this. There should have been nothing to fear about wearing and operating a machine, but Kuklo's anxiety was growing with each word Xenophon spoke. Something like a sixth sense was detecting danger and sounding an alarm.

"By the way, what's this guy for? Is he a spare?" Xenophon asked, turning to Cardina with unabashed curiosity.

"I think he's confusing me for a machine part…"

Cardina's complaint wasn't far off the mark. Xenophon was a man who walked many fine lines as a mad engineer of sorts. At the same time, he had managed to climb his way up to workshop chief, so he was clearly somebody—even if he seemed to have traded something in for his talent.

"I'm going to be taking care of them," Jorge warned.

"Hmph. So you're going to work them like dogs as recruits? I'd be tempted to pity them…but I'm sure they can handle it."

"Why do you say that?" Kuklo inquired.

"You were able to return alive despite being chased by Titans. That's more than enough experience under your belt."

"The greenhorns don't even compare."

Neither Jorge nor Xenophon's faith in him assuaged Kuklo.

I was just lucky… It would be one thing if he'd exercised his wits, hatched a plan, and relied on his physical capabilities to escape from the Titans. Overcoming the situation and returning to the interior on his own would have been extremely difficult. *Or rather, impossible.*

If Sharle had not entreated Carlo, and if Carlo had not spoken to Jorge, Kuklo would have ended up in a Titan's stomach alongside Cardina.

"By the way, what about the training equipment I requested?"

"Oh, *that*? It will arrive soon enough. Learning to manage it promises to be next to impossible, though."

Jorge and Xenophon continued their conversation, but what interested Kuklo was neither the Vertical Maneuvering Equipment nor his own potential as a recruit. Just as he was getting impatient that the two weren't turning to the main issue at hand, his ears picked up a slight sound.

That's…

He knew this sound that approached him with a steady rhythm. They were footsteps. Before the image of the person making them could even form in his mind, the door to the workshop chief's office burst open. Everyone's eyes turned to settle on the girl who stood at the entrance.

"Kuklo!" With that lively cry, she leapt into his chest. Then she clung to him, and that was how anxious she'd been. "I'm so glad you're all right," breathed Sharle.

Kuklo felt shocked at his own recklessness, rather belatedly, and relieved from the bottom of his heart that he'd made it back.

I'm lucky just to be alive. No sooner than he let out a sigh, a wave of fatigue came crashing down on him. He was hardly to blame. Tossed out of the walls before sunrise, he'd danced with a Titan. If anything, he deserved a pat on the shoulder for not keeling over.

"Oh dear. We'd planned out such a moving reunion, but you couldn't wait and just had to jump the gun…" Xenophon grimaced and scratched his head. "I suppose you could say this is moving in its own way."

"I know it seems like everyone wants to leave the young couple to themselves, but do you think you could introduce us first?" Cardina asked Kuklo, grinning. He seemed to be enjoying the situation.

He's acting like he's a stranger… In truth, Cardina had a connection to Sharle. As the heads of the Inocencio family and the Baumeister family were now departed, their engagement had to be moot; it seemed unlikely that Cardina would be interested in courting her, certainly not at this stage, but this was delicate stuff.

"You don't need to be introduced," Kuklo stated.

"Not for my sake. But, you know, because the young lady doesn't know who I am?"

Sharle had regained her composure while Kuklo and Cardina chatted. She stood up straight, turned to Cardina, and bowed her head. "My name is Sharle Inocencio."

"How polite of you. I'm Cardina Baumeister. Nice to meet you,"

Cardina replied innocently, glancing at Sharle to catch her reaction.

As he expected, it was extreme. She dashed around Kuklo to hide.

"You don't need to worry, *that* business isn't valid anymore. I'd opposed my father's plans, anyway, so I think that makes us something like friends."

"Friends?" The word seemed to calm Sharle. She looked relieved.

"I might have been spared a prison sentence if I'd stayed in the Training Corps like a good boy."

As luck would have it, Cardina had left the Training Corps just as Bruno, his father, had walked into a trap laid by his political opponents. He'd probably have avoided a sojourn behind bars simply by sweating his days away as a recruit. Even politicians couldn't touch a member of the Training Corps, which was overseen by the Military Police Brigade.

Jorge would never have allowed it, either, Kuklo reasoned. The instructor hoped to see the Vertical Maneuvering Equipment in action, and training new recruits was his first priority. Besides, Cardina had been talented enough to contend for the top ten. There was not a chance Jorge would have surrendered him to politicians.

"So! Can I finally start talking about the Vertical Maneuvering Equipment?" Xenophon intervened with a forced cough in a blatant attempt to change the topic. He was so impatient to introduce the Vertical Maneuvering Equipment that his eyes glimmered like a child's.

He was met by resistance from none other than Jorge. "I think this is enough for today. Both of you must be tired, yes?"

Kuklo and Cardina seconded this without a moment's hesitation.

Xenophon looked displeased. "It would be helpful if you could provide feedback on how the Vertical Maneuvering Equipment handles," he insisted.

Defeated by everyone else's silence, he threw up his arms.

***

Sharle had been assigned a small room measuring less than ten square meters. It had served as a nap room for craftsmen, a breed who loved their work more than their daily bread, so all it afforded was a place to sleep. The impression was reinforced by the fact that the beds occupied over half of the room. It reminded Kuklo of life in the underground city, but there was a skylight so it wasn't suffocating. Despite the incessant echoes of craftwork, only the sensitive would have trouble sleeping here. Compared to life in the underground city, life in the workshop was heaven.

"I'm relieved," Kuklo muttered, gazing about the room. He had no idea how Sharle had fared after Shiganshina, but the workshop seemed to be treating her well.

I'm not so sure about Xenophon, though. Even then, next to the likes of Xavi and Dario, the workshop chief was decent.

"I think I'm a lot more relieved than you are," Sharle accused with a dry laugh, then sat down on one of the beds. "I'm shocked you were with someone from the Baumeister family, though. Where did you two meet?"

"In prison," Kuklo replied, eliciting an *oh* and a nod of understanding from Sharle. Rumors of the Baumeister family's fate had been circulating in the underground city, so the outcome was no surprise. "Believe it or not, he used to be in the Training Corps," Kuklo told her.

"He was a recruit?!" No doubt having pegged him as a spoiled heir, Sharle's eyes went wide with surprise. Her reaction was worth a chuckle, but Kuklo had received a similar first impression.

"He isn't a bad person."

"Well, yes, I can tell, somehow," Sharle answered with a smile, but her face soon darkened. "The Training Corps..."

"Is something the matter?"

"You're going to enter the training academy, aren't you?"

"I suppose," Kuklo said noncommittally. He hadn't made the

choice for himself so he was hardly to blame, but that wasn't what bugged Sharle.

"If you join, that means you'll be with my brother…"

So that's what. Sharle's complaint wasn't that Kuklo wanted to become a soldier. It was that he'd be reunited with Xavi. Her anxiety was only natural considering how the two had parted ways.

"It's not as though we'll be alone," Kuklo reassured her. Meeting Xavi back in the shed would be one thing, but the academy hosted many trainees. Xavi couldn't attempt anything rash. *Things aren't like they were then, either.*

Kuklo's eye fell on his wrists. The sensation of the shackles once on his arms and legs still remained with him. Though seldom aware of it, listening closely now he even heard the metallic jingling of the chains, and just like that, he was brought back to the days of abuse he'd suffered as a Titan's son. The countless wounds engraved on his body began to throb.

Kuklo balled his fists tight and drove the memories out of his mind.

Nothing holds me down now. He wouldn't let Xavi pull ahead of him, either. "Apparently he's good enough to apply to become an MP," he said.

"My brother?"

"I can't imagine him as one, though." The Military Police were the elite who stood at the top of the military. The majestic figure that Jorge cut sufficed to convey their special status. Kuklo couldn't imagine Xavi wearing the unicorn emblem on his back; letting him do so would jeopardize the Brigade's dignity.

"It's because he's weirdly confident," Sharle noted.

"Confident?"

"Well, he thinks he beat a Titan's son."

"Oh. I see…"

It was a truly annoying thing for Kuklo to hear, but subduing a Titan's son did seem like an invaluable experience for a recruit. One could say Dario's scenario had worked out well for Xavi.

"In any case, this is the last foolish thing I do," Kuklo said, sitting down next to Sharle.

"I'm betting you'll never stop."

"I will, really. I know exactly what my goal is."

"Your goal?"

"Killing Ogre."

Sharle looked inquiringly at Kuklo, and he began to explain his connection to the Titan. Ogre and Kuklo's family were bound by chains of misfortune.

"That's why I have to kill Ogre with the Vertical Maneuvering Equipment. That will be what finally severs our bond."

"Ogre…" Sharle briefly sank into thought before speaking again. "I may have seen that Titan."

"Seen it? Where?!"

"It was a long time ago—" Sharle began, telling Kuklo of the time she climbed atop Wall Maria on a family trip. The Titan she saw then was large, a ten-meter-class, and resembled a skinny twenty year old. The most lasting impression, though, was its smile. It sounded a lot like Ogre, the Titan that was Kuklo's sworn enemy. "I'll never forget what it looked like," she said, finishing her story.

"Yeah." The Titan was frightening enough to give Kuklo nightmares, so it was a given that a young Sharle would fear it.

"But I guess I should thank that Titan in some small way," she said.

"Why is that?"

"If I'd never seen it, I wouldn't have been able to tell that you weren't a Titan's son." Sharle took out a familiar object from her pocket. It was the Iron Bamboo paring knife she kept as a charm.

That's why I didn't have to get killed that night… Sharle, knife in hand, had visited him with an intent to do harm the first time they'd met in the shed. If she hadn't seen the Titan from the wall, she might have mistaken Kuklo for a genuine child of the monsters.

"You hold on to this, Kuklo. I'm sure it'll come in handy."

Sharle held out the knife and Kuklo took it from her. Right away, he clutched the sheath and pulled out the blade. Its sharpness evident, the knife that could rend even Titan flesh shone an unclouded silver. Kuklo had no idea how effective it was as a charm, but already having saved him more than once, the weapon was worthy of his trust.

Maybe it can sever my ties to the Titans, too. Perhaps a knife alone wasn't sufficient for felling a Titan, but if he learned from Jorge and mastered the Vertical Maneuvering Equipment, it didn't seem impossible, either.

Then again, Kuklo didn't have much of a clue about the machine. Not the faintest...

***

His first sound night of sleep in what felt like ages revitalized Kuklo. Muscles all over his body hurt after being harnessed to the limit against a Titan the previous day, but it wasn't as though he couldn't move. In fact, he felt refreshed thanks to his unbroken respite. Come to think of it, he'd never before gone to bed neither monitored nor pursued. It was no surprise that he felt so rested.

While a good part of him hoped he could just sleep in, Xenophon summoned him before he could relax even a little more.

"Can't I at least spend one day in bed?"

Kuklo couldn't but grumble, but he was in Xenophon and the workshop's debt for a night's room and board. Given what they had done for Sharle too, he couldn't simply refuse.

I do want to see the Vertical Maneuvering Equipment. Said to be the definitive anti-Titan armament but known for remaining completely unused, the Vertical Maneuvering Equipment was a fascinating tool indeed. For Kuklo, who wished to sever his bond to the Titans, it promised to be an indispensable device.

Though excitement filled him, he felt just as anxious. The reason was simple. *The workshop chief created it.*

The Vertical Maneuvering Equipment was an invention co-developed by Xenophon and Angel based on the Equipment. While Jorge had given it his guarantee, its performance seemed questionable in more ways than one. Kuklo's doubts were backed up by the fact that no one had been able to control the machine.

It worries me, but... If he needed it in order to defeat the Titans, he had no choice but to master the tool.

As soon as he opened the door to the chief's office, Xenophon greeted Kuklo, applauding. The blazing glint in the chief's eyes more than hinted at his jubilance that the Vertical Maneuvering Equipment was going to be tested out.

Also present were Cardina, Jorge, and Sharle.

"Now that our leading man is here, why don't we have him get dressed?" the workshop chief cut to the chase, pointing to the soldier's uniform lying on a table. It consisted of three pieces: a shirt, trousers, and a jacket. The khaki jacket bore the emblem of the Training Corps, two crossed swords. "It should be the right size. Try it on."

Kuklo followed Xenophon's instructions and put on the shirt and trousers. The cotton clothes, light yet warm, fit him so well they felt like a part of his body.

"Hey, you look pretty good in those," Cardina observed.

"When were you able to get these, though?"

It was Jorge who answered Kuklo. "I had a hunch you'd want to become a soldier. I ordered them in advance."

"These fit awfully well..." The uniform felt like an extension of his own skin, yet they had never taken his measurements. He felt completely unrestricted.

Sharle answered next, but not with words. She simply looked away from Kuklo, but her reaction was enough.

So that's what. She knew his measurements. Xenophon must have gotten all sorts of information out of her.

"You seem to have seen the light, so could you try wearing this next?" Xenophon took the harness off of the mannequin it sat on and presented it to Kuklo.

The harness stretched from the shoulders to the back and the legs, even down to the toes. On first sight, it resembled a straightjacket. Somewhat distrustfully, Kuklo began to strap it to his body.

"The harness is like a bit and bridle. A rider controls the bridle to stimulate the bit and make a horse follow orders. If we translate this to the Vertical Maneuvering Equipment, you could say the harness is the bit and bridle, while the equipment itself is the horse," Xenophon explained as he attached the machine's main unit to Kuklo's waist. "And these things placed on both sides of your hips are for firing anchors."

Kuklo looked at his waist and saw contraptions that looked like saddlebags.

"You've already experienced that feature."

"What do you mean?"

"That's what pulled us up from outside the wall," Cardina assisted.

"That thing came from one of these?"

"They fire anchors into targets and pull your body along by reeling in the wires attached to them. These controllers are used to manage them."

Xenophon handed Kuklo two devices that looked like saber hilts. Instead of a hand guard, the controllers had levers that could be used to reel in wires. As with the old Equipment, the controls were so simple that even Kuklo could understand them without having to ask twice. "It's quite simple," he ventured.

"Of course it is!" Xenophon said, his chest puffed out with pride. "The machine's structure may be complex, but make it as simple as possible to control. Inventions come from a desire to simplify difficult operations, after all."

Kuklo got that, but one thing still troubled him and he pointed it out: "I can't attack if both of my hands are full." Even if he made use of the controllers to move freely in space, he'd never be able to defeat

Titans if he had no way of attacking them.

"That was actually one problem with the old Equipment." Xenophon seemed to have been expecting the question, as his tone grew lively without skipping a beat. "The controllers look like sword hilts because they also act as weapons."

"Weapons? These?" Kuklo checked them out again, but they just looked like saber hilts missing their blades. He didn't detect any special machinery in them, either.

"Please place the controllers in the scabbards."

As soon as Kuklo placed them in the scabbards at his sides as Xenophon instructed, there was a clicking sound and a slight vibration in his palms. Some feature seemed to have been activated. When Kuklo looked at Xenophon, the chief nodded back as if to say, *You'll see when you pull them out.*

Kuklo gripped the hilts once again and drew them slowly. Two thin blades appeared, each with regularly spaced notches on them.

"Those are single-edged swords made from Ultrahard Steel."

"They look kind of weak…" While it was clear that Xenophon held the single-edged swords in the highest esteem, the thin blades seemed quite unreliable. They flexed at the slightest application of force and would surely snap in a sword fight.

"Don't let looks deceive you. Their sharpness is second to none."

"Will they even work against Titans?"

"Of course! They're specially made to be used against them," Xenophon shot back. "They were made in order to cut through Titan flesh. Specifically, they're weapons made to slice out their weak point, the medulla oblongata." The blades described a gentle curve and flexed like willow trees for that same reason. "While the drawback is that they break rather easily, the scabbard holds many replacement blades so that shouldn't pose a problem. And of course, I guarantee their sharpness."

"I see," Kuklo said, returning the blades to their scabbards and placing the controllers back into the cases on each side of his body.

They looked exactly like holsters.

"That's all you have to wear. Less bulky than you thought, right?"

Just as Xenophon said, the Vertical Maneuvering Equipment had been kept relatively compact. It seemed to weigh only two or three kilograms. While it would be difficult to move around unrestricted while wearing it, it had not been designed with land-based combat in mind, so its weight was unlikely to be a hindrance.

"All right, everyone. Let us now to the stage where Kuklo will be making his debut!" Ushering them in high style, Xenophon exited the room, a skip in his steps. He seemed uncontrollably happy that someone was about to operate the machine.

"I have a bad feeling about this." The more gleeful Xenophon grew, the more Kuklo's sense of unease deepened.

But it was no time to falter. Kuklo and company nodded to one another and left the chief's office.

***

Xenophon brought the group to a lot in the rear of the workshop. It was being used as a storehouse for materials, and heaps of raw ore and Iron Bamboo stood high. Something else caught their attention, though.

"That's—"

As soon as Kuklo saw it, his body stiffened, and a chill came over him like a splash of ice water. A humanoid form over five meters in height towered over him.

Why is one of those monsters here?!

Even as Kuklo reached for the controllers sitting in his holsters, confused, he realized that the figure poised as if to pounce on him was a paper Titan. It seemed to be made of some kind of wood product. He noticed a grain-like texture on its skin when he looked more closely.

"Pretty well made, isn't it? I thought we'd be able to use it for training purposes," Xenophon bragged. A terror-inducing level of finish seemed like overdoing it. Still, even though a crude caricature would have done, perhaps a target that closely resembled a Titan was preferable for simulating real combat. Five meters weren't even enough; Ogre was twice as large as the dummy. That fact drove home what an incredible monster it was.

"All right, now try out the Vertical Maneuvering Equipment," prompted Xenophon.

"You say that like it's nothing..." Kuklo pulled the controllers from their holsters and looked up at the dummy. While it had flustered him just moments ago, the imitation was nothing like the real thing now that he observed it calmly. Even then, it was imposing, and Kuklo felt oppressed and outmatched by it merely as it sat there.

"Maneuvering in all three dimensions will be tough, but going in a straight line shouldn't be beyond you," Xenophon encouraged matter-of-factly, hardly putting Kuklo at ease.

I can't kill Ogre without this, though. In order to strike at a Titan's medulla oblongata, its weakness, he had to overcome the problem of height. Even more so in face of a ten-meter-class Titan.

"By the way, the machine uses gas extracted from Iceburst Stone as fuel. Those cylinders attached to your scabbards send fuel to the main unit."

Kuklo looked at the scabbards on both sides and noticed cylinders ending in valves.

"This goes without saying, but it stops working if you run out of gas. Be quite careful not to run out—though I guess it won't be an issue if you never get the hang of it."

"I'll try." Kuklo put his fingers on the controllers' levers and looked up at the towering Titan.

All right. The second he gathered his resolve and pulled the levers, the Vertical Maneuvering Equipment on his hips let out a bestial howl. Before he had a chance to be surprised, it ejected compressed gas to send two anchors flying like bullets from the devices attached to each side of him. It was almost like an air gun. Like a fang the left anchor bit firmly into the tip of the dummy Titan's chin, but the right anchor just barely missed its mark.

"You might have hit the target if your right eye was fine. You basically have to eyeball it," Xenophon quipped. He nodded with a satisfied look on his face, so it must have been a good result for a first attempt.

"I wasn't aiming for anything in particular…"

"The harness attached to your body works in sync with the firing mechanism."

"It aims on its own?"

"You just need to look at your target and work the levers on your controllers."

In other words, the Vertical Maneuvering Equipment would do all the busywork for him. Kuklo returned the anchors to the firing mechanisms and glared once again at the Titan dummy. Though he might not be acquiring his target perfectly without his right eye, he felt he could compensate by making minor adjustments based on where the anchors landed before.

Kuklo stared at the tip of the Titan's chin and pressed the levers. Both anchors shot out and hit the dummy's chin, the taut wires attached to them giving him solid feedback.

I'm managing, but that's all. He wouldn't have time to modify his aim in a real battle. Using the Vertical Maneuvering Equipment against a Titan would require ever-perfect shots. If an anchor missed its target, he'd either lose his balance and fall to his death, or a Titan would grab and eat him.

As soon as he returned the levers to their original position, the machine began reeling in the wires at a fierce rate. Guided by the anchors, Kuklo soared into the air and headed toward the Titan dummy. The lightning velocity was such that his face distorted from the strain as his body was carried away. A moment's lapse in concentration and he'd black out for sure.

"Nkk…" Despite letting out a groan, Kuklo gritted his teeth and kept looking ahead. The Titan dummy was already in front of him, and he needed to act right away to avoid a collision. He worked the levers in a panic, but his momentum not letting up, he continued to head straight into the dummy.

Damn it! he cursed and braced himself for impact. An instant later, a shock ran through his body as if a horse had galloped headlong into him.

"Ow…" The force of it seemed capable of pulverizing every bone in his body, but his injuries were not so bad as to render him immobile. Kuklo grimaced and tried moving his limbs and did not notice any problems in particular. His body was surely starting to bruise, but that was all.

I guess you can call that a success… It was, so long as the goal was to travel to a high place.

"You're pretty good at it!"

Cardina clapped in praise, but Kuklo's performance was hardly expert, given that he was now swinging in the air five meters above the ground. Unable to pilot the machine, he had simply been jerked up by it. A baby bird did a better job of flying.

But I can kill Titans with this. The issue was getting to their weakness. Getting behind a rampaging Titan and wielding his single-edged swords to carve out its medulla oblongata necessitated making full use of the Vertical Maneuvering Equipment.

Kuklo began to consider the details of defeating a Titan, but high in the air was no place to be tackling the subject. When he tried to loosen the wires to return to the ground, however, heaven and earth abruptly switched places. He started plunging headfirst before this even sank into him.

Oops… As soon as he noticed, he squirmed his body around like a cat. While the landing was not on his head, it was not a soft one, either. Kuklo rolled along the ground.

"Are you all right?!" Sharle asked in a panicked tone.

Kuklo replied with a smile, but the tumble had covered his fresh uniform in dust. He could expect more fresh bruises to form on his body, too.

"If you'd fallen on your head, you'd have been greeted by an angel instead of us. Being sent to heaven by Angel-made gear," Xenophon deadpanned the grim words, "would be no laughing matter."

"You'll lose your balance and flip over unless you maintain your posture using your entire body," Jorge said. "It's fundamentally different from fighting on the ground. Hammer that into your mind."

The problem, though, was that putting the idea into practice promised to be a challenge, as Xenophon elaborated: "Your senses need to adapt to coping with all three dimensions. Humans live on the ground, so we end up thinking about everything from a ground-based perspective. Naturally. But if you're going to use the Vertical Maneuvering Equipment, you have to toss all of those notions out."

"I think I get it. Or maybe not..."

"Well, it is a revolutionary change I'm asking you to make. Getting the hang of it will require some trigger."

"Like what?"

"I think the fastest way is to learn with your body. And fortunately, yours seems durable."

"It'll break before I ever learn."

"Well, yes, it would be inconvenient if the Vertical Maneuvering Equipment broke."

"No, I meant my body."

Kuklo sighed and looked again at the Titan statue, a fake only five meters in height whose oppressive presence still reminded him of the real deal.

Ogre is twice as big as this thing, too... Not only that, his enemy's movements were quick, its stamina inexhaustible. Add to that powers of regeneration in a league of their own and you had a truly irrational monster. Standing against one was nothing short of reckless.

But I have to. And to do so he needed to be able to impose his will on the wild stallion that was the Vertical Maneuvering Equipment.

Rising to his feet, Kuklo stared daggers at the Titan dummy and gripped his controllers tight. Without pause, he kicked off of the ground and leapt into the air, then pressed the controller levers.

***

It was morning, and a full week since Kuklo and Cardina's arrival in the factory city.

For Kuklo, who'd lived in wretched conditions for so long, the seven days passed in what felt like the blink of an eye. His fatigue, however, vanished thanks to the calm and tranquil days, his body feeling so light he felt like he'd undergone an exorcism.

In their Training Corps uniforms, Kuklo and Cardina waited in front of the factory for the carriage that would take them to the academy for new recruit training. Only Sharle was there to see them off. Jorge had returned to the training academy ahead of them, while Xenophon was not the type for proper goodbyes.

"You know, my plan was to lead a life of debauchery," Cardina muttered with regret. Apparently the possibility of going back to the training academy hadn't occurred in his wildest dreams.

"It's not like you can go home anymore."

"Right, I wouldn't want people thinking I'm going to take over the family business…" If Cardina returned to Wall Sheena, he'd be noticed by political enemies. They believed he had died outside the walls, and it was best to let them think so. "I don't have any cash right now, either."

He must have decided that at least he wouldn't go hungry as a recruit. His politician father's blood ran through him, and he could become a merchant if he exercised his natural gift for speech, but it was nearly impossible to imagine Cardina hard at work. He was the sort who hoped for a life of debauchery after all.

"Trying to get into the Military Police Brigade wouldn't be bad, though. It was what my father wanted me to do, anyway."

"For revenge?"

"His enemies did plot his death, and I might clear my family's name with a proper investigation." Becoming an MP would allow him to do that, but Cardina's expression didn't hint at any resolve, and his tone was flat. The idea didn't seem to speak to him.

"He wasn't a hard person to dig up dirt on," Cardina added as if to explain, "but enough about me."

With a smile laden with meaning, Cardina nudged Kuklo in the side with his elbow, and Kuklo followed his gaze. There he found Sharle, looking uneasy. It was clear that while in no way happy about his joining the Training Corps, she understood and was trying not to protest.

Sharle had decided to stay at the workshop as Xenophon's assistant. She couldn't depend on family, so she had no choice but to acquire some skills. Although life in the male-dominated world of the workshop would be difficult for someone of her refined upbringing, she was confident she'd make it. The reason was simple. Angel Aaltonen, the creator of the Equipment and one of the developers of the Vertical Maneuvering Equipment, had had a girl as his assistant, too.

"I guess I won't meet her again until I graduate."

"We'll be entering during the rush of the second half of training, so about three months from now. I'm sure it'll go by before we know it."

"That's assuming I graduate." Kuklo had no idea what the Training Corps curriculum was like but it couldn't be a breeze, especially if it involved mastering the Vertical Maneuvering Equipment.

"You'll be fine. You have both the Survey Corps commander and the instructor's seal of approval. I believe in you, too."

"I wonder…" Kuklo cast a dubious look at Cardina.

As the two chatted away, they noticed a carriage approaching them that appeared to be their ride. Its driver was not Jorge, but a different male soldier who must have been assigned to the Training

Corps.

"Looks like it's here," Cardina said. "To be honest, I don't feel like doing this."

"You don't know when to give up, do you?" Kuklo pushed him into the carriage, which had pulled up next to them, then got in himself.

"Um… Please don't do anything crazy," Sharle pleaded, unable to silence her worries.

Kuklo nodded and asked her, "Is there something I should say to Xavi?"

Sharle just shook her head.

Of course not… Sharle's brother might try to use her if he learned that she was still alive. It seemed best to leave her whereabouts unknown to him.

Judging that they had put an end to their goodbyes, the driver whipped his horse. It reacted by trotting off with a sure gait.

"I guess I'm off."

"Be safe."

As Sharle waved and saw them off with a smile, the carriage gradually picked up speed.

***

The training academy that stood between Trost District and Wall Sheena was a sizable facility encompassing a square kilometer. Surrounded by rich, green foliage, the location itself was entirely unremarkable. On the premises were a school building, where lectures primarily took place, a dormitory where the recruits slept, and nothing else. The majority of the land was taken up by fields for practical training. It would be safe to say that the facility was dedicated solely to turning recruits into soldiers. The idea of amusement seemed foreign to it.

The military did not rely on conscription, but rather on volunteers. Anyone over the age of twelve with a sound body and mind could apply. There was no set maximum enrollment, but about a thousand individuals volunteered every year, and half dropped out before making it to graduation. While the number seemed small, it was not a problem as their ranks never suffered from extreme drops in size. The Titan invasion fifteen years ago had been a unique case.

There were no recruits anywhere on the grounds, and the place was eerily still.

"They don't seem to be in the middle of classes, either. Maybe they're off on a run?"

Kuklo was unable to answer Cardina's question, but someone who could was waiting for them in front of the school building. The stalwart figure straddling a warhorse was none other than their instructor, Jorge.

"You're late. Everyone else has already left." Jorge pointed to the east, but only thick woods were visible in that direction.

"Left?" "To where?!" Kuklo and Cardina got off the carriage and immediately began questioning Jorge.

He tossed two knapsacks off his mount, directly onto the ground, and headed off with a simple: "Just go and you'll see."

"Okay. Straight to training, huh…" Cardina shouldered the knapsack, sighed, and began to chase after Jorge.

Kuklo grabbed his own knapsack and prepared to follow him, but it was far heavier than it looked. He thought his shoulder might give.

What is in this? It weighed a shocking amount as though it were full of stones. As Kuklo stood there puzzled, Cardina and Jorge trekked off.

This might be harder than I thought… Though Kuklo felt a tinge of unease, he'd experienced the hellish world outside of the wall and returned, surviving by the skin of his teeth. When he considered that, he realized there was no need to fear any training devised by humans. Slinging his knapsack, Kuklo chased after Cardina and Jorge.

Catching up to the two wasn't difficult, but matching a horse's pace was. What was a mere trot for the fleet-footed mount forced

Kuklo and Cardina to run to keep up.

"What kind of training is this?" Kuklo asked Cardina.

"Logistics."

"What's that?"

"You could call it service support. Assisting soldiers working on the front line."

The duties would be wide-ranging. While transporting supplies was a given, it also entailed other obviously important tasks such as maintaining weapons and warhorses, constructing and quartering camps, and more. Without soldiers to provide rear support, no force could hold out on the front lines. One day, humanity would push out beyond the walls to retake lands that had been ceded to the Titans. Even Kuklo saw how crucial logistics training was.

"There's food to eat all over the place. Grass, bugs," he remarked nonetheless.

"You're just about the only person who'd be satisfied with that kind of a diet…" Cardina shrugged in resignation.

"Are these full of food supplies?"

"They're heavy in order to simulate that. They're full of sand."

"It's dead weight?"

"Just pretend that they're packed full of essences that soldiering requires."

That passed over Kuklo's head, but he supposed he simply needed to run to his destination with the knapsack on his back. "Where do I need to go?" he asked.

"Wherever the instructor says to go. Sometimes we march for a full day."

"That's ridiculous…"

"I wouldn't say so," Jorge interrupted, apparently having overheard their conversation. "I don't want to say it's all about willpower, but we're up against enemies that are beyond the pale. There's no point in a lukewarm regimen."

Even if a recruit could overcome the absurdly strenuous training, taking on a Titan was an even wilder challenge. It followed that a soldier unable to endure this much wasn't qualified to stand against a Titan.

Jorge began to lead the two into a woodland path. It was time for logistics training.

***

After a couple of hours of running through the forest trail, a gaggle of what looked like recruits came into sight. A small group of about six running in double-file formation, they appeared to have fallen about ten meters behind the rest. Perhaps they'd slipped to the tail end unable to keep up thanks to their below-average stamina, as they showed no signs of shrinking the distance.

Stragglers? wondered Kuklo. The recruits ran dispassionately and showed no signs of fatigue, to judge from behind. Their knapsacks did look heftier than the ones carried by the recruits ahead, but the impression must have been due to differences in build. The lagging runners were about Kuklo's size if not smaller, putting them on the low end among troops. They didn't conform to the line of thinking holding sway that soldiers ought to be large and impressively muscled.

But running at the tail end didn't necessarily make them inferior. Kuklo, who was built like them, didn't slow down. His breathing was audible and his body hot, but he was not at his physical limits.

I'm not sure if I could do this all day… Yet if he paced himself well, it wasn't impossible.

Cardina, running beside Kuklo, also seemed to have energy to spare. As a former recruit, he no doubt knew how to ration his strength.

The distance between them and the stragglers continued to shrink.

Ahead of the two, Jorge pointed a finger at the tail end group and said, "They're receiving special Vertical Maneuvering Equipment training."

Them? Even though they're at the very back?! Kuklo tilted his head, unable to understand Jorge's selection criteria.

"It's not recognized as part of the official curriculum, so it's had to take the form of remedial lessons…"

"The other recruits who don't know call them flunkers," Cardina said in a rather self-mocking tone.

"As you can see, they lack somewhat in stamina compared to the rest, but they're far more nimble, and they know how to persevere. In other words, they have the perfect bodies for learning how to master the Vertical Maneuvering Equipment."

So that's why… Utilizing it was the major premise for the next generation of soldiers as Jorge imagined them. A large frame or a bulging armor-like musculature would only be a hindrance.

The muscles required were vastly different ones, anyway. Controlling the Vertical Maneuvering Equipment also called for dexterity, in order to properly operate machinery. Furthermore, superhuman balance and spatial recognition were required to move with ease in three dimensions.

So the old ways won't do. Kuklo had tried to aim for the back of the Titan dummy many times while in the factory city, but all he had to show for it were bruises that covered his body. The only thing he felt more confidence in after his practice was his ability to move vertically.

A revolutionary change… Xenophon had compared it to a revolution, and in fact, one seemed likely to come. Kuklo had no idea when or how, but he felt that training would take him there, whether gradually or in some flash akin to a divine revelation. If a revolution was needed, Kuklo felt he could start one, and he knew what it would feel like.

I've experienced one. That revolution had been acquiring language, something that turned his world upside down. *Sharle gave me the opportunity then.*

He felt he could master the Vertical Maneuvering Equipment once he got the knack of it. *This time, the practice equipment might be my opportunity.*

Having caught up to the group, Kuklo and Cardina joined the end of the line. The remedial students turned to look with surprised expressions, not expecting anyone to show up from behind them.

What truly shocked them, though, seemed to be Cardina.

And why not… The guy was supposed to have quit the corps, yet here he was in a soldier's uniform. They couldn't be blamed for doubting their eyes. After all, Cardina himself hadn't expected to return to the Training Corps. He wore an expression of embarrassed resignation right there beside Kuklo.

What surprised Kuklo were the faces of the recruits running at the back of the group. He sensed strong willpower in their sharp eyes. While he'd wondered if they were straggling, they'd endured their training thus far and evidently had what it took to become soldiers. Jorge had handpicked them, too, so they had to have some spine.

Are the other recruits the same way? Unlike the ones he was now among, the recruits who ran slightly ahead were burly. That was the current standard for soldiers, indicative of the doctrine that the Titans should be met with brawn.

Even though that's pointless. For Kuklo, who was familiar with the Titans, large muscles were like fat, worthless.

Jorge's efforts to introduce the Vertical Maneuvering Equipment derived from his understanding that the Titans could not be defeated as things stood. The man responsible for a Titan falling to the Equipment had to know that truth well. It explained his impatience with the status quo.

Kuklo stared closely at the main group ahead of him.

Xavi is in there, too. He was Kuklo's natural enemy, so to speak. Unlike when Kuklo was shackled, he wouldn't let Xavi beat him mercilessly, but he still wanted to avoid dealing with the guy. If Kuklo could choose never to meet him again, he would, but now that he was a recruit, they'd come face to face sooner or later.

He can shoot for MP, huh. Jorge evaluated him highly as a soldier, but Xavi seemed far from praiseworthy in light of the hardship he'd inflicted on Kuklo. Xavi was what he was now only because he'd built his confidence by tormenting a Titan's son. Giving such a person any credit was unthinkable.

As soon as Kuklo thought of Xavi, he began to wonder what the guy might be like now.

Half a year has passed... It felt like ages since he'd parted ways with Xavi on that stormy night, but it wasn't long enough for any dramatic transformation. Regardless of outward appearances, it was doubtful that any change had overtaken him.

Kuklo's right eye began to ache and throb as if in response to his enemy's presence.

To get rid of these feelings... He increased his pitch, surprising Cardina.

"Where're you going? We're in the middle of training!"

"To meet Xavi."

"Excuse me?" Cardina's voice cracked in surprise, but Kuklo continued ahead, paying no heed.

He wasn't out to clear his years of pent-up resentment. Nor did he mean to so much as call out to the guy. What Kuklo wanted was to see what Xavi looked like now.

My goal is to kill Ogre. Compared to that, his grudge against Xavi was trivial. It did upset him, but he could turn a blind eye. What did trouble him was Xavi possibly standing in his way. Kuklo knew the guy's personality well, so it was an all-too-plausible scenario. He had to know what Xavi was like now to predict what was to come.

Cardina needn't worry.

Of course, it would be a different story if Xavi came at him.

***

Cardina watched from behind with a dumbfounded expression as Kuklo dashed off. Kuklo's extraordinary physical ability was amply clear from the chain of events that had brought him here, but calmly running ahead with his burden despite having no training was still stunning.

Cardina hadn't fared well after his first logistics training session. Unable to get food down his throat, anything he did manage to eat he'd thrown back up. The other recruits had met similar fates, with many even blacking out, and Cardina came to realize that it was a way of screening unfit candidates. Kuklo's instant adaptation testified to his astounding stamina; he didn't even seem to be suffering.

Kuklo's harsh upbringing had indeed granted him exceptional vitality. It wouldn't have been an exaggeration to call him a beast in human clothes, or a feral child. Not only that, in his veins ran the blood of his father Heath, a Survey Corps team leader. Kuklo was cut out to be a soldier, and he could even come to embody the next generation of soldiers that Jorge sought to turn out.

If there's one problem... Cardina watched Kuklo pulling farther and farther away. *Should I stop him or not?*

At this rate, Kuklo might cause a row mere minutes after joining the Training Corps. It would damage his impression.

Unsure of what to do, Cardina looked to Jorge, but the instructor issued no reprimand even though Kuklo's behavior clearly posed a problem.

"Are you just letting him go?" Cardina asked, unable to hold his tongue.

Maintaining his indifference, Jorge simply stated, "I'll leave this to you."

Leave this to me? Being entrusted with the situation limited Cardina's choices. *Actually, there's only one thing I can do.*

As soon as Cardina reached this conclusion, he realized what Jorge's intentions were. This was rough medicine to make Kuklo conform to life as a recruit.

I do feel like I've pulled the short straw here, though. Cardina couldn't hold back a bitter grin, but his expression soon stiffened as clamors came drifting from the front of the group. He hardly needed to wonder why.

"Sheesh, I should have had Sharle teach me how to handle the kid," lamented Cardina. He put a hand to his forehead, let out a groan, and dashed forth, prepared for the worst.

***

Kuklo single-mindedly charged ahead. He closed the gap between him and the rear of the main group in an instant, then charged through the recruits who were running in an orderly double-file formation. He was trying to get to the very front.

I know he'll be up there. From his earliest days as a person, Kuklo had been with Xavi. It was easy to imagine him running at the head, eagerly feeding his conceit.

All right! Kuklo roused himself and continued to plunge forward with forceful steps.

Not expecting to be passed by anyone who'd been trailing them, the recruits clamored as he left them behind, but Kuklo kept running, paying them no mind.

The frontrunner sped about three hundred meters ahead, and it was the exact person Kuklo expected to see. Even from behind, he would never mistake Xavi for anyone else. Kuklo even remembered the sound of Xavi's feet hitting the ground.

As soon as he recognized Xavi, Kuklo's days in the shed replayed themselves in his mind. It sent a chill through his heated body, but he only increased his speed as if to shake off the memories.

Xavi's body had always been imposing, but it was now incomparably larger, thanks either to the training having built his muscles or to a growth spurt. He stood out even among the other recruits, and if one were to judge by his physique alone, he could pass as a competent soldier. Since he ran at the front of the group, he was reasonably able too, as much as Kuklo didn't wish to concede the point.

Swiftly closing the distance to Xavi, he began running alongside him. This seemed to bother Xavi, who clicked his tongue and glanced at Kuklo with an annoyed look on his face.

"Wha…"

Xavi's expression turned absolutely befuddled; his eyes couldn't have opened wider. It must have seemed to him that Kuklo had come back from hell. Though Xavi's cheeks should have been flush with blood, his face looked almost pale.

"You… Weren't they supposed to execute you?" He seemed to know about the verdict handed to Kuklo.

Xavi must have been informed of all the details as the victim's relative, up to and including the execution of the sentence. While the method, banishment, may have been covered up, it made sense for him to believe that Kuklo was dead since the sentence had been carried out. Kuklo felt like taunting him further, but just seeing Xavi so flabbergasted was soothing.

As Kuklo gloated, he heard Cardina's footsteps come drumming toward him from behind. Maybe he feared Kuklo would get violent, but he bore no such intention. Shocking the hell out of Xavi was plenty satisfying.

Right as Kuklo turned around to assure him, Cardina yelled, "Look out!" At the same time, he sensed a wave of malice.

"Why are you still alive?!" came the enraged scream, along with a powerful, log-like arm.

Angling his head to dodge the approaching right fist, Kuklo snapped a kick into Xavi's defenseless left flank.

"Guhh…" Xavi stopped in his tracks and groaned, holding his side. The menacing gleam that his eyes still gave off proved that the kick hadn't done much.

It isn't like before. Some time had passed since Kuklo last confronted Xavi, and the present standoff was very different. There were no chains restricting his movement, nor was there a precious person he needed to protect. He wasn't going to stand there taking punches.

Now that Xavi, the leader of the pack, had stopped, the entire group of pacesetters halted their march. The effect, quickly passing down the line, interrupted the entire exercise in logistics before long.

"Ack, now you've really done it…"

Cardina, catching up to them, cast a desperate look heavenward. Despite his exaggerated reaction, it was Xavi, not Kuklo, who had caused a scene. Kuklo didn't see how he could be blamed.

"I've done nothing."

"That's not true. Take a look," Cardina asserted, turning his gaze on the line of recruits from Xavi on down.

Knitting his eyebrows, Kuklo did the same to find countless pairs of hate-filled eyes looking back at him. *This is…*

Every recruit he saw was visibly upset, and about ten of them were inching toward him. They exchanged glances with Xavi and closed in on Kuklo with the kind of caution hunters might show. They must have been Xavi's lackeys. By the time Kuklo realized this, he had already been surrounded. Xavi's henchmen would surely all swoop in on their target at once on their boss' signal. Their eyes intended harm, and a fight was unavoidable.

Can I do it?

Kuklo balled his fists and carefully watched his enemies' movements. Knocking out every one of them would be difficult, but they were only human, nothing compared to a Titan. Besides, Kuklo wasn't beyond the walls but inside them. He could always retreat without having to worry about being attacked by strange monsters.

Just as he was preparing to fight, he heard a voice.

"No. Put down your fists." Cardina put his hand on Kuklo's and forced them down. "They're our allies, not our enemies."

"But I didn't attack first…" Kuklo said, and would have continued, "he did," but Cardina didn't let him finish.

"We can talk about what happened later. For now, I want you to apologize to them," Cardina whispered, but Kuklo could hardly consent to this. Even if he did have a legitimate reason to lower his head to Xavi, he still wouldn't.

As their exchange played out, Xavi and his underlings continued to close in. Unless he did something, Kuklo would fall prey to the venom that was Xavi's gang.

Even if they're on our side... If they bared fangs at him, there was nothing else but to fight back with everything he had. He clenched his fists anew, getting in the mood for it.

"You have to hold back. Touch them, and you lose," Cardina admonished, as if he'd sensed Kuklo's bellicose thoughts. Yet Kuklo could not bring himself to apologize as Cardina insisted, even with empty words.

Kuklo kicked off the ground and charged at Xavi, who took a large leap backwards, apparently having anticipated the move. In his place, Xavi's henchmen closed in on Kuklo. Unlike the Titans, who moved in straight lines, they came at him from both sides in freely shifting ways that he couldn't anticipate. When he reached for them, he was sidestepped, and even when he succeeded, he was brushed off. It was as though the recruits and Kuklo used their bodies in completely different ways.

I'm no different from a Titan like this. To the extent that his actions were guided by sheer instinct, he truly was the same. Just as the unpleasant notion crossed his mind, one of the recruits moved in. Ready to send him back shorn, Kuklo grabbed at him but found his own body floating up and his vision turned upside down. He had no idea what had happened, but the recruit who'd dashed into his range must have thrown him. Kuklo turned his body mid-air to land safely before he could crash, but other recruits were waiting for him and soon pinned him down.

Damn it! Kuklo writhed in protest, but there was nothing he could do with all four limbs immobilized. He lay on the ground face-up as though crucified.

Then came Xavi, who'd bided his time. Kuklo held up his head, the one part of his body with some freedom left, and glared at him.

"You should have stayed dead," Xavi spat. Then he delivered a powerful kick to Kuklo's face.

"Gah…" The powerful impact felt like a blow from a club, and Kuklo's face twisted in anguish. His vision wavered like he was looking through water, and he could tell that he was rapidly losing consciousness.

But Kuklo didn't stop glaring. He flatly refused to submit to Xavi.

Opening his eye wide, he blacked out staring at his sworn enemy.

CHAPTER FIVE

He shivered from the cold. It felt as though the heat was escaping from his body into whatever surface he was lying on, perhaps a stone floor.

The temperature was low, and Kuklo breathed what looked like white steam out at a regular rhythm. While much of his body's heat had been robbed from him, his clothes seemed to keep him from being frozen stiff. After all, Kuklo had once spent his days being drenched by cold water while completely naked. This was no life threatening crisis, and he felt relaxed enough to change his posture and go back to sleep. If he held his knees to his body and curled up into a ball, he'd be able to minimize the loss of heat.

But there was something he had to find out before succumbing to his drowsiness.

Where am I? He was surrounded by complete silence and couldn't detect anyone else. He concentrated on his sense of hearing but only sensed the wind, the chirping of insects, and other sounds of nature. Fortunately, there seemed to be nothing malicious nearby.

Kuklo squinted his eye open to look carefully around him, but he could see nothing through the pitch darkness. Nevertheless, he cautiously surveyed the area, and in time his eye adjusted and gradually conveyed his surroundings to him.

He was lying in a cramped room just barely large enough to sprawl in. There was nothing resembling furniture, only a toilet and a small window for lighting with bars over it. With only stars and pale moonlight on the other side, no clue offered up his current location. The telltale silence could only belong to the dead of night, however. The sturdy metal door in the entryway featured a slit that could be used to observe the room's interior.

"This is a—" Kuklo frowned at his sense of déjà vu. Although he didn't know where he was, the room's setup was familiar to him.

Why am I in jail?! Kuklo trembled at the accursed sight and his absurd plight, but soon gathered himself, rose off the floor, and stood on guard to be ready for anything. Just as he did, a dull pain shot across his skull.

"Ow!" He grimaced and put a hand to his forehead and felt a bump on it. He must have taken a blow to the head. He wanted to know why but didn't have the time to sit back and think—his sensitive ears had registered a faint noise.

Something is here. Kuklo strained to hear what it was, focusing his attention on the noise coming from the other side of the door. It wasn't the sound of a small animal's steps, nor the flutter of a bug's wings.

The sound of clothes… In other words, the rustling of cloth against cloth. *A person's here.* Friend or foe, he was sure of that.

A jailer? Considering his surroundings, it was a reasonable guess. His life didn't seem to be threatened for the moment, but he couldn't let down his guard.

What now?! Just as Kuklo was thinking about his next move, a familiar male voice broke the silence.

"So, are you finally up?"

"Cardina?"

"Yes. Doesn't it suck to be us?"

"Are you in a cage, too?"

"Why would I be in a cage? I'm not an animal." There was a hint of a chuckle in Cardina's voice, and he was surely smiling as wryly as ever.

"We've been put into nice little disciplinary cells."

"Dis-ci-pli-nary? What does that mean?"

"Let's just say it's where people who break the rules are deposited to urge them to reflect on what they've done," Cardina explained in what he thought was a straightforward fashion, failing to enlighten Kuklo. "Don't you remember the fight with Xavi during logistics training?"

"Oh. Yes. I was kicked by Xavi..." Kuklo finally recalled, arriving at the cause of the bump on his head at the same time.

"You probably don't remember, but training was aborted after that. We all came back to the academy."

"So this place is inside the academy?"

"Yes. It's rarely used, though. Actually, I'm not sure I've ever heard of it being used before." Cardina sighed and added, "For that matter, I've never heard of training being aborted before, either. By a brawl, at that, so I suppose we deserve this."

"Was it such a bad thing to do?"

"Of course. Acting on your own is a big problem once you're a member of the corps."

"Why?"

"Troops act as one. That's why it's called a corps. One might even say that there is zero room for independent behavior. Basically, whatever you're concerned about is secondary. Operations can't be carried out if soldiers decide to act on their own."

Cardina's point reminded Kuklo of a certain event, a scene from the time he'd snuck along on the Survey Corps' expedition. *If the corps had abandoned the wagon, it would have been easier for them to return safely.* What Cardina described sounded similar.

"By the way, the smallest unit of soldiers employed in carrying out missions is the eight-person team. Your father was a team leader, which means he had seven soldiers under him."

"So the reason the recruits were running in such an orderly way..."

"Is because that's part of training, too. Logistics training isn't meant to be a competition. I told you, didn't I? Those knapsacks were full of essences that soldiering requires." Cardina explained that logistics training not only bolstered knowledge, technique, and physical abilities but also fostered a spirit of cooperation. In other words, clockwork order was a must. Kuklo didn't have to search his mind to recall that only he and Cardina had passed other recruits.

Thinking back, the Survey Corps were advancing in an orderly line, too. While nowhere near as spectacular, the recruits' logistics training did resemble the Survey Corps' march.

"Is he here too, then?"

"Xavi? No, he's probably curled up in his bed right about now."

"Wha?!" Shocked, Kuklo actually bent forward. "But—"

"Whoa, don't ask me why. I don't know," Cardina interrupted. "The one thing I can tell you is that Xavi handled himself well out there. He could say he was teaching a lesson to a chap who was flaunting military discipline. His violence would take on some legitimacy."

While the explanation did make sense, something kept Kuklo from being fully satisfied. *Why didn't he tell me?*

If Jorge had explained how the corps worked, Kuklo probably wouldn't have acted so rashly. It wouldn't have done away with his desire to know what Xavi was now like, but he could have avoided causing an incident that merited his landing in a disciplinary cell.

"He didn't tell you on purpose."

"Why?"

"It's just a few months until graduation. He doesn't have time to guide you through the alphabet. Rather than teach you using words, he probably intends to have you learn first-hand. And honestly, I think you have, no?"

True, Kuklo's body might absorb the lessons, but that didn't make Jorge's method of instruction any less rough.

That's why he didn't stop me. Jorge had stood by and watched Kuklo and Xavi's scuffle on purpose then, to teach Kuklo the rules in an efficient manner. There had to be better ways, but the instructor must have decided that the method suited Kuklo best.

I definitely won't be forgetting while this pain lasts, Kuklo admitted with a wry smile, rubbing the bump on his forehead.

"When can we leave here?"

"In two or three days, probably."

Kuklo's stomach grumbled as soon as he heard Cardina's estimate. "What about food?"

"The point is for us to think about what we've done. Why would we get any?"

"Nothing to eat, then..."

Knowing that he wouldn't be getting a meal made him want one even more. Still, he was only mildly hungry and could bear it. He'd fought against hunger for most of his life. A two or three day fast would certainly affect him but hardly make him throw in the towel. If he was desperate for food, he should be able to find some by searching his cell diligently. A few days were a mere blink of the eye.

Kuklo got on all fours like a beast, then closed his eye to cut off his sense of sight. With no information coming from his eye, his hearing grew sharper. He could hear footsteps.

"Someone's coming—" Kuklo whispered and quickly lay back down, pretending to be asleep. Of course, that was not all he was doing. He had his ear to the ground, trying to do whatever he could to find out more.

While the footsteps were clearly approaching the disciplinary cells, the question was to whom they belonged. Kuklo was on alert at first because it could be a raid by Xavi, but the rhythm of the footsteps indicated that it wasn't him. Given where they were, it could be an instructor on patrol. The footfalls were awfully soft for that, though, and the span of the steps suggested that it was a woman, not a man. *Probably around Sharle's...*

Whoever it was stopped in front of his cell. Kuklo could sense he was being watched, perhaps through the slit on the door, but the observer didn't seem to bear any harmful designs. Just moments later, the eyes were no longer on him, and the presence left the door.

The person who'd been watching Kuklo began walking to Cardina's cell. This time, there was a small knock.

"Are you awake, Cardina?" The voice had to be the visitor's. It was a woman's, and a whisper.

"Is that you, Rosa? What business do you have down here?"

"Just saying hello. And I should be asking you that." The woman Cardina had called Rosa sounded rather vexed. "I don't know what you were thinking, but everyone's talking about you now."

Cardina breathed a deep sigh. "I guess that was about as flashy of a greeting as you could get, wasn't it..."

Are the two friends? Their casual back-and-forth suggested that Cardina and Rosa knew one another.

"I hadn't planned on coming back to the academy, but...I guess you could say fate played a little trick on me."

"You mean rejoining the corps right as everyone thought you'd left, then getting put in a disciplinary cell before even saying hello?"

"I meant all the stuff that led to this."

"Like what?" Rosa did not seem aware of the misfortunes that had visited Cardina. The training academy was in a location isolated from the outside world, so it was no surprise she hadn't heard. The only people in the Training Corps who knew everything had to be Kuklo, Cardina, and Jorge. The other instructors, perhaps privy to bits and pieces, probably had to keep them under wraps considering the sentence's nature.

After another deep sigh, Cardina spoke to Kuklo. "This is Rosa Carlstedt. She's one of the recruits receiving special training from Instructor Jorge."

"Those remedial lessons? You're training to use the Vertical Maneuvering Equipment?!"

"Huh?!" the woman named Rosa let out in surprise. She must not have expected Kuklo to be only feigning sleep.

Kuklo was surprised, too, but by something else: the fact that a woman was attempting to master the Vertical Maneuvering Equipment. Since the machinery guided its user to wherever she needed to go, steering it didn't require formidable muscles. In fact, they only got in the way of three-dimensional movement. Yet no matter how hard Kuklo tried to imagine it, he couldn't picture a woman heading toward a Titan using the Vertical Maneuvering Equipment, and the reason was simple. He kept being reminded of Sharle.

"I kind of owed him for something, so I swallowed my pride and decided to come back."

"Whatever it is that happened, can I assume that you intend to graduate this time?"

"Reluctantly, yes."

"Really?"

"I seem to have lost a lot of credibility."

Rosa sighed in response. "Of course you have." Cardina's departure from the Training Corps must have been sudden, and she couldn't be blamed for being skeptical.

"Sorry, I should have introduced you earlier—the talk of the town, Kuklo."

"Kuklo? I think I've heard that name somewhere…"

"That's because you probably have. He's the Titan's son that Xavi claims to have punished."

What exactly Xavi had said about the "Titan's son" was unclear, but it was easy to imagine him gleefully spinning yarns of his heroics. Yet Xavi probably knew little about his Titan's son, nor, in all likeliness, did he care to. The fact that he'd defeated a Titan's son sufficed, though even that was no fact. In reality, Xavi knew practically nothing about Kuklo.

"He's the Titan's son…" Rosa said pensively, as though it concerned her.

"Aren't you scared of me?"

"Scared? Because you're a Titan son?!"

"Yes."

"I may still be in training, but I'm a soldier. We learn about Titans. It's not hard to figure out what's true and what's not."

"*He* had us confused for a while, though," Cardina said of Xavi. His bragging must have commenced as soon as he'd joined the

Training Corps.

"Child-sized Titans exist, but there are no records of a Titan ever giving birth," Rosa explained matter-of-factly. "Still, to think you were with the famous Titan's son."

"It's a long story. He came here on Instructor Jorge and Commander Carlo's recommendations."

"Killing Ogre. That is my goal."

"Ogre?"

"That's the name of the Titan that ruined his life," Cardina supplemented.

"I need the Vertical Maneuvering Equipment if I'm to kill a Titan. That's why I came here."

"So you have an actual goal in mind, unlike Cardina."

"Such a mean way to put it."

"Well, you earned it. He seems to have potential, though. He has a lot to learn as a soldier, but he must have what it takes if Instructor Jorge recommended him. And—" Rosa suddenly cut herself off. "Anyway, I see that you two mean it."

"And you came all the way here to find out?"

"Of course I'd want to know. There's a strong chance we'll be in the same team."

"I see. So you're the one leading up the flunkers now."

"Yes, because a certain someone actually dropped out."

Cardina grunted, the barb finding its mark.

"Well, I should get going..." Rosa opened the slit at the bottom of the door and shoved a piece of bread torn in half and an apple through it. "It's probably not enough, but you did cause a problem large enough to land you in a disciplinary cell. I hope you think about what you've done." With that, she closed the slit and walked away.

"Always so serious. Why can't she relax a little?"

"I think there is such a thing as being too relaxed, too," Kuklo noted with some dismay.

He bit into the dried-out piece of bread.

***

Xavi Inocencio was terribly addled. Because he was together with his fellow recruits, he took care not to betray his agitation, but his pulse was elevated, and a cold sweat covered his body.

Even after returning to his bed in the barracks, having finished training and bathed, he couldn't rid himself of his growing anxiety. Unable to sit still, he writhed in secret on his bed.

He was supposed to have died. It was Kuklo's continued existence that bewildered Xavi. Sentenced to death for the crime of murdering Dario Inocencio as well as the cultists, Kuklo should never have shown himself again. Not only that, the execution had taken place a week ago. Though Xavi was not there to witness it, he'd received a report from the Military Police, so he was certain of it. *Why is he alive?*

Until now, everything had gone exactly as Xavi had planned. He had provided false testimony to the Military Police in order to finally rid himself of the eyesore that was Kuklo, and doing so had even resulted in a death sentence. His scheme had been flawless. Except, of course, for the fact that Kuklo was still alive. It was an utter paradox. It was impossible.

Could it be someone else who happens to look like him?! But Xavi immediately rejected the idea. *The cut on his right eye. I did that to him.* Even without the wound, Xavi would never mistake someone else for Kuklo. And vice versa. *He came to show himself to me… He wanted me to know he was alive.*

Xavi had deemed his plan perfect, but something must have managed to upend it. He had no idea what that thing was, nor did he know why the Military Police wasn't apprehending Kuklo anew, but it seemed as though the devil's own luck had worked to miraculously save the Titan's son.

This is bad. Very bad. Kuklo's existence was nothing short of a threat to Xavi. If Kuklo told the truth, Xavi faced ruin. Not only would his path to the Military Police be cut off, he'd be thrown into a dark prison and left to rot, his remaining days a bleak gray. Sharle, his younger sister, knew the truth, too, but she'd kept her silence until now and promised to be harmless. Perhaps she was no longer of this world to begin with. It wasn't one that a girl with her sheltered upbringing could navigate.

Even more was on Xavi's mind. *Why is he in the Training Corps?* He could tell by the emblem on Kuklo's jacket that he belonged to the academy. *But why?!*

Kuklo still being alive could be chalked up to some sort of twisted luck, as Xavi forced to persuade himself… Kuklo joining the corps as a recruit, on the other hand, was unthinkable. Not only that, he was with Cardina, who was supposed to have left.

The unexpected developments sat in Xavi's mind like a ball of tangled threads. It was all he could do to keep from panicking. There was one thing, however, that he understood in his confusion.

They're definitely going to be a menace. Both Kuklo's very presence and Cardina's abilities as a soldier endangered Xavi's standing. Cardina returning to become a recruit meant, quite simply, that one seat on the Military Police was gone. Kuklo's abilities were still an unknown, but he was the Titan's son. He could be hiding incredible power within him. Xavi couldn't help but fear that his road to the Military Police was receding.

I'm the one who'll be applying to be an MP! he nearly screamed the words without thinking, but grit his teeth to hold them back.

Xavi had established his current position by winning over potential rivals with money. Those stubborn enough to resist him he subjugated by force. Even then, it was unlikely that he could graduate at the top of his class, so he'd resorted to any and all measures to secure his spot in the top ten.

"You think you can get in my way?"

His body atremble, Xavi searched for a way to make sure that only he found happiness.

***

Roughly five hundred recruits stood in rows on the athletic grounds. The sight of the orderly lines of stern faces seemed almost like a work of art, the result of days after days of training.

Yet they were most certainly not there as decoration. Though still in training, they were indeed soldiers. In an emergency, they would be sent into battle as a matter of course to protect the citizenry. While no records spoke of the Training Corps engaging in actual combat, its members were absolutely ready to be tapped. That much was clear from their expressions.

Their collective attention was on two recruits who stood facing them: Kuklo and Cardina, freshly out of their disciplinary cells that morning. Since they'd been placed in their cells before they could introduce themselves as classmates, Jorge was giving them a chance to do exactly that.

Due perhaps to the earlier incident, the pair were receiving a less than hearty welcome, as was clear from the tension in the air and the askance looks, as if the two brought bad luck. Graduation was now in sight, making this an important period. Any unnecessary trouble had to be shunned like the plague. In particular, Xavi, who stood in the front row, had murder in his eyes as he gazed at Kuklo.

So many enemies, I see. But this neither inconvenienced nor upset Kuklo. He'd come to the training academy to learn how to use the Vertical Maneuvering Equipment in order to kill Ogre. He wasn't here to be chummy or to make friends.

"I didn't think I'd ever have to wear fatigues again," Cardina moped beside Kuklo.

"Better than a death sentence."

"Now, that would shut me up, wouldn't it?" Cardina scratched his head and smiled bitterly.

"This is Kuklo and Cardina. They'll be joining you as of today.

There's not much time until graduation, but I'd like you to work with one another as you aim to better yourselves. For the king, for the country, and for the people," Jorge succinctly informed the wall of recruits. Then he looked at Kuklo and Cardina. He seemed to want them to introduce themselves.

What do I talk about? Kuklo couldn't think of anything worth telling the group.

As he stood there confused, Cardina boldly stepped forward. Placing his right fist to the left side of his chest, he hollered, so loudly his voice seemed to echo into the farthest corners of the grounds, "Cardina Baumeister! Due to certain reasons, I have returned!! I intend to make up for every day I have missed by devoting every drop of sweat I have to my training! Thank you all!!"

Kuklo blinked and turned a surprised look at Cardina, not expecting anyone so low-keyed to bellow from so deep in his stomach. Nevertheless, standing straight as an arrow and saluting, Cardina was the very picture of a soldier ready to sacrifice his life for the king, the country, and the people. He had just been moping so it was hard to tell what was in his heart, and maybe it was all for show.

It was Kuklo's turn next. Following Cardina's lead, he took a step forward. He hadn't come up with anything to say, and he lacked Cardina's glibness to make do with platitudes.

I came here for one reason. His only choice was to tell them the plain truth.

"I am going to slay a Titan!"

Kuklo's declaration caused a stir among the recruits.

***

There were many skills the recruits needed to acquire. Of course, there were the combat arts like swordsmanship and wrestling, but other know-how and classroom learning required of soldiers—tactics, medicine, and such—were beaten into the recruits from sunrise to sunset until it became their flesh and blood.

While the term "combat arts" seemed self-explanatory, it covered a wide array of techniques including swordsmanship, marksmanship, wrestling, roping, horsemanship, and more. It went without saying that these were founded on certain basic physical abilities. Likewise for classroom learning.

The recruits applied themselves to all subjects, but differences in aptitude existed to varying degrees. Roughly speaking, the Training Corps consisted of two types: physically gifted soldiers who were good at combat and mentally gifted soldiers who excelled in the classroom. The ones with the top grades needed for applying to the Military Police tended to be nearly perfect in both aspects, and both Cardina and Xavi counted themselves among that group. It was a natural result of their upbringings. Educated well from a young age and endowed with a wealth of knowledge, they'd been schooled and trained as elites precisely so that they might join the Brigade.

Meanwhile, Kuklo's grades were poor. While everyone recognized his great potential, he relied on sensibility alone, and his self-taught ways didn't pass muster. He was like raw ore, no different from stone unless he was processed and polished. Far from adept at reading and writing, he also suffered in the classroom, but what he lacked most in comparison to his corpsmates had to be life experience. His uncooperative streak and deficient imagination revealed as much.

So I couldn't beat Xavi back there because I'm not experienced? As soon as the thought distracted him, his feet were taken out from under him, and he tumbled to the ground. He reflexively shot out his right hand for a soft landing—not a moment too soon, as he'd have smashed his back against the earth and been left gasping.

"You're getting thrown because you keep spacing out," a petite female recruit in fatigues told him as she reached out her arm.

The striking young lady with glossy, short black hair was none other than Rosa, whom Kuklo had met in the brig. She was also the one who'd just caught him with a double leg takedown. Kuklo took

Rosa's hand and stood up slowly.

"We're in training so no one's going to finish you off, but you'd be a goner if this were a real fight," Rosa said, looking up at Kuklo with her obsidian eyes. As the angle of her head indicated, she was only as tall as the bottom of Kuklo's jaw and the shortest soldier in the entire Training Corps.

I can't believe she managed to throw me... Not particularly muscular, Rosa didn't look strong enough to throw a guy, but she'd done exactly that to Kuklo. While he doubted he was weaker than her physically speaking, their differences in skill and experience had determined the round's outcome.

That's why I couldn't match up to Xavi. Moreover, Xavi's hangers-on had made winning impossible from the outset that time.

Looking around, Kuklo saw recruits sparring with partners across the athletic grounds. He could tell from their movements that the bouts weren't being decided by size or strength.

"Soft and fair goes far. You may think that being small is a disadvantage, but a world of possibilities opens up if you see it as a weapon instead."

"So I just have to practice."

"That's certainly the quickest way. You have the raw talent, all you need to do is have faith and keep at it."

Perhaps speaking from personal experience, Rosa sounded confident. She also seemed to believe wholeheartedly in the teachings of Jorge, her instructor. In fact, she posted above average grades, and while the practicals dragged her down, she was completely capable when it mattered. She'd serve quite fine as a soldier out of the academy.

If she stayed inside the walls, of course. But Rosa was taking Vertical Maneuvering Equipment lessons, which meant she wanted to join the Survey Corps.

"Why did you become a recruit, Rosa?" Kuklo asked her. Even if she'd been handpicked by a hero like Jorge, going outside the walls took some serious resolve.

Rosa replied by telling him about her parents, both of whom had been soldiers. "My father died before I was born, though, and my mother's retired."

"So you followed in their footsteps?"

"I guess you could say that."

"But why learn to use the Vertical Maneuvering Equipment?"

Instead of answering him, Rosa squared off against Kuklo as though to remind him that they were in the middle of training.

I see. Kuklo adjusted his posture and began sparring freely with her.

"My dad was killed by a Titan," Rosa said.

"You want to avenge him?"

"I don't feel like it's anything as admirable as that, but maybe his blood is guiding me."

"Was he in the Survey Corps?"

"Yeah. In the team your father led."

"Heath's?" Kuklo let out in surprise.

I see. That's why she was quick to trust me... His father's identity must have steered her to accept him without preliminaries when they met in the brig.

"I was interested in the Vertical Maneuvering Equipment, too. After all, the guy who made it lives with my mom," Rosa remarked with a shrug.

Then she sent Kuklo's body flying through the air.

***

Training finished just as the sky began to turn crimson.

Betraying a mix of fatigue and relief, the recruits retired to their barracks with whatever friends each had. Soon they'd wash the dirt from their bodies in the baths, eat in the mess room, and enjoy their free time, but it was a different story for Kuklo and the others who received remedial lessons. The day was only now starting for them, their training so far merely a warm-up. More tired than prepared, their bodies covered in sweat and dust, it certainly didn't look that way though.

Since Vertical Maneuvering Equipment training was not part of the regular curriculum for recruits, the sessions, considered remedial, took place after hours. In other words, it ate into Kuklo's free time. Everyone knew about the old Equipment, but the Survey Corps slaying a Titan under Jorge's command didn't prove the efficacy of the Vertical Maneuvering Equipment.

It could be used to approach a Titan's weak point so as to slice out the meat around its medulla oblongata with single-edged swords—this, however, was nothing more than a theoretical possibility. The Titans' weakness had been discovered and the armaments existed to destroy it, but if no one could put them to use, it was pointless. The brass refused to add Vertical Maneuvering Equipment training as an official subject as a result. If it weren't for Jorge, even the remedial lessons might not have been tolerated, the invention shelved, never to see the light of day. Yet the same brass couldn't reject a national hero's proposal outright. Ignorant of the political two-step, the recruits simply saw fellow students receiving "remedial" lessons. The unjustified label of "flunkers" had spread unchecked.

The special training did not take part in the athletic grounds but in the nearby woods. Pulling oneself up with the Vertical Maneuvering Equipment involved firing anchors into targets and winding the wires back in. The targets were trees. While anchors might be lodged into a Titan's body to approach its weakness, the enemy—an avatar of destruction—seemed unlikely to stand stock-still. A target on a rampage made maneuvering difficult, whereas trees were ideal.

The world outside of the walls was mostly an expansive wasteland, but it wasn't entirely barren. Resilient flora that weren't picky about soil quality grew here and there, and oases where trees flourished, though rare, also dotted the area. Forests offered advantageous terrain that drew out the Vertical Maneuvering Equipment's full potential. The best setting not just for offense, they'd surely come in handy in the event of a retreat.

While training took place in the woods with actual combat in mind, the old Equipment was used for the lessons. Identical in concept if functionally inferior to the Vertical Maneuvering Equipment, it was suited for training since it allowed adapting to a third dimension and simulated the feel of handling the improved model.

The truth, however, was that continued use of the old Equipment, which only permitted movement along one axis, barely established a foothold for mastering the Vertical Maneuvering Equipment.

***

After their special training, Kuklo and the others headed back to the barracks and straight toward the mess hall. It was a large room filled with orderly lines of simple, wooden tables.

There were about a hundred seats there, so recruits ate in shifts, but over two hours had passed since the end of regular training, leaving the hall empty. They had the place to themselves, but this meant plating their own chow since the recruits on cafeteria duty were gone too.

Of course, the meals did not consist of the colorful fare one might find in a town canteen. The food was little better than rations; not only that, these were their fellow students' leftovers. Naturally it was cold. Though it would fill their stomachs, that was about it.

Looking displeased, Cardina shrugged and said, "I really hope they hurry up and elevate it to an official subject." He bit into his bread.

"I doubt that'll happen during our time here."

This blunt assertion came from Rose, who sat next to Kuklo. Vertical Maneuvering Equipment training wouldn't be added as an official subject until someone mastered it and proved its usefulness to the brass. Even if things went smoothly, providing proof in the course of their studies was a tall order. They had no choice but to put up with leftovers for dinner.

"This doesn't bother me, you know?" opined Kuklo. For him these leftovers amounted to a feast. There was nothing about the situation he found unsatisfactory.

"Well, maybe not you," Cardina said, sighing conspicuously, "but not everyone's as tough as you." He then looked around at everyone at the table.

Only Kuklo, Cardina, and Rosa had enough strength left to get food down their throats. All of the others were just barely sipping soup, their stomachs unable to handle the solid fare—a struggle Kuklo found impossible to understand.

You can't be sure there will be food tomorrow. Therefore, eat when you can. That was Kuklo's creed, and leaving food on a plate was unthinkable.

He bit into his bread and moistened his throat with soup. There was no hurry, but he hastily brought the corn beef to his mouth, which was growing full from whatever he could shovel in.

"Are you a squirrel or something?" Cardina looked appalled, but Kuklo, true to his credo, continued to stuff his face, very much like a squirrel storing acorns in its cheeks. Cardina changed the topic. "Still, we don't seem to be getting the best results from the special training, though we're mastering the old Equipment at least."

"I see how the Vertical Maneuvering Equipment works, but using it is another story… I can't even imagine myself flying around with that thing," Rosa agreed. The sight of their special training barely simulated the advanced version's operations. Shrugging, she concluded, "We need to make a breakthrough soon. I don't want to leave this place a flunker."

"Xenophon spoke about a change that's like a revolution. It takes some trigger," Kuklo said.

"Like what?" asked Rosa.

"I don't know."

Rosa sighed in grief. "What if it turns out that it's not the kind of machine humans can ever master?"

"No one has learned to use it yet," Cardina pointed out. "That possibility is there…"

"I respect what the instructor says and I do believe in the brilliance of its inventors, but there's no guarantee that we have what it takes to do the job."

"Does it pain you to not be making progress?" Kuklo asked.

"It does," Rosa admitted frankly. "Making so little headway ends up sowing doubt. Sometimes I think that maybe it'd be better just to use the old model rather than the Vertical Maneuvering Equipment…"

"It did manage to bring down a Titan in the past," Cardina reminded.

"But Uncle Angel insists that the old Equipment is defective, so it must be inadequate as anti-Titan gear."

"So our only option is to master the Vertical Maneuvering Equipment?" Kuklo pressed.

Rosa nodded and replied yes, but her voice sank and she seemed lost. Perhaps the lack of results and her impatience over it was affecting her motivation.

The conversation drifted away from the topic of training, and they each worked on their dinner at their own pace. It was then that Kuklo's ears detected ominous footsteps approaching the mess hall.

That's… Kuklo didn't have to concentrate on them to tell who they belonged to. *Xavi!*

He seemed to have his entourage with him, as Kuklo could hear multiple pairs of feet. It was most likely a small group of four or five including Xavi, perhaps the same gang that had taken Kuklo down during logistics training. In any case, Kuklo was certain he'd get dragged into trouble if they met.

Suddenly tense, he felt his pulse quickening.

I knew I was right about eating. Kuklo gulped down all the food that was in his mouth, then pointed at the mess hall's exit. "We're done eating. Everyone go to their rooms now."

"Done? We're still in the middle of—"

"Do we have company?" Cardina interrupted an upset Rosa. No doubt he could tell from Kuklo's demeanor, thanks to the time they'd spent together, that unwanted guests were about to arrive. "Sheesh, I'd rather not have to go back to one of those cells…"

"Oh, I see," Rosa read the situation.

"He has business with me."

"So we should get out of here? That would be like abandoning a comrade in enemy territory."

"This is your opportunity to learn what being a soldier means."

Cardina and Rosa seemed to have no intention of running, nor did the other recruits at the table.

"He really does seem bothered that you joined, though," Cardina said, his voice free of any nerves. "I guess that's normal when someone you counted off as dead shows up."

"What do you mean by that?" Rosa asked, puzzled.

"Some things are better left unknown. You don't want to be disappeared by a suspicious organization, do you?"

Cardina is right…

Leaving aside the bit about suspicious organizations, a punishment as inhumane as exile could only exist in the shadows. Nearly all soldiers would be in the dark about its existence, let alone any civilians. It was not something to bring up lightly. Furthermore, it was a trump card ensuring Kuklo and Cardina's personal safety. It kept the royal government from making facile moves against them.

"Whatever happens, you can't fight back. That's exactly what they want us to do," Cardina whispered. Careless behavior was to be avoided if the scuffle during logistics training were any indication.

The disciplinary cell was not a particularly frightening place for Kuklo, but rather like home. For the others, though, it would be worthy of its name, and he was reluctant to send them there with him.

"Just leave this to me. There's nothing they can do," offered Cardina.

"Nothing they can do?!"

"Yes. I have a magic word that can silence him," Cardina winked. He was brimming with confidence.

In time, the topic of their discussion entered. Unexpectedly, Xavi was alone, his entourage apparently waiting outside. As far as they could tell, he was unarmed.

"What a surprise to find you flunkers here. You must be tired from such a long day of training," Xavi spoke snidely the first thing, striding towards Kuklo.

"Is there something you're here for?" Cardina responded as though to a close friend.

"We're in the middle of a meeting, so could you make it short?" Rosa requested. Despite her small frame, she was plucky and didn't so much as flinch in face of the bear-like Xavi. Perhaps she, like Kuklo, took after her father.

"I'm here for this monster. Mind leaving me and the Titan's son to ourselves?" Xavi said, gesturing toward the exit of the mess hall with his chin.

"Is it some kind of problem if we're here?"

"This doesn't have to do with any of you."

"Did you bring lookouts so no one would get in your way?" Cardina accused.

Xavi's right cheek twitched. There was no reply, but his reaction revealed that it was the truth. Not only that, they had already heard his lackeys' footsteps.

With Cardina and the others gone, the mess hall would be a locked room of sorts. There'd be no way of knowing what took place. In the worst case, even if Kuklo's corpse were discovered, Xavi would have an alibi if he and his cohort stuck to their guns.

"Anyway, you're all in my way. Scram," Xavi tried to intimidate them.

Cardina just smirked and scratched his head. "That's something we can't do. He's one of us, you see."

"A Titan's son? One of you?! What kind of freak are you?!" Xavi's face relaxed and he bared his teeth as he broke into laughter, but his eyes weren't smiling. Flaming hatred dwelled in the long, sharp slits of his eyes.

At this rate... Xavi was like a volcano on the verge of erupting. The slightest thing could cause him to explode. Kuklo balled his fists and braced for a fight, ready for anything to happen. His crass enemy shrank from no means to accomplish his goals, and inattention could prove fatal. Kuklo's body grew hot, his blood pumping through him at an increased rate. Already in combat mode, he was poised to spring forth at any moment.

Rosa, who sat next to him, put a hand on his fist as if to pacify him. She shook her head slightly and muttered, "Be patient."

If I get in a fight here it will be the same as last time... Exhaling, Kuklo quietly unclenched his fists.

Cardina and Xavi continued trading words.

"That thing is a monster, not something you can make friends with."

"I don't see any Titan's son in here."

"Excuse me?"

"As you're aware, the Titan's son was executed. He's no longer of this world."

"Where the hell did you hear that..." Xavi's eyes opened wide. He must not have expected Cardina to know about the death sentence.

He was not the only one who was surprised. All the others, including Rosa, looked bewildered. A criminal heinous enough to be sentenced to death couldn't have joined their team.

But there was a contradiction at play. *That is why Xavi came to meet me.* He no doubt wanted to know why Kuklo was still alive and kicking when he'd been executed.

"Let me repeat myself. There's no Titan's son here."

"But…"

"Or would you rather have the case reopened? They might always discover some new evidence they missed the first time." Cardina grinned knowingly at Xavi, who grimly ground his teeth.

I see. That's what he meant. "Reopened"—that was Cardina's magic word to silence Xavi.

If the case were reopened, Xavi's false testimony to the Military Police might come to light, a fatal blow for someone attempting to join the Brigade. He couldn't press the issue of Kuklo's death sentence.

Of course, Jorge already knew all the details, so Xavi had been rendered powerless on this front long ago. Cornering the guy didn't interest Kuklo, though.

What matters is learning how to use the Vertical Maneuvering Equipment to kill Ogre. Therefore he had no time at all to waste on Xavi.

The Inocencio heir glared at Kuklo spitefully, clicked his tongue, and turned around.

"See? Didn't that go well?" Cardina bragged, puffing his chest out. "Now he shouldn't be able to bother us."

"I hope not…" Since they knew his weakness, he'd surely refrain from taking overt action. Still, this was Xavi. He wasn't one to meekly back down.

"What's all this about executions and reopening cases?" Rosa posed the obvious question, but Kuklo and Cardina just looked at one another and refused to answer. The reason why went without saying.

"Some things are better left unknown." "You don't want to be disappeared by a suspicious organization, do you?"

Kuklo and Cardina spoke the words as if they were telepathically linked, and Rosa could only sigh in response.

***

A week had passed since starting his life as a recruit.

For Kuklo, who had spent most of his life alone, everything about his time at the training academy seemed fresh. He ate together and slept together with five hundred other recruits, and that alone qualified as a dramatic change in environment. While it was a constricting one since he wasn't accustomed to matching the pace of others, Kuklo didn't cause too much friction thanks to Cardina and Rosa helping him along. To begin with, the other recruits didn't go out of their way to accost him given Xavi's proclamations that he was a Titan's son.

Kuklo's life was proceeding without a hitch. If he continued to train hard, he would no doubt post adequate grades. He might not make the Military Police, but a stable life as a soldier was nearly guaranteed.

Meanwhile, the Vertical Maneuvering Equipment training failed to put up any results to speak of. They tried everything they could imagine, but the gains were always trivial and resembled nothing like a breakthrough. Time passed idly by, and a fretful mood hovered over the team. Perhaps it just wasn't possible.

It was when Kuklo and the others strapped on the Equipment to head toward the forest, the day's classes over, that Jorge announced to them, "Today's training is canceled. We're all going outside today."

"Outside to where?" Kuklo asked, to which Jorge replied, "Wall Maria."

"Shopping in Shiganshina District?"

"There's something I want to show all of you."

"I assume it's for our Vertical Maneuvering Equipment training."

"You're right, Rosa," Jorge admitted, without divulging any details. He seemed to want it to be a surprise until they arrived, but it wasn't as if keeping it a secret buoyed his students' hearts.

"You're not going to make us run to Wall Maria, are you?"

"We'll go by carriage. You're free to run if you want to build some stamina."

"I'll take the carriage, please," Cardina took back his joke. He dashed straight to the stables, eager to prepare a carriage before Jorge could change his mind.

Wall Maria… Only half a month earlier, Kuklo had barely made it back from beyond the walls after being banished from the country. *It feels like so long ago.* Two short weeks felt like years thanks to a string of events that had changed his outlook on life.

"Kuklo!"

The yell cut short his train of thought. He hadn't noticed, but Rosa and the others were already walking toward the stables and beckoning him to follow.

I should go. Kuklo nodded and hurried to them.

***

Jorge Piquer drove his carriage southward down an artery road, his students on board.

All around him was enveloped in pitch darkness. Driving with neither street lamps nor moonlight was difficult even for a man of his experience. If not for his lantern lighting the path, he wouldn't have been able to proceed.

Though the major route was full of carriages during the day, it was now deserted, with only the occasional patrolling soldier or diligent merchant passing by. It was not an ideal time to travel.

Jorge's students were asleep in the wagon, tired from their training, leaving only him, the driver, awake. Vertical Maneuvering Equipment training was not an official subject, which meant it received no assistance from the corps. He had to prepare anything and everything himself. Normally, it was unthinkable for an instructor to sit reins in hand on the driver's seat and personally transport recruits.

I should just be happy they're allowing the training to take place… If he had not accomplished the incredible feat of defeating a Titan as commander of the Survey Corps, even that permission would not have been forthcoming from the brass. *I have to prove the Vertical Maneuvering Equipment isn't plain junk if I want it to be recognized as a subject.*

While his students were working hard, they were stuck in a long tunnel with no exit in sight. They had yet to lose heart, but he knew it was going gradually downhill. Their doubts about the Vertical Maneuvering Equipment were sapping their spirits.

I hope this becomes the trigger... He hadn't told them, but they were headed to the top of Wall Maria. The Survey Corps would be going on an expedition the next morning, and he wanted his students to watch.

Yet, it wasn't the brave figure of the Survey Corps venturing outside the walls that he wanted to show them, but the opposite spectacle.

Carlo Piquer, Jorge's son and the current commander of the Survey Corps, was the one to suggest an observational lesson upon hearing about the Vertical Maneuvering Equipment training's status. Witnessing what went on in the field might help undo their stagnation. Envisioning a battle with a Titan might help them make free use of the gadget.

It was a different approach, but that was exactly why Jorge considered it necessary.

But it might also cause them to lose heart. While Kuklo and Cardina had already seen hell outside the walls, Rosa and the others had not. Though they knew from lectures the gist of what awaited them, it was ultimately nothing more than second-hand knowledge. The cruelty of the lands outside the walls could not be conveyed in words, and that was especially true when it came to the irrationality called the Titans. Jorge had seen the wills of scores of soldiers snapped in two by them.

"Shall I take the reins?" Rosa asked, peeking out from the wagon. She didn't seem to have just woken up, so she must have been resting her body but not asleep.

"I'll be okay. You're the one who ought to rest."

"I'm fine, too," Rosa smiled. She moved to the driver's seat, next to Jorge.

"You took after your mother. Considerate, in just the same way."

"You know my mother?"

"Of course."

Rosa's father, Solm Hume, had served under Jorge in the Survey Corps. Jorge knew his fiancée, Maria Carlstedt—though they only met for the first time at Solm's funeral.

"Maria was once called Wall Maria's guardian angel."

"I've never heard that before."

"I would assume not. It was just something whispered among the Survey Corps."

It was natural for his troops to search for special significance in a Garrison soldier named Maria. No one knew who first said it, but there had been a rumor that a corpsman who saw her before an expedition would return uninjured. Of course, it was nothing more than a superstition, but it was adhered to by countless men who hoped to glimpse her as they passed through the gates. In a way, that was how cruel the world outside the walls was. How ironic that others were able to return alive when Solm, her fiancé, died on an expedition.

"Maria doesn't seem to be very happy that you're going to become a soldier."

"It's because I want to join the Survey Corps."

"So she doesn't want Solm's fate to be yours."

"I don't plan for that to happen," Rosa replied firmly. "But I do see what they mean by 'Like father, like daughter.'"

"How so?"

"It's like I was guided by my father's blood coursing through me. But maybe it's just my imagination."

"Solm was a talented soldier. Were he still alive, I'm sure my son would find his presence reassuring."

The reformed Survey Corps was undeniably inferior to the corps under Jorge's command. Troop quality could only deteriorate after avoiding actual combat for fifteen years. It was a grave problem and the reason Jorge couldn't step down from active service.

Kuklo. He might be the same, too. It seemed too perfect a coincidence that Kuklo was in the Training Corps under Jorge. Heath had been appointed as team leader when Jorge was still commander. Carlo and Solm were in his team, and Carlo would later discover Kuklo in a Titan's vomit.

Destiny, I suppose. The Survey Corps had resumed their expeditions as if they'd been waiting for Kuklo to come on stage. The Vertical Maneuvering Equipment had lurked in the wings as well. It only seemed right to call it destiny.

In that case, he'll soon learn to use the Vertical Maneuvering Equipment. Perhaps thanks to his newfound confidence, Jorge's mouth loosened into the slightest of smiles.

"Is something the matter?"

"Oh, I was simply thinking about what I'll do when I retire."

"What's that?!"

"Just talking to myself."

Jorge cleared his throat and cracked his whip.

***

Shiganshina District was bustling with energy. Filled with pedestrians, the avenue that ran from north to south through the center of town was so alive that one might be forgiven for thinking it a festival day. There were no roadside stalls, but the people walking down the avenue wore excited smiles on their faces.

Shiganshina District was a gigantic town that boasted the largest population of any inside the country. It was also the nation's center of trade. While it was full of energy even on a regular day, today's commotion was something special.

Kuklo and the others had not made it in time, but the Survey Corps had left on an expedition that morning. In other words, the men and women on the street were spectators, and their unusual enthusiasm was due to the Survey Corps' imminent return.

Dumbfounded, Cardina watched the spectators in front of the

main gate. "It's like some festival."

"An expedition is a festival for them. They're here for the return parade to the barracks," Kuklo said.

"You seem to know a lot about this. Have you been in one of these crowds before?"

"I was in a parade with the Survey Corps."

"That's quite a valuable experience there…"

The town only grew more restive, and the area around the gate became jammed full of people trying to secure front-row seats. At the moment, though, their attention was focused on Kuklo and the rest of his group. The crowd was used to seeing soldiers, but recruits must have been an uncommon sight. That fact alone may not have garnered their attention, but Kuklo and the others wore the old Equipment. The strange armament naturally drew eyes toward them.

Wearing the Equipment was a part of their training, meant to get their bodies used to the machinery.

"Nothing wrong with being looked at," Cardina welcomed sarcastically, but Rosa and the others looked stiff. Perhaps they were excited and afraid of the outside world in equal measure, for their faces bore an inscrutable mix of emotions.

The classes might be part of the problem, Kuklo suspected. While knowledge was necessary to survive beyond the walls, it was counter-productive if the lectures planted fear in the recruits' hearts. Even so, fears rooted in knowledge rather than experience wasn't true fear.

Kuklo looked at the towering wall and concentrated on what was on the other side. *No Titans nearby…*

Just as he confirmed this, Jorge returned from speaking to a Garrison soldier. "Okay, let's go up," he said, pointing to the top of the wall. He pulled out the Equipment controller from its holster on his waist.

"We're not going up there using *these*, are we?"

"Of course we are," Jorge disabused Cardina. Then he fixed his aim and pushed down on the controller's lever. An anchor flew from its muzzle and sank into the top of the wall. "This is the perfect opportunity for you to display the fruits of your training. Make a good impression here and it'll be easier for me to talk to the higher-ups, too."

Jorge smiled fearlessly as he returned the controller's lever to its original position. The machine on his back howled and rewound its wire at a fierce rate. Jorge's body flew into the air and approached the top of the wall almost instantly, causing spectators to cheer in amazement. After grabbing the edge of the wall to pull himself up, he motioned to Kuklo and the others to follow.

"That's the instructor for you. I guess he had this all planned out from the beginning," Cardina marveled.

"He seems like he'd do fine out there, too," Rosa said, sounding just as surprised.

Jorge had moved with such fluidity and grace that it was hard to believe he was a veteran who'd stepped away from the front lines. If anyone dared to spar with him, he would end things quickly after amusing himself, no doubt.

Kuklo grabbed his own controller and followed Jorge's lead, sinking an anchor into the top of the wall. The taut wire provided him with solid feedback; the Equipment would be able to support his body. Having made sure, Kuklo used the lever, and the Equipment roared in response. His body shook off gravity and suddenly flew into the sky, guided by the anchor. He was nearly to the top just a moment later, and he let off speed to make a soft landing. As soon as he did, he grabbed the edge and moved onto the wall.

One by one, the others followed.

"Looks like all that practice is paying off," Jorge nodded, looking satisfied. Still, that didn't keep him from adding a pointed reminder. "The goal is to learn to control the Vertical Maneuvering Equipment. Don't forget that."

The top of Wall Maria was full of soldiers at work. With an expedition in progress, they had to bring their A-game and be ready for anything.

Jorge and his students moved to a watchtower, and from there they could see the world beyond the walls alongside the lookouts.

The tower was perfect for getting a panoramic view of the outside world. Of course, all they saw was an expanse of unused, barren land, with little of note. Kuklo cast a quick glance across the area but found nothing more than a dreary wasteland stretching to the horizon. No Titans seemed to be nearby.

But they have to be somewhere... He could be sure of that.

"You know, though, the more I see it, the worse it looks," Cardina said with some feeling, perhaps reminded of his dash through the outside world. Kuklo didn't care to play another life-or-death game of tag with a Titan, but it was inevitable if he wished to take one on.

Rosa spoke next. "I can't believe that people used to live there..."

"Without humans there to tend the land, it ends up looking like that."

That was especially true where the Titans roamed. When they rushed through a town, it was enough to turn buildings into rubble.

Only one Titan had entered Shiganshina, but it had razed half the district, leaving countless people dead or injured. It was said that hundreds of Titans existed—perhaps thousands. If a horde of them descended on a town, it would collapse almost instantly.

The soldiers burst into activity. A lookout had spotted something beyond the walls through his binoculars.

That's... Kuklo focused on the direction the soldier was pointing. He saw black smoke in the sky a few kilometers ahead. It was a beacon. The menacing puff made it clear that something had happened.

"The Survey Corps is coming back."

The black smoke that polluted the sky was from a signal flare fired by a soldier. A "Black Star" indicated that the Survey Corps was heading back with a Titan in tow.

This was followed by a Yellow Star. It seemed the Survey Corps was being followed by a considerable number of Titans.

Before long, dots that appeared to be the Survey Corps emerged from beyond the horizon. They seemed to be advancing at full speed, their warhorses kicking up a storm of dust. At second sight, that was not all. The cloud was also due to grand, human-shaped creatures that madly pursued the Survey Corps.

"Titans…"

Only their silhouettes were visible through the cloud of dust, but there seemed to be ten at the very least. While varying in size, they were all easily larger than any human. That their shapes were clear despite the distance was proof.

"Burn this sight into your memories. Never forget what those Titans look like."

Jorge's instructions were superfluous, as his students all had their eyes glued on the monstrosities. Rosa, who was seeing a Titan for the first time, had her eyes opened especially wide. She was trembling, but the reaction was natural. It was hard to stay cool and collected in the face of monsters that defied human comprehension. Everything she thought she knew about the world had to be crashing down around her.

This was the trial Jorge wished to impose on his students. It was his way of screening them. If a recruit couldn't weather it, he or she was incapable of challenging a Titan. It wasn't a sign of Jorge's severity—just the opposite.

Fortunately, Rosa and the others seemed to have conquered their fear. They stood firm, even if their faces had turned sickly pale…

As they watched, the Survey Corps grew closer and closer. The Titans were now clearly visible, too, and while initially there seemed to be around ten, the true count, including some smaller Titans, approximated twenty.

It was a dreadful sight, like something out of a nightmare. The Titans were about five hundred meters away from the Survey Corps. Though not slim enough to be covered instantly, the gap was nonetheless rapidly closing. It would only be a matter of time before the Titans caught up.

With the Survey Corps drawing near, the gigantic, ten-meter-tall gate began to open.

Commander Carlo brought up the rear as the group closed in on the gate, their horses neighing. His sharp gaze stared straight forward, and he skillfully used his reins to spur his mount.

"Fire!!"

The order came from a soldier who'd been gauging the situation from up high. The cannons placed on top of the wall spewed flames, and balls of fire shot out of their muzzles and into the ground a few hundred meters ahead. Amidst explosions, giant pillars of flame flared up from the ground, engulfing the bodies of multiple nearby Titans. Still, that did not stop the attack of the Titans. They seemed to know no fear, and they all continued to charge savagely forward, expressions unchanged.

The bombardment continued, blowing Titans away and bathing them in hellfire. It still wasn't enough to incapacitate them, but it did pin them down, providing one Survey Corps soldier after another the chance to pass through Wall Maria.

"Close the gates! Close the gates!"

The portal shut almost as soon as a soldier shouted the command. Perhaps noticing that their prey had vanished, the Titans halted their attack.

After that, the monsters began to act erratically. While some wandered off, others stood in place as if they were reluctant to part. Unlike when they were chasing after the Survey Corps, they seemed to have no clear goal in mind. Eating humans was the only thing that interested them.

The Titans that had been knocked over by the shelling rose up. Though they should have been missing limbs, these had been restored, and their hideously burned skin had finished regenerating as well. Having recovered completely in just a few minutes, the monsters began roaming the land as though nothing had happened. The bombardment must not have so much as tickled them.

Kuklo balled his fists and glared at these implacable enemies of mankind. Perhaps noticing his impassioned stare, a familiar Titan, tall and lean, approached with a smile.

"Ogre..."

The Garrison soldiers did nothing to the sluggish figure. With the gates closed, Titans had no way of breaching Wall Maria. Perhaps the understanding was that it was safe to ignore them. The wall was thick enough to repel Titans and tall enough to be unscalable. A misguided strike damaging Wall Maria posed a bigger threat than any of the Titans outside of it.

"So, is that one your nemesis? Quite a fine young man, isn't he?" Cardina joked, but his face was stern.

Rosa stood next to him, her expression no less stiff. "Did you see those monsters? How do you even..."

"As you saw, they can't be defeated by orthodox means," Jorge replied. "I doubt the current Survey Corps, which still relies on the same old tactics, can ever down a Titan." Despite the Garrison soldiers around him, the instructor openly criticized the prevailing doctrine. Only Jorge, who'd defeated a Titan, could get away with that.

"To defeat them we need the Vertical Maneuvering Equipment," Kuklo said.

"That's right."

"What if that doesn't work?"

"Then humanity will gradually decline."

Xenophon might come up with a groundbreaking new weapon, but waiting wasn't the answer.

At a tortoise's pace, Ogre ambled to a spot right below the watchtower. Then it looked up at Kuklo.

The more Kuklo looked at Ogre, the more it resembled a person. Aside from its size, it was nearly identical to a human, and this was what made Titans all the more repulsive. As if to greet Kuklo, it opened its mouth, a slit that stretched form ear to ear.

"Laugh while you still can," Kuklo spat at the Titan. If he'd been

holding explosives, he'd have thrown them into the Titan's mouth, but unfortunately he was empty-handed. While he couldn't settle things just yet, he believed he'd have the chance soon.

Kuklo heard the cries celebrating the Survey Corps' return from inside the walls.

***

Xenophon Harkimo soaked in satisfaction on the training academy's athletic grounds. Four giant machines resembling swings had been installed on one side, and he'd just finished making final adjustments. While it looked like playground equipment at first sight, the apparatus had been manufactured for Vertical Maneuvering Equipment training purposes as per Jorge's request. In truth, it may have been too low-tech to be called an "apparatus," as it neither used special materials in its construction nor possessed any newfangled features. Built with three support pillars each, it resembled a towering tripod. Two bungee cables stretched from the top of the pillars, and users could simply strap one to each side of their hips in place of the Vertical Maneuvering Equipment. After that, they'd have to rely on their senses to maintain their posture mid-air.

In other words, these machines were made to cultivate a sense of balance, without which wielding the Vertical Maneuvering Equipment was a pipe dream.

"It took me a bit of time, but…they look good," Xenophon sang his own praises, nodding over and over with satisfaction.

Since the machines were of simple construction, they'd taken no more than three hours to set up. Xenophon had only supervised, leaving the actual work to his subordinates, but they finished before noon, more or less on target.

He might have made a more groundbreaking machine… Comparing himself to Angel was a bad habit of Xenophon's that he couldn't kick. *Well, no point in asking for what you can't get.*

Grimacing and scratching his scraggly hair, he complained, "They're late, though. It'd be nice if they decided to show up soon." Looking around the grounds he saw greenhorns doing sprints, but Xenophon wasn't waiting for any run-of-the-mill recruits. He awaited the elite selected by Jorge. The others were no more than part of the scenery, extras who wouldn't be missed.

He's probably whipping away at a horse right about now. The gang for whom Xenophon was impatient still hadn't returned from their excursion. If all had gone according to plan, the viewing of the expedition was over and they were heading back to the academy. They'd be arriving before he became downright irritated.

Just as he thought this, a carriage approached with Jorge in the driver's seat. Xenophon called out, "You kept me waiting for quite a while. I was about to take a nap out of boredom."

"I think we're exactly on time, are we not?"

Jorge's dubious look forced Xenophon to notice. "I must have finished a little too early..."

"Are you fishing for praise?"

"Perish the thought," Xenophon shooed, but he did feel fairly satisfied. "Anyway, here are your machines."

When he introduced the freshly completed machine to Jorge and his students, they all looked at it blankly, confused as to how it worked, but Xenophon had expected this reaction.

"It would be fastest if you just used it. You, my spare. Try it out." The workshop chief grabbed Cardina, who'd just exited the wagon, and guided him to the machine.

"Um... What exactly is this shifty contraption?!"

"It turned out wonderful, didn't it? Save the praise for later, though."

"Hold on, I'm asking you how to use this thing..."

Cardina looked bewildered, but his words went in Xenophon's right ear and straight out the left. What was important was getting the fellow to use the machine, not anything he had to say.

"This thing has been tested, right?"

"It's flawless. At least, it worked without a hitch in my mind." True, none of the experiments using his subordinates had met with success, and a few were in a hospital now. Regardless, Xenophon deemed it to be working as intended. The only problem was the difference in athletic ability between military recruits and craftsmen. Most importantly, it functioned perfectly in his mind, so any problems rested with the users. *Probably.*

Upon hearing this, Cardina's face filled with the gloom of a condemned man standing on the gallows. Before he could resist, he was hooked up to the machine and pulled up in the air. All that supported him now were the cables attached to his hips and the hands of one of Xenophon's men. Cardina's feet were fully thirty centimeters off the ground. Though the craftsman supported his body for the time being, if he let go, Cardina would have to rely on his sense of balance alone.

"I'm very unstable up here…"

"Just like using the Vertical Maneuvering Equipment, isn't it? If you can control your posture on this, then some day you'll be able to master the Vertical Maneuvering Equipment! Or maybe not! It might at least trigger a breakthrough."

"Okay."

Having persuaded Cardina, Xenophon locked eyes with his subordinate. The craftsman nodded and let go.

"Gwuh?!" Cardina let out a wild cry as he lost his balance. He flipped upside down and hung in mid-air.

"If you had been using the Vertical Maneuvering Equipment, you'd have fallen and hurt yourself just now."

"I guess you could call that a silver lining…" Cardina half-laughed, half-spat, suspended.

"I want to try it out," Kuklo volunteered.

With no reason to say no, Xenophon quickly instructed his men to hook him up to a machine. "I'd love to see you master this," he said to Kuklo, who was now connected to the practice apparatus. The words were honest ones. Someone had to master the Vertical Maneuvering Equipment to prove its utility to the upper echelons of the military. Having an epochal invention consigned to the warehouse would shame Xenophon as a craftsman.

The subordinate let go. Unlike Cardina, Kuklo held his posture without falling over. His sense of balance must have been better. Still, it was clear to everyone that deprived of the stability of standing on his feet, Kuklo was making use of all the muscles in his body to maintain his posture.

I see it's placing too much of a strain on the body. Trying to tame the Vertical Maneuvering Equipment by force could end in torn muscles or dislocated joints, even broken bones—mid-air at that. The fate awaiting such an operator was as clear as day. Posture control needed to become as natural as breathing.

"Maintaining your posture on your first try? Impressive." Though not totally satisfied by the performance, Xenophon clapped and praised Kuklo. If one person got the knack and learned to handle the machine, others might use him as a model, raising the floor for all. The same logic held for the Vertical Maneuvering Equipment, and Kuklo was the most likely model.

While I do feel sorry about his background, I can't help but be grateful to it right now. It was true that Kuklo's abilities were outstanding, but he wasn't superhuman. He didn't possess powers beyond the ken of mere mortals unlike the Titans. Rather, harsh conditions had brought out his potential, and a comparable aptitude surely slumbered in the others. If Kuklo could learn to master the Vertical Maneuvering Equipment, anyone could with enough effort.

Whatever the case, I'm going to need him to work hard. Briskly walking up to Kuklo, Xenophon said, "I forgot I had a message for you from the young lady."

"From Sharle?" Kuklo's body twitched and shook as he tried to maintain his posture.

"She says, 'Please don't do anything too crazy, okay?'" Xenophon said, imitating Sharle's tone, then kicked one of the pillars hard.

The slight vibration this caused rippled out to the entire machine, affecting Kuklo, who struggled to use his entire body to keep his posture intact. He pawed at the air as if he were paddling water in a desperate attempt to stabilize himself, but regaining his balance after losing it was not an easy task. He began to fall over, face-up.

"Agh!"

Despite his cry he kept trying, but his exceptional physical abilities now worked against him. As if hoping to land like a cat, he twisted his body reflexively. While this would have narrowly saved him in actual combat, his body was connected to bungee cords. Flipping over in an awkward position, he slammed his head against the ground and passed out.

"Didn't I just pass on Sharle's message not to do anything crazy? You're going to make her sad, you know." Xenophon shrugged and sighed, ignoring his own culpability.

It seemed as though a bit of time would be needed before the Vertical Maneuvering Equipment could be mastered.

***

Xenophon's practice apparatus was producing the desired result. Unlike the earlier blind attempts at training, all questionable in their efficacy, the machine had been developed to help its users master the Vertical Maneuvering Equipment, and that was exactly what it was doing.

Kuklo and the others—who had the required specs, so to speak—quickly took to the machinery and handled it well enough within a few days. By the time a week had passed, they moved in it freely. Once they had the knack down, their bodies reacted without the assistance of conscious thought. They'd probably be spared any more head-butting the ground and blacking out.

The skills mastered during this training worked for the Vertical

Maneuvering Equipment. Though they couldn't quite fly around with total freedom, they were able to move up, down, left, and right. Tight turns and precise motions still eluded them, however, and they were by no means ready to be sent into combat.

I'm like an ape in this. Using the Vertical Maneuvering Equipment, Kuklo weaved his way between trees. Behind him were Cardina and Rosa, and behind them followed the rest of the team. Compared to back when all they did was move up and down repeatedly, this was a dramatic improvement indeed. Yet, Kuklo still wasn't tracing the trajectories that his mind's eye drew. *Something is lacking... What is it?*

"Monkeys on the move," the other recruits derided, and in fact Kuklo's team hopping through the woods must have looked like nothing more. Kuklo bore the mockery since he felt much the same way. Right now, he needed to devote every waking moment to the Vertical Maneuvering Equipment.

He looked straight forward and glimpsed a giant mannequin fifty meters ahead of him.

There! Kuklo inserted both of his controllers into the scabbards hanging on either side of him. He felt a slight but certain sensation in his palms. *All right!*

He nodded and pulled the controllers back out to reveal slender silver-gray blades—single-edged swords. Their shockingly sharp edges justified Xenophon bragging about them. Kuklo cut away the twigs and branches in his way as he continued to charge forward.

Soon the giant mannequin came into view in its entirety. A large dummy about five meters tall, it was the same Titan mockup Kuklo had taken on in the factory city. Upon hearing that the recruits were now wielding the Vertical Maneuvering Equipment, Xenophon had brought it for them to train with.

Scanning the area around the Titan dummy, Kuklo hammered the positions of everything he saw into his head. Approaching the target wasn't enough. He had to attack it, then escape safely, and that required a route. More than one route, actually. He needed to prepare multiple paths in the blink of an eye. Unlike the dummy, a Titan wouldn't stand still for him.

Although Kuklo managed nothing close to his intended trajectory, he somehow found himself closing in on the Titan's back. He dealt its neck a single blow on his pass and disengaged. His fellow recruits followed suit.

This won't do. Straying from the path he had in mind meant that in a real fight, he would have exposed himself. Against a Titan, that equaled death. He needed to be able to move more precisely as well as swiftly if he were to ever slay a Titan.

Kuklo picked a towering tree ahead of him, sinking in an anchor and moving in its direction. Managing his controllers and maintaining proper balance, he shot toward one of the branches that stretched from the trunk and landed with ease as if he were stepping over a puddle. The others followed him, each choosing a branch.

The world they saw from ten meters off the ground was breathtakingly beautiful. While the scenery from the top of Wall Maria was pretty grand, getting to where they were on their own via the Vertical Maneuvering Equipment offered a special joy.

"Honestly, I never thought I'd be able to use this thing so well," Cardina shared from the branch below.

"I guess you can say your hard work paid off," Rosa chimed in from a different tree.

"The training machine was the trigger we needed. Without it, we never would have been able to graduate from the old Equipment."

Cardina was absolutely right, but there had to be more to the machine. Wielding it to get to the top of a tree was a major achievement, but not a game changer. *The revolution Xenophon talked about hasn't happened.*

"Not yet. I can't defeat Ogre like this," Kuklo spat, jumping off his branch without hesitation.

"Hey, hold on! We need to move as a group!" Rosa yelled after him.

But there was no stopping him now. Kuklo set his sights on a nearby tree and pressed a controller lever.

***

With graduation a month away, the recruits were training more intensely than ever. Moreover, royal government officials and military brass had been invited to a contest to be held in a week's time. The recruits were all eager to pitch themselves.

The reason for their fervor was clear: they wanted to apply to the Military Police Brigade. While graduating recruits could only apply to the Brigade if their grades put them in the top ten, making a good impression on the brass during an inspection match offered a plausible way in. Recruits naturally dreamed of joining the Brigade.

One particularly fervent aspirant was Xavi, a shoo-in for the top ten. Nevertheless, he didn't feel relaxed at all and fretted mightily. The cause of his angst was the contest, or to be more precise, the reason it was being held in the first place. Officials and officers wouldn't care to sit through a contest among recruits. Nor were there any records of such an event being held in the past. In other words, something had happened that necessitated it, and the flunkers with their Vertical Maneuvering Equipment were the most likely culprits.

Why them? Xavi grumbled in his heart, his face a picture of raging frustration. Though he was on guard about Kuklo and Cardina, the flunkers were just a bunch of losers who meant absolutely nothing to him. Just the other day, he'd seen them going from tree to tree and mocked them, comparing them to apes. The other recruits all did the same.

And yet! The situation had been reversed, and the flunkers and their remedial lessons were the talk of the academy. It was even rumored—though it was nothing more than a rumor—that they were almost certain to be among the top ten.

I'm the one who'll be applying to the Military Police! Clenching his fists, Xavi tiptoed through the darkness.

It was late at night and the barracks were silent, with only the occasional snore wafting out of a room. No other recruits would be awake at such an hour provided they hadn't slacked off during the day's training. If they'd taxed their bodies, they were simply too overcome with drowsiness by the time they returned to their rooms after dinner.

He had to be the only one prowling around the barracks. Of course, as someone aiming to join the Military Police Brigade, Xavi had given his training his all. He was tired, and he felt sleepy. Still, there was something he had to do.

He headed to the locker room in the barracks. The soldiers changed into their uniforms and put on their equipment there before heading to training, and Kuklo's band was no exception. The only difference between them and the other recruits was the harnesses they wore to control the Vertical Maneuvering Equipment.

Xavi reached the locker room without encountering another soul. Once there, he quietly opened the door and stepped into the room. It was filled with a thick, tangible darkness, and he couldn't see everything in it even though his eyes were adjusted to the dark.

But he was familiar with the room. As long as he minded his steps, he'd reach his target without trouble.

Xavi halted once he arrived in front of a specific locker. He suddenly grew tense and gulped down a glob of saliva. The locker in front of him was not his own. The plate on it read "Kuklo."

Xavi placed his hand on its handle and carefully opened the door. He examined the locker's contents and immediately found what he sought: the harness. Grabbing it, he pulled out a knife he'd hidden on himself.

"You're an eyesore, all right?" Using his knife he cut into a part of the harness. "There we go. There…"

CHAPTER SIX

Kuklo and the others applied themselves to their training even harder than before, especially in light of the decision to unveil the Vertical Maneuvering Equipment at the contest. They couldn't let such a golden opportunity to push the training up to an official subject get away.

Yet, their skills hadn't improved decisively. Facing a Titan still seemed like a pipe dream, and beating a hasty retreat was all that the device seemed good for.

At the same time, it wasn't as if they hadn't honed their techniques at all. It was just that the thing took a while to master. Titans had to wait until after graduation, but showing off what the Vertical Maneuvering Equipment could do at the contest was well within their reach.

To begin with, perhaps they shouldn't be rushing to graduate. Middling technique did them no good, and heading to the battlefield as they were spelled death. Waiting until they were adept seemed acceptable to them. While repeating a year would be unusual, an academy first in fact, it was nothing to be ashamed of. If anything, it was the right decision, and Jorge, their instructor, agreed. They'd surely be granted a second year of training as a special measure if they could show off the Vertical Maneuvering Equipment's capabilities at the inspection matches.

Their curricular training done for the day, Kuklo and the others equipped their machines and walked to the usual woods off the athletic grounds. What wasn't usual was the presence of other recruits who'd come to watch.

"How distracting…" grumbled Rosa.

"There's a few more every day. Looks like we're popular." Cardina chuckled and glanced at the recruits observing them from a distance.

Following his gaze, Kuklo counted about thirty absorbed spectators following their every movement, perhaps hoping to steal some techniques.

While Cardina and the others seemed to find the gallery distracting, Kuklo, used to being watched, felt nothing. They aimed no hostility or hatred toward him, so he considered them as harmless as the vegetation around him. Thinking about them was a waste of time and energy.

He pulled his controllers from the holsters and looked at the sea of trees ahead of him. Full of thriving cedars, pines, and cypress trees over twenty meters tall, the setting drew out the full potential of the Vertical Maneuvering Equipment. The Titans needed to be lured onto similar terrain if they were to be felled. While there were only a few such places outside the walls, the oases featured a decent density of trees.

Okay! Kuklo fired himself up and stared at a thirty-meter-class cypress that soared before him. He set his sights ten meters up it and used his controller's lever to fire an anchor. He missed his target slightly, but the anchor dug itself into the tree more or less where he wanted. *I guess that's fine.*

Accuracy was somewhat of an issue for Kuklo, who was missing his right eye. But that was nothing new. He could make minor adjustments on the fly, so there was no need to disassemble the gear to make mechanical adjustments.

Kuklo returned the controller lever to its original position and leapt into the air. The wire quickly reeled back in, sending his body flying with ease. Cardina, Rosa, and the others all sank anchors into other trees and began to move. Repeated practice had rewarded them with both bruised bodies and newfound skill, and their movements were as smooth as silk.

The audience oohed. Their reaction testified to the impressive possibilities hidden in the Vertical Maneuvering Equipment.

Kuklo and company weaved through the trees at a relaxed pace as if they were jogging.

"How self-serving, though." Cardina seemed bewildered by the other recruits' change in attitude.

"I have a feeling they'll have another change of heart if we don't do well at the contest," Rosa offered her cool, realistic take. "But thanks to them, rumors about the Vertical Maneuvering Equipment will spread. We need to show them everything it can do." She began increasing her speed.

Cardina followed after her, bantering, "Honestly, I think we already stand out."

Though they only expressed anxiety and discontent, they were proud of the daily growth in popularity the Vertical Maneuvering Equipment was enjoying. Kuklo, on the other hand, couldn't care less what others thought.

All I care about is killing Ogre. The Vertical Maneuvering Equipment was attracting attention on his way to that goal, nothing more.

Likewise, he needed to perform well at the inspection matches in order to defeat the Titan. He hadn't been moved by Jorge's passion, nor was he concerned about the future of humanity. What drove him was utterly personal. He wanted to sever his ties to the Titans. But whatever it was that motivated Kuklo, no one would object if he put up some results. He was certainly putting in the required effort.

It happened when he was fine-tuning the placement of his anchors even as he proceeded among the trees. A shot from his right firing mechanism strayed far from its target and missed.

"Wha?!" Kuklo opened his eye wide in surprise. It seemed like a mechanical malfunction. Having lost its mark, the anchor descended in a parabolic arc.

He clicked his tongue and quickly tried to reel the wire back in, but the right controller linked to it didn't respond. He pressed the lever again and again, to no avail.

Oh no... Kuklo's wires were his mode of transportation as well as his lifeline. When they failed, he was essentially throwing himself off of a tree. *What now? What do I do?!*

His left wire having been reeled in, Kuklo's body was flying forward from the momentum. Normally, his right anchor would grab its target and stabilize his body, but now...

Kuklo quickly looked around him but spotted no branches that might save him. His body began to decelerate and lose balance. He found himself overtaken by a strange, floating sensation.

I'm going to fall... Just as Kuklo thought this, his body began hurtling toward the earth.

Ten meters to the ground. He could see a verdant rug below him, but it seemed unlikely to catch his body gently. His scattered blood would turn the flowers into crimson mementos.

"Kuklo!" Cardina and Rosa yelled almost simultaneously.

"Damn it!" Kuklo spat, gripping his left controller. Dying thanks to a tool meant to kill Titans was no way to go. *No thanks!*

He had options left, too. While his right controller wasn't functioning, thankfully his left one still did. While he could no longer maneuver in three dimensions, he could still move up and down. In other words, he just had to imagine that he was using the old Equipment.

The only problem was his sense of direction, which had been scrambled thanks to his rapid descent. His inner ears seemed not to be working, and he couldn't even tell which way was up.

He'd crash into the ground unless he did something, but just then, his eye caught a nearby tree.

Here! Kuklo immediately used the lever on his controller. An anchor shot from the firing mechanism and went straight into its target.

Far from a miracle arising from exceptional instincts, it was a conditioned reflex, the sort of feat that became possible only through grueling practice. He had learned how to move his body in his wrestling classes, and he'd fostered his sense of balance using Xenophon's practice apparatus. Thanks to the old Equipment, he'd grown familiar with his gear's workings. His response was the summation of all of this training and not a matter of chance.

Just a meter away from the ground, an intense force ripped through his body and he came to a sudden stop. The harness spread the impact out to some degree but didn't eliminate the stress altogether. Kuklo quickly started losing consciousness.

While he'd narrowly missed hitting the ground, that was not the end of his troubles. The impact also affected his anchor, which pulled itself out of the tree trunk, unable to support his body.

This time, Kuklo did fall to the ground, and that was when he blacked out.

***

Cardina watched, befuddled, as Kuklo hurtled to the ground. Kuklo, who was more skilled and twice as hardworking as any of the others, wouldn't ever fall.

But that was exactly what he was seeing.

Fortunately, Kuklo's superhuman nimbleness had kept him from falling all the way down, but he was surely hurt. He was now face-up and flat on the ground, completely still.

He couldn't be... The worst of all outcomes crossed Cardina's mind, but he shook his head, denying the possibility.

"Cardina!" Rosa yelled out to him and descended to Kuklo's side before he could. His classmates followed.

I was just jumping to conclusions. Cardina breathed a deep sigh and quickly shot out a wire to head back to the ground. He landed, recovered his anchor, then rushed over to where Kuklo lay spread out.

"He's just unconscious. It doesn't look like he's particularly hurt."

Just as Rosa diagnosed, Kuklo seemed to be okay. He had no noticeable injuries and his breathing was normal. He would be bruised the next day, but they were confident he'd come to soon.

"In any case, I can't believe how tough he is." Cardina was genuinely stunned.

"It might not be appropriate to say this, but I'm kind of relieved."

"Why?"

"Now I know he's human, too."

"Ah, I take your meaning."

Kuklo had been known as the Titan's son, and his body was hardy enough to give credence to the label. Rosa could be forgiven for harboring a faint, lingering suspicion.

"As you can see, Kuklo is just a regular human. Though he is tougher than most people need to be." Cardina shrugged his shoulders. "Still, I can't believe he'd fall... What could have happened?"

"I was in the air a little behind him..." Rosa looked pensive for a short while but continued, "His anchor flew off in a weird direction, so it could have been a mechanical malfunction."

If the error was due to the Vertical Maneuvering Equipment not working properly, then even Kuklo could not avoid falling.

Could that really be it, though? It had been developed by Xenophon and Angel. They wouldn't overlook such a flaw, but if an anchor flew in a direction its user didn't intend, there had to be some cause.

Cardina looked at the parts in question, the right controller and firing mechanism.

Well, I don't see any damage. He couldn't be sure until he took it apart, but an amateur like him probably wouldn't be able to pinpoint the problem anyway. Since the left anchor worked properly, the main unit of the Vertical Maneuvering Equipment had to be fine. *The cylinders are full of gas, too.*

Cardina performed a quick check of all the equipment on Kuklo's body but found nothing that could have caused a malfunction.

We'll probably have to learn how to service these things sooner or later. Having to call the craftsmen every time something broke wouldn't do in an emergency. At the very least, they needed to learn how to disassemble the machinery, study its parts, and reassemble it.

"Let's carry him back to the barracks for now. It could be that he's sick." Though Cardina didn't really think Kuklo was ill, a medic needed to see him, just in case.

He took the Vertical Maneuvering Equipment off of Kuklo's body, then moved on to the harness. When he was nearly done, a section of it snapped and tore off.

Rosa looked at the split harness. "So this was the problem…"

"The machinery must not have registered his movements because this part was coming loose. It makes sense that an anchor flew in the wrong direction."

Cardina sighed in relief now that he had a satisfactory answer. Rosa, however, continued to stare at the harness with a grave expression.

"Is something bothering you?" he asked her.

Rosa nodded and pointed to the severed part. Carved into it was an unnatural notch. "If it tore itself apart, there would be fraying. But this…"

"Yes. It's like someone used a sharp blade to make a cut there."

"Did someone tamper with his harness?"

"I hope not…"

Yet the artificial slice made it clear that someone had meddled with it. It must have been left mostly intact just so it'd fail in the air. In other words, the cut was like a time bomb.

Did someone try to kill Kuklo?! It was a natural conclusion, considering the Vertical Maneuvering Equipment's purpose. A chill ran down Cardina's spine.

"But who would do such a thing…" Despite the words that spilled out of his mouth, he didn't need to whittle down a long list of suspects in order to name the culprit. Kuklo had an enemy, and the answer was obvious.

"I think we might know who our criminal is." Rosa seemed to be thinking of the same individual. "So, what do we do?"

"Let's consult with the instructor first. This isn't the first time *that guy* has done something evil."

"Not the first time?! Why let someone like that join the Training Corps?" Rosa demanded, visibly distrustful.

Oops, I said too much there. But it was too late for him to take it back. "There'd been a certain situation," Cardina said evasively.

Rosa looked even more doubtful. "Are you going to spout some bullshit about suspicious organizations again?"

"Please, let's just leave it at that. I'll tell you about it once we get everything sorted out." Given the nature of the matter, however, that time might never arrive.

Cardina hoisted Kuklo up with his teammates and returned the way they came.

***

Kuklo's body screamed the moment he turned in his sleep. The pain was severe, as though every muscle in him was cramping, and since he was hurting from head to toe he hardly dared budge. He had yet to look over his body, but it promised to be an ugly sight. His chest ached just from breathing. Groaning, he forced open his eyelid. It felt as heavy as lead.

"Where am I…" A familiar ceiling came into Kuklo's view, and he knew right away: he was lying sideways on his own bed in the barracks.

"How do you feel," Cardina asked, peering into his face. Behind him stood Jorge.

"How do I feel?" Kuklo was still groggy, just having woken up, but he soon remembered something important. "Oh, yes. I was using the Vertical Maneuvering Equipment when I—"

Since he was still alive, he'd just barely avoided crashing into the ground. His body was in pain because he'd pushed himself to the limit to survive. He could have been left with muscle injuries, tears in the worst case, but it seemed as though he hadn't moved in overly extreme ways. His pain was within manageable bounds, and he'd recover in a few days.

But that was not what was important. He needed to focus on the chain of events that began with a mechanical malfunction and ended with a nearly fatal dive.

It took place over just a few seconds, but in that brief moment Kuklo had considered many things and settled on a course of action. It felt as though he'd applied all of the skills he'd learned.

As soon as he came to this realization, his heart filled with a sense of accomplishment. *I handled the Vertical Maneuvering Equipment perfectly during that split second.*

"Anyway, about the accident..." Cardina said, looking serious. "There was actually a problem with the harness you were using."

"I see..." Kuklo balled his fist. His euphoria seemed to be acting as an analgesic, and he felt no pain.

"This doesn't leave this room, but there were signs that your harness was tampered with."

"Someone did that, then..."

"Oh, so you've figured it out. Please take a look." Cardina brought the harness out in front of Kuklo and pointed at the torn area. "We believe that someone made a notch here with a blade. The culprit is most likely—"

Waving his hand to cut him off, Kuklo said, "Enough about that, listen to me!"

"What? This is important, you know?" Cardina looked quite nonplussed.

"The revolution! It's happened!" Kuklo exclaimed.

"What are you talking about?"

"I think I've mastered the Vertical Maneuvering Equipment."

"Really?!"

Kuklo nodded, then explained why he thought so to Cardina and Jorge.

"Perhaps being on the brink of death drew out new possibilities," mused Cardina.

"And thanks to an ambush of sorts. All of your disparate skills combined as one due to an accident, the machine failure," Jorge remarked with a look of understanding.

"So now we know what the revolution we need is…"

"An ambush can't be the only way, Cardina. It must be one of many methods."

"But we found one," Kuklo said.

"Yes, a rather dangerous method…" Cardina's cheeks had grown stiff. He clearly preferred a different method. Reacting in the wrong way could lead to a fatal fall or a career-ending injury, so he was hardly to blame.

"A small price to pay for mastering the Vertical Maneuvering Equipment," Kuklo insisted.

"I don't think so. Live to fight another day, and all that," Cardina countered.

"An ambush is definitely dangerous," the instructor admitted. "But if you can't overcome one, then sooner or later, you will drop out. I don't mean to pressure anyone, of course."

"I was the one who decided to stick with him, so I'll try my best, but… Please don't get your hopes up."

"Don't worry. You can do it too, Cardina. So can everyone else." Kuklo was certain of it, though he couldn't explain why in words.

Jorge expressed his agreement. "If Kuklo can master it, everyone else should be able to. You have a tendency to underestimate yourselves, but you're all completing the same training. You can be more confident."

"I sure hope so…" Cardina sighed. "Getting back to the harness, what should we do?"

"Do?"

"Weren't you listening to me at all?!" Cardina put a hand to his forehead and groaned. "Someone tampered with your harness. Don't you think you need to question him?"

"So that's why my Vertical Maneuvering Equipment was strange?"

"Yes."

Kuklo immediately had an idea of who had done it, but he was not interested in hunting down the perpetrator, nor did he feel the desire to expose him and see him ruined.

I don't care about that stuff. It was a waste of time.

In fact, it was thanks to this perpetrator that Kuklo could now use the Vertical Maneuvering Equipment. He felt like he needed to thank him if anything.

"He'd regret it, and his face would turn red, if he heard you say that," Cardina said chuckling.

***

"How? How is this the result…" Xavi mumbled, dumbfounded. His eyes were fixed on the flunkers leaping through the forest's trees. More specifically, he was watching Kuklo make deft use of the Vertical Maneuvering Equipment.

Kuklo ought to have suffered major injuries during a training accident a few days ago. Yet, he was the picture of health with no noticeable after-effect. In fact, his movements were more agile and exact than before. Did he now have complete mastery over the Vertical Maneuvering Equipment?

The same was true for the other flunkers. Advancing smoothly as though they were marching on the ground, they looked like full-fledged servicemen. The only difference was that the sky was their stage, not the earth. There was no longer a trace of apishness.

There's no way he could be fine. They trained twenty meters in the air. Anyone falling from that height would suffer grave injuries, and there were in fact rumors that Kuklo had been dealt a fatal one. After all, Xavi had prepared the cause of the accident and foreseen the calamity that befell Kuklo.

A debilitating injury at the very least. Preferably, death…

Yet, contrary to Xavi's expectations, Kuklo was brimming with energy. At this point, Xavi had to question the source of the rumors.

I have to murder him. There's no other way… Dirtying his hands was undeniably risky, but the only option left was to watch Kuklo die with his own eyes. Unless he committed the deed personally, Kuklo would come back to life again and again, just like a Titan, to stand in Xavi's way. *I have to put an end to it myself...*

But killing Kuklo would inevitably generate suspicion—a dire problem for Xavi, who wished to join the ranks of the Military Police Brigade. He had to figure out a way to not only kill Kuklo but to come out of it clean. He was asking for too much, but he needed to make it happen.

Fortunately for him, an event where he might do exactly that was going to be held in two days. If he proceeded boldly yet carefully, he should be able to slaughter Kuklo once and for all.

Glaring at his enemy among the branches, Xavi began to consider the necessary steps.

***

Ten tree-like posts had been set up on the athletic grounds. Each about ten meters tall, they were for the Vertical Maneuvering Equipment's unveiling prior to the inspection matches. With footholds in place of branches, these simple substitutes, less than half as tall as actual trees, seemed unreliable. As long as there were places to sink in the anchors, however, Kuklo and the others could take to the skies. The posts had to serve for their demonstration.

Unlike the gallant expeditions of the Survey Corps, everything about the contest seemed plain. The audience consisted only of government officials, military brass, and a few other concerned parties. All in all, they numbered only about fifty people, but it sufficed for publicizing the Vertical Maneuvering Equipment to keypersons.

Kuklo and company came very first on the program. They would be making practice runs in the way of unveiling the Vertical Maneuvering Equipment. A large dummy sat on the grounds in place of a Titan.

How would the Vertical Maneuvering Equipment alter anti-Titan combat? Could they really beat the Titans to begin with? Kuklo and the others' mission was to answer these questions definitively with their demonstration.

"Don't overthink it. You don't need to try to show them anything special. Just do what you always do, and you'll provide the results we need," Jorge instructed the recruits.

Putting aside Kuklo, who was used to being observed, Cardina, Rosa, and the others were all nervous to varying degrees. Failure was not an option, so it was little wonder they couldn't relax.

"You'll stop worrying once you're up high," Kuklo declared flatly. The demonstration wasn't taking place on the ground. Though the posts were only ten meters high, the view from them would be drastically different. From that height, the spectators would blend into the scenery where they could be ignored.

"Then I'll just pretend they're potatoes or something," Cardina said, scratching his head.

"That's probably the right approach," Rosa seconded. "We have an inspection match waiting after this, so we need to save some of our strength."

While the run was all that mattered to Kuklo's team, the mock battles to be held afterwards offered the other recruits a final chance to self-promote. The matches were crucial to them, especially if they were aiming to join the Military Police.

It doesn't matter one way or another to me. Still, Kuklo planned to go all-out in the match to gauge where his abilities stood.

"Let's go." He pulled his controllers out of his holsters.

"Did you check your harness?" Cardina teased.

"Just don't fall. It'd be shameful to see," Rosa said.

"I'm okay."

After Kuklo's accident, they made a point of inspecting their harnesses before wearing them. Going forward, the plan was to add inspections and maintenance of the Vertical Maneuvering Equipment to the routine.

Kuklo turned his attention to the top of a post, then fired an anchor using his controller. Feeling much like a bird, he rushed into the air. His visual field suddenly opened up and the world transformed.

They really could be potatoes. With his bird's-eye view ten meters off the ground, the people below him seemed like a simple mob. From up there, differences in social status and talent meant nothing, government officials and recruits all potatoes. Nothing about them could put anyone on edge.

As if to chase after him, Kuklo's comrades sped to the same heights. They split into two groups, each rotating around their target, the dummy. One group went clockwise while the other went counterclockwise. Both made sure to vary their altitudes as well.

The audience let out cries on the ground, but the wind whooshing past the recruits' ears blocked the exact words. The reaction didn't sound bad at all, though.

After maneuvering for a time, the team shifted to attack mode. Appending single-edged swords onto their controllers, they confirmed the location of their target, the Titan dummy, and settled on routes to its weak point, the medulla oblongata. Approaches weren't hard to deduce against a stationary target.

Kuklo lifted his body to a point higher than the Titan, then moved horizontally to swing around to its back, bringing the nape of the dummy's neck in sight.

There! Locking in on the Titan's weakness, Kuklo began swooping down toward it. He moved from upper right to lower left in a slashing motion as if he himself had become his blade.

He aimed strictly at the Titan's nape and not its body. An attack anywhere else yielded nothing more than a tactical advantage. Forming a V with the single-edged swords he held in each of his hands, Kuklo slashed at the Titan dummy as if to slice away its medulla oblongata. True to their mark, the blades gouged it out.

Cardina, Rosa, and the rest of the recruits followed in succession

toward the dummy. They came from above to below, from below to above, or on the level, and sliced. This proved their ability to strike a Titan's weak point from any angle. The team exchanged glances, finished their run, and returned to the ground.

Though buttoned down compared to how Survey Corps expeditions were welcomed back, the audience response, the whole point, was quite favorable. The Vertical Maneuvering Equipment's capabilities had been conveyed well enough. Jorge's satisfied expression reinforced the impression. All that was left was for a political decision to be made, and Kuklo would have no say in that. He just had to believe in Jorge and wait.

The team saluted the audience and retreated, with light steps, to the athletic grounds' outer edges, where the numerous recruits awaiting their turns cast envious gazes upon them—except for Xavi, whose expression was rather one of rage.

"I let you out of sight for a while, and look how good you get."

A man who looked like the very picture of manliness approached Kuklo as he sat on the ground resting. The soldier in his mid-thirties had a beast's penetrating glare. On his uniform was a winged emblem, the symbol of the Survey Corps.

Carlo Piquer—that was the soldier's name. The current commander of the Survey Corps and the very man who'd discovered Kuklo's raw talent and recommended his recruitment, Carlo was Kuklo's savior. If it hadn't been for him, Kuklo would have died in exile, devoured by a Titan.

"So you came."

"Of course. I needed to see if the Vertical Maneuvering Equipment is worth using in combat."

Bowled over by the sudden presence of the Survey Corps commander, the other recruits began to stir. He practically existed on a different plane, so their reaction was natural.

"And what did you think?"

"It passes with flying colors," Carlo replied immediately. "However,

Titans and Titan dummies are two different things, as I'm sure you're aware."

"It'll be hard to aim for their weak spot. I know that." Having been chased by Titans before, Kuklo wasn't letting his results against the dummy get to his head. The other recruits showed the same reserve. Seeing the Titans first-hand from atop Wall Maria had paid off.

"I felt like I was watching the future of the corps when I saw all of you. Old soldiers like me are probably going to be shown the door soon."

"It's not too late. You just need to train."

"I would if I could, but I'm a slow learner, you see. It's too late for me to change my ways."

Carlo added that the same went for his troops. Their style of combat had seeped into their marrows, and embracing novelties would be difficult.

"I'll be going, then. Keep at it until graduation." Carlo began to walk way with confident steps, but he turned around once to say, "The next time we speak, it'll be as fellow soldiers."

"Wow, I guess you need to be a force of nature to be the Survey Corps commander." Cardina was just being honest.

Kuklo felt the same way. Many recruits boasted impressive physiques, including Xavi, but not the aura around Carlo forged by countless battles and brushes with death. Cardina likened the quality to a force of nature, but whatever it was, Carlo had something that attracted others to him. Perhaps it was his largeness as a person.

Rosa had tilted her head now and again, unable to get over her puzzlement. "First the instructor, now the commander. How in the world do you know such people?"

Kuklo had no answer for her, but if he had to come up with one, it was fate.

Because I was the Titan's son. Burdened with a curse from before he was born, he endured horrible treatment, but as a result he came across people he might not otherwise. When he thought of it that way, his days of abuse seemed to have meaning. Of course, this in no way inclined him to speak any words of thanks to Xavi.

Meanwhile, the preparations for the inspection matches had been completed. The bouts would take place between teams, eight on eight. The recruits would marshal the gamut of the combat techniques they'd acquired to try to disable the opposition. Arms were allowed, but the short swords would feature regular bamboo blades rather than sharp Iron Bamboo edges. As for firearms, toy guns replaced carbines. Both weapons were capable of imparting bruises but not fatal blows.

Ten mock battles would take place at once, with the soldiers switching out for a total of three rounds. Kuklo's team wasn't up until the second round, but they had no time to dawdle since the bouts would be decided quickly.

"It'd be so easy if we could use the Vertical Maneuvering Equipment," Cardina sighed as he looked at the grounds. Ten pairs of teams, a total of a hundred and sixty recruits, braced for battle. Simulated or not, it was quite a spectacle.

"It wouldn't be a fair fight if we could," Rosa said, and she wasn't exaggerating or bragging. She only spoke the truth.

The Vertical Maneuvering Equipment would allow them to move freely through the air. They could just blast away with their toy guns from up above to make the match one-sided. Thus, Kuklo's team was to engage in the mock battle equipped with just the standard gear. The one difference was that they would each carry two fake blades. Having gotten used to dual wielding, they felt uneasy with just one sword.

The first round of battles finished in about ten minutes, and it was now Kuklo's team's turn. Having prioritized their earlier demonstration, they were somewhat tired. They still had some stamina, however, and felt perfectly capable of fighting. They certainly didn't plan on losing.

Kuklo's team walked to its designated position on the field.

"Hm? It looks like the big shots are going," Cardina said. The officers, including Carlo, and the bureaucrats started to leave the grounds, apparently tired of watching recruits spar.

"Maybe they just wanted to see what the Vertical Maneuvering Equipment could do," Rosa reasoned. She was probably right.

While this served Kuklo's team, who'd only wanted to promote the device, it had to be vexing for the other recruits who'd hoped to make an impression. In the end, the quickest way to the Military Police was through honest and steady progress.

"This will probably demotivate our opponents," Cardina said sympathetically.

"Not true. Let your guard down and they'll get you," Kuklo said, noticing the naked hostility on their counterparts' faces. In the center of the opposing team stood Xavi.

"I see, you're right. One careless moment could sink us." Perhaps the usually frivolous Cardina sensed that a fierce battle was coming; his expression suddenly turned grim.

"This doesn't feel like chance," Rosa said.

"He could have asked for it," Cardina agreed.

Whatever the reason, they were in for a tough fight. They needed to be ready.

As for Xavi, wasting no time, he issued malicious threats. "An eyesore is what you are. I'll crush you."

They had no effect on Kuklo. While he faced a formidable enemy, he wasn't exactly afraid, and the same went for his teammates. None other than Xavi had created the opportunity for Kuklo's team to grow so bold. Having incorporated surprise attacks into their training, they had all flirted with death time after time. Each of them could brush off Xavi's threats like so many specks of dust.

"We're not going down easily."

"You want to crush us? You'd better be ready for what's about to happen then."

With those fighting words, Cardina and Rosa drew their dual practice swords.

Xavi still seemed to look down on them, and his face was as red as hot steel. "You're nothing but flunkers…"

"We're no flunkers." Kuklo drew his swords. "We're soldiers!"

He returned Xavi's glare, and just as their fighting spirits reached a peak, the instructor gave the command: "Commence combat!"

Kicking against the ground, Kuklo quickly closed the distance and slashed sideways with his swords. Xavi stepped back to evade the attack, but it didn't miss him entirely, the tips of the swords grazing the bottom of his jacket's collar. If the blades had been made of metal, his uniform would have been damaged; had they been the usual single-edged swords, the material would have torn. Kuklo stepped forward again and thrust his swords, but Xavi swayed to avoid them.

Defeating him won't be simple. Kuklo knew that much. Among the pool of recruits, Xavi was a highly talented soldier. Jorge conceded the fact, so it had to be true.

Kuklo and Xavi stood apart from each other, both of them glaring at the other.

"I'll kill you… I swear, I'll kill you…" Xavi opened his eyes wide and slowly unsheathed the sword at his waist. What emerged was a blade shining silver-white.

That— Right as the blade's suspicious gleam gave Kuklo a bad feeling, Xavi brandished the short sword and stormed forth.

While Kuklo craved a straight fight, Xavi's powerful arms would deal bludgeoning strikes. Pitting his strength against Xavi's could only end in Kuklo being overpowered and crushed. Given Kuklo's agility, it would be easy to dodge Xavi's attacks, but going head to head with an opponent who was all about brawn and defeating him had its special appeal. It would surely leave Xavi's pride in tatters.

Xavi brought down the short sword he'd raised above his head. The vicious blade sliced through the air, heading toward Kuklo with enough force to snap a bamboo sword in two. Rather than naively try to catch the blow head-on, Kuklo took advantage of his blade's curvature to deflect it. But something else happened.

This… Kuklo's eye opened wide. Far from deflecting his opponent's blade, his practice sword broke cleanly in two, and one look at the damage revealed that it hadn't been caused by blunt force. His sword had been severed by a sharp edge. In other words, the silvery-white weapon rushing toward Kuklo's head was a live blade.

No wonder he'd had a bad feeling about it.

So Xavi really meant to kill Kuklo, and he intended to do it in front of a crowd. Yet, considering the guy's personality, it couldn't simply be a desperate and reckless act. He had to have some underhanded plan to get himself out of it.

It was too late to evade the blow. Trying to dodge to either side would get him cut down, and jumping back promised the same outcome.

The circumstances couldn't have been any worse, in fact were panic-inducing, but Kuklo's mind was as still as a lake. Yes, he had a fear of blades. When he was still in the sideshow, he'd been dealt knife cuts and nearly died from them. Now, though, he had the ability to overcome his fear, to maintain his composure, and to contemplate his next move.

I don't need to dodge it.

Kuklo lunged forward, straight into Xavi's space.

Escaping the range of the sword called for distance, but overcoming his fear and stepping in nullified his opponent's attacks. Since a pummeling at close quarters couldn't be ruled out, Kuklo had to stay on his toes, but his first priority was to avoid lethal injury.

Sticking close to neutralize the swing, Kuklo drove the pommel of his practice sword into Xavi's exposed solar plexus.

"Gah." A moan forced its way out of Xavi's mouth, the blow having struck a vital point.

Seeing his chance, Kuklo swiftly hurled Xavi's body away. After being tossed again and again by Rosa during wrestling training, Kuklo knew first-hand that with the right leverage even larger opponents could be thrown.

Xavi must have been knocked nearly unconscious by the initial blow. When Kuklo made a clean, textbook-worthy throw, Xavi didn't even try to land safely and ended up splayed on the ground. The whites of his eyes showed, and it was clear that he'd passed out.

Kuklo breathed a sigh and looked to the rest of his team, whom he'd nearly forgotten.

"Call it a difference in experience," joked Cardina, having already downed his enemy.

All of Kuklo's other teammates had also knocked out their opponents while he'd taken his sweet time. None looked particularly tired or were breathing hard after what must have been child's play.

Throwing a glance at Xavi's unconscious figure, Kuklo picked up the short sword that had fallen near him. It was a live, standard-issue Iron Bamboo sword, the notoriously effective real deal.

"An 'accident' during the fight, I guess."

"Huh?"

Cardina pointed to the short sword Kuklo held. "He tried to kill you, didn't he?"

"Maybe he thought you'd falter if you saw a real one. Like that'd work," Rosa said without a hint of drama. She probably would have charged straight into Xavi and unleashed one of her flawless throws.

"So, what do we do with him? This guy won't stop hustling until you're dead."

"You can only turn the other cheek so many times, we need to take care of him. He's a threat to military discipline, to say the least."

Cardina and Rosa were in agreement that Xavi needed to be handed over.

Meanwhile, Kuklo didn't care either way. It was safe to ignore Xavi, who could do him neither good nor ill. The problem, if anything, was the hassle that handing him over might entail.

Before long, the other teams put up their own results, and the second round of inspection matches was declared over.

***

The demonstration that unveiled the Vertical Maneuvering Equipment at the contest brought about a more than satisfactory result. There was now an inquiry into making Vertical Maneuvering Equipment training a part of the official curriculum. The final verdict wouldn't be out until after graduation, but there were already rumors that the Training Corps had placed an order for more units with the workshop, and the common view was that it was a done deal.

The Vertical Maneuvering Equipment's battlefield debut was still some way down the line, but Kuklo and the rest of his team had definitely done their part.

Though the Training Corps wasn't deciding until after their graduation, Kuklo's team did reap some benefits. Their special training had once come at the cost of their free time, but it was now considered a part of regular training. This was a dramatic change. Finishing at the same time as everyone else meant they could eat something other than leftovers. This meant little to Kuklo, whose sense of taste was nearly nonexistent, but a lot to his comrades. More so than their improved diet, it was being treated like everyone else that pleased them, a natural reaction after being groundlessly branded as flunkers for so long. In a telling shift, the remedial lessons were now synonymous with honest effort.

While the erstwhile flunkers' stock rose rapidly, Xavi was fading into the background. His crushing defeat to Kuklo at the matches hadn't gone unnoticed. There was hardly any room for sympathy since he deserved his comeuppance.

Only two weeks remained until graduation. Kuklo and the other recruits kept at their training without slacking off.

Soon. We'll meet soon, Kuklo muttered in his heart as he squeezed his controller. Then, imagining the soaring cypress tree in front of him to be Ogre, he pulled the lever.

A crystal-clear blue sky spread as far as the eye could see. The rays of the calm morning sun poured onto the athletic grounds with not a cloud in sight. The entire day seemed guaranteed to be beautiful after such a refreshing morning.

About five hundred recruits stood in neat, orderly lines on the grounds. Every one of them wore a tense expression, and they listened closely to the address being delivered by the headmaster from atop the stage.

Thirty minutes had passed since the beginning of the Training Corps graduation ceremony. The headmaster went on tirelessly about his own struggles during his years on active duty. Most of his stories were simple bragging meant to prove his brilliance. In a nutshell, his point was that he belonged to the Military Police Brigade because he was indeed that good. The ceremony was like a final lesson intended to test the recruits' fortitude, but Kuklo was barely listening in the first place.

"—You recruits graduating today have three options. The Survey Corps, the Garrison, or the Military Police Brigade." The headmaster continued in his resonant voice, "Of course, only the ten students with the highest grades announced earlier are allowed to apply for the Military Police Brigade."

In other words, any recruits who didn't stand head and shoulders above the rest wouldn't be able to enter the Military Police as fresh recruits. To do so, they needed to produce results as active soldiers. In Jorge's case, he'd been deemed worthy after many an expedition as the Survey Corps commander and for bringing down a Titan.

"Am I in the top ten, too?" Kuklo whispered to Cardina, who stood on his right.

"Yes. Everyone in our team. The Vertical Maneuvering Equipment must have left that strong of an impression."

"The Military Police, eh…"

"Do I hear you sounding interested? You work in the interior and get a lot of authority, so you could act important for the rest of your life."

That much was clear from watching the headmaster, but the Brigade was also home to soldiers like Jorge who gave their all to the nation. Ultimately, it was down to your personality. Inconveniently, an individual with a problematic one had scored well enough to end up in the top ten.

"Xavi's in the top ten, too…"

"He is talented, after all," Rosa, who stood to Kuklo's left, replied to his muttered words. "Let's just pray he doesn't take the country in the wrong direction."

"Right," Kuklo said, but in reality, nothing would come of Xavi joining the Military Police. Kuklo knew this intuitively as a result of butting heads with him. If he'd felt even the slightest bit threatened by Xavi, he would have done something after the attempts on his life. He hadn't even felt the need, which meant that Xavi no longer affected him in any way.

As Kuklo chatted with Rosa and Cardina, the headmaster brought his speech to an end. "This concludes the Training Corps graduation ceremony. We will now move on to the recruitment ceremony."

Taking the place of the headmaster, who had finished bragging about his exploits through his so-called address, Carlo briskly walked up to the stage.

"I am Carlo Piquer, and I have been entrusted with the position of commander of the Survey Corps," he began. The recruits quickly started whispering amongst themselves. If the commander of the Survey Corps was taking the stage at the recruitment ceremony, it could only mean one thing. "As I'm sure even you recruits know, the Survey Corps, recently reformed, suffers from a perennial lack of personnel. After this ceremony, you will be asked which branch you wish to join. When that happens, I want you to think about us, the Survey Corps."

Carlo spoke with passion. He was wooing the newly minted soldiers for exactly the reason he gave. More than anything, what the Survey Corps lacked was quality. Putting aside exactly how capable it had been in bygone days, it certainly seemed to fall far short of Carlo's ideals in its current state. Kuklo, who had snuck along on an expedition, knew this well.

Moreover, because the Survey Corps took on the unique duty of embarking on expeditions, their members were far more likely to die than those in the other branches. A new soldier only had a seventy percent chance of survival on an expedition. While the level of risk differed drastically depending on the nature of the foray and whether or not they encountered a Titan, it was clearly a harsher assignment than working within the walls. Joining them was not a decision to make lightly. Not even the strongest sense of purpose warded off sudden death.

The Survey Corps was like that. Naturally, few recruits volunteered to join them. No one wanted to die. Hoping to provide the last push to anyone who might be just a step away from applying, Carlo himself had come on stage to court them.

"We plan to have recruits from this year join us in an expedition to take place a month from now. If you learn the truth about this world, you will understand why the Survey Corps exists."

Whispers ran through the recruits once again.

"There is no guarantee that you'll return alive. If you, knowing this, still want to put your life on the line and venture beyond the walls, stay here. All of you who want to join a different branch, you are dismissed. That is all."

The moment Carlo finished his speech, the grounds grew quiet, but only for a moment. When one new soldier began to walk away hurriedly, it put the whole crowd in motion. Recruits began leaving one after the other as if an avalanche had been set off.

Cardina said as he watched the recruits practically fleeing the grounds, "That's no surprise. Why go out of your way to choose a dangerous path?"

"You're all okay with it? Even after snagging the right to join the Military Police?" Rosa asked everyone.

"I came here to kill Ogre."

"And I decided to tag along with him… But if he decides he just has to join the Military Police Brigade, I'm not opposed to the idea."

"I'm only interested in the Survey Corps."

Cardina slumped his shoulders. "That's what I thought."

The recruits continued to disappear before their eyes even as they talked. In the end, only one score of them remained on the grounds. Whether that number was large or small was in the eye of the beholder, but Carlo seemed satisfied.

"You're brave soldiers. I respect you from the bottom of my heart," Carlo said calmly to the faces that remained. "Well then, I welcome those standing here into the ranks of the Survey Corps. That is all!"

With that, the recruitment ceremony came to an end.

"Did I join the Survey Corps?" Kuklo asked to make sure.

"I think it's pretty clear we just did," answered Rosa.

"Sheesh. Rejecting the Military Police to join the Survey Corps? My father must be rolling in his grave," Cardina mumbled with palpable regret as one who only wished for a life of debauchery.

"Time to give up," Kuklo chided.

"Resign yourself," Rosa said appalled.

"You're not the only ones who've turned down the Military Police," a voice said. This one belonged to Jorge. "It looks like he's doing the same to join the Survey Corps," he said before shifting his gaze.

Kuklo's eye followed it only to fall upon someone so unexpected that his jaw dropped. "Xavi."

Among the recruits staying on the grounds was Xavi, who could have exercised his right to join the Military Police. His expression was terribly grim, and his large frame seemed to be shaking a little. The life seemed to have been sucked out from his face, and he seemed unsteady and ready to faint at any moment. Clearly, Xavi's true wish wasn't to join the Survey Corps.

"Wasn't he going to become an MP?" asked Kuklo.

"I thought so, too, but something made him reconsider," Jorge said, though Kuklo had no idea what could have. "Putting that aside, let's talk about your future," the instructor cut to the chase, facing toward his pupils. "As Carlo informed you, you'll be taking part in the expedition occurring a month from now. And of course, you'll do so wearing the Vertical Maneuvering Equipment."

"Will we be killing Titans?" Kuklo asked.

"That will depend. While you have all received plenty of training, you have close to zero combat experience. It will probably be hard for you to take on Titans from the get-go." Jorge said "close to zero" rather than "zero" only because of Kuklo and Cardina's skirmish of an encounter. Simply being chased by a Titan beyond the walls was a valuable experience.

"So what should we do, then?" Cardina asked.

"For now, just join the expedition."

"To get used to it?" Rosa said with a look of understanding.

"Your first mission is to return alive no matter what. You hear me?"

Kuklo and the others nodded in reply.

"The next time I meet you, it will be a month from now. I'll be watching you from the top of Wall Maria." With that, Jorge walked off without any further parting words.

"So he wants to meet us in Shiganshina District after we've returned alive?" Cardina threw out.

"Probably."

"Okay. Well, we can't let him down."

While Cardina and Rosa continued to chat, Kuklo was interested in something unrelated to his own safe return. He stared at Xavi, who stood there stock-still.

Why would he join the Survey Corps? Xavi hungered for power more than any of the others. Kuklo still couldn't bring himself to believe that the guy had joined the Survey Corps after all. He had to have some ulterior motive. *But what is it?*

There was only one way to find out.

Kuklo approached the dazed-looking Xavi and asked him, "Why

the Survey Corps?"

"It's your fault..." Xavi's voice and body were both trembling. "I'm going to join the Military Police. I'm going to gain power and become greater than my father ever dared to be!"

"Then why not apply to the Military Police?"

"I can't keep losing to you! I'll join the Military Police after I settle the score!!" Xavi yelled, glaring at Kuklo with all he had. He looked ready to pounce at any moment, and Kuklo was naturally put on guard by the tense mood, but rather than raise his fists Xavi spun and stormed off.

Chuckling, Cardina walked toward Kuklo. "You know, he might have some promise after all."

Rosa tilted her head, mystified. "Maybe he wasn't actually rotten to the core. Or maybe he was reborn after his thorough beating."

Some change of heart must have visited Xavi, indeed. Yet it was unlikely to affect Kuklo in any way.

Taking his eye off of Xavi's receding back, Kuklo gazed up at the sky. It looked calm—a perfect day for thinking about the future.

Of course, thinking guaranteed no flash of inspiration, nor was it his part to use his head.

Kuklo simply voiced his desire. "I wanna fly..."

***

Though it was still bright out, the saloon was full of energy. Every one of the hundred-plus seats taken, the place was brimming with the smell of liquor, tobacco, and assorted dishes. Add the heat emanating from the guests and the air was thick enough to choke on. Most of the patrons were affiliated with the military, and half were Survey Corps soldiers there to raise their spirits with a drink.

The lively discussions mainly concerned the expedition waiting for them the next day: having encountered Titans in certain locations; needing to alter the route this time; getting their hopes up for the new crop of recruits; and so on. The most popular topic of all, however, was the Vertical Maneuvering Equipment. The free movement through the sky it enabled seemed to defy common sense, and even the grizzled veterans present couldn't help but show some interest. Still, corpsmen had absolute confidence in their tough, honed bodies, which meant that more than a few were doubtful of the Vertical Maneuvering Equipment's capabilities.

"I guess we need to show them what it can do," Cardina started in, having eavesdropped on the barroom gossip.

Rosa, who sat next to him, shrugged. "We might not get the chance to use the Vertical Maneuvering Equipment." Reaching for her glass of amber fruit wine, she took it from the table.

"I'll be happy just as long as you all come back okay." This came from Sharle, who sat on the opposite side of the table. She was in her work clothes. The next day's expedition was reason enough for her to take a day off to travel to Shiganshina District, where the Survey Corps was stationed.

"Jorge did say that our first mission was to return alive," Kuklo, who was sitting next to her, mumbled through stuffed cheeks.

"It isn't a good idea to rush straight into battle. We first need to get used to the environment," Cardina said.

"I can't imagine getting used to it," Rosa confessed, shivering a bit at her recollection of the world outside the walls.

Sharle felt the same way. "I don't think you need to. If you're just a little nervous, and are hoping to come back alive, you might even get better results."

"It beats letting your guard down," Cardina agreed.

"Oh, that's right. Mister Xenophon had a message for all of you. If you get to fight a Titan, he says to please tell him how the Vertical Maneuvering Equipment handled in actual combat."

"He should come with us. I bet he'd manage to survive," Kuklo said.

"He said he had the chance once but turned it down because he was scared."

"How did he ever develop the Vertical Maneuvering Equipment, with such a mindset?"

"It's because Uncle Angel went in his place with the old Equipment," Rosa explained, drawing nods from everyone.

"By the way, the emblem on your clothes changed," Sharle said pointing at Kuklo's chest. The new soldiers all wore a fresh set of fatigues that displayed the winged emblem of the Survey Corps.

"It'll help us become popular with the townspeople," Cardina joked, but the residents did indeed notice men and women of the Survey Corps. Soldiers who braved the outside world for the sake of humanity in spite of the danger were like heroes to them.

"Except we're a bunch of greenhorns who've never been on an expedition," Rosa reminded him.

"Ah yes, our spanking new uniforms, a sign that we're not regular soldiers yet."

"I've heard that appearances matter for Survey Corps troops, though," the workshop chief's assistant said.

"Well, the residents expect a lot from us. I guess raggedy uniforms wouldn't cut it."

"It's hard to move in," Kuklo complained, rolling his shoulders. Though it didn't really restrict him, the newly tailored uniform felt somewhat strange on him.

"Want to move around in it a bit later?" Rosa suggested. "I'm sure you'll get used to it in no time."

"Let's."

"Hold on, hold on. Tomorrow's the expedition. Why not take it easy today?" Cardina grumbled, but Kuklo was already fidgeting. Cardina put his hand to his forehead and groaned, "I can't believe it. How addicted to training are you idiots?"

***

While their plan was to work up a quick sweat, their training session turned into a full battle simulation before they knew it. The turn of events vindicated Cardina's earlier complaints, but somehow he too was covered in sweat. In the end, he was as much of an idiot as his teammates. Poor Sharle had been forced to tag along.

Still, thanks to their thorough workout, Kuklo's new uniform now felt natural on him. Outside the walls, he'd be able to fully concentrate on the expedition.

"Oh dear. Did we overdo it a little?" Cardina looked around scratching his head.

He'd been too focused to notice, but it was already dusk. They must have been at it for a few hours. The scarlet rays that filtered through the leaves said as much.

They'd been practicing in a forest a short walk away from Shiganshina District. It was where they always conducted their neverending training.

"I think that's enough for me and Rosa." "Why don't you two take a little stroll first?" Cardina and Rosa teased and walked off before Kuklo could reply.

"Stroll? Through these woods?"

"I guess it's the right hour, though," Sharle addressed Kuklo's puzzlement with a wry smile.

Kuklo gazed through the branches to find the sky a blazing red. He pulled his right-hand controller from its holster and sized up a nearby cedar tree. He estimated it to be about thirty meters tall. Focusing on one of its branches, he fired an anchor at it.

"What are you doing?" Sharle said, tilting her head.

Kuklo embraced her with his left arm. Then, using the Vertical Maneuvering Equipment as an elevator, he brought them up among the boughs and alighted on one.

Despite her surprise and fear, Sharle seemed to enjoy the view from up in the trees. "So this is how you see the world. You spread your wings to make up for all the time you spent trapped."

"My chains are gone." Though he couldn't say since when, so was that annoying phantom sensation of still being manacled. It was proof that nothing held him back now.

But there's still one thing left. The strange tie that had formed between himself and Ogre—he could not be truly free until he severed that bond. But now the machine he'd mastered promised to let him do just that.

"So tomorrow is the day," Sharle said.

"Yes."

"What will you do once you settle everything?"

"Everything?"

"Once you defeat Ogre."

"Well…" Kuklo had gone to the training academy and learned how to use the Vertical Maneuvering Equipment in order to defeat the Titan. He'd given no thought to what might follow. "I'll think about it once I come back."

"That's one more reason you need to come back safe. Promise me, okay?"

"I know."

"Good." Sharle gave a satisfied nod, but her expression suddenly darkened. "I heard my brother joined the Survey Corps…"

"He could've joined the Military Police but turned them down. He said he couldn't keep losing to me."

"I see…"

"Are you worried?"

"We're siblings, after all," Sharle admitted.

"I don't like him, but he's strong. He won't die so easily."

"I suppose you're right…" Sharle's expression remained clouded, her worries hardly banished.

"It's okay."

"Huh?"

"If it comes down to it, I will save him."

The old Kuklo never would have spoken those words, but he had it in him now. *I bet Xavi would be mad if he heard me, though...* He'd surely fly into a rage and yell that he didn't need Kuklo's help.

"Thank you," Sharle perked up and smiled. "I'll be praying for all of you to come back safe."

"Yup." With a nod, Kuklo turned to look at the town enveloped in twilight.

***

A shrill cockcrow pierced through the gloom as if to drive off darkness, but the cloud-filled sky failed to oblige. The thick leaden cover sat there ominously, ready to burst into rain at any moment.

The east sky was gradually growing brighter so the sun must have been rising. The clouds yet refused to budge. The biting-cold outside air turned breaths as white as steam; any precipitation might take the form of snow. The soldiers' cloaks and hoods kept them from feeling too cold, but their body heat was slowly but surely being sapped away.

It's almost time... Kuklo looked out at the orderly file of Survey Corps troops from atop his warhorse. At the head of the group was their commander, Carlo Piquer, and the two deputy commanders who assisted him. After them came a column of ten teams, each headed by a team leader.

Kuklo was in Team Ten at the end of the line. All eight of its members wore the Vertical Maneuvering Equipment. In other words, the team consisted entirely of the training academy's former flunkers, with Rosa Carlstedt serving as leader. The position was normally filled by an experienced and capable soldier, but since no such troops could use the Vertical Maneuvering Equipment, Rosa had been selected as the best overall pick.

To begin with, a team consisting only of first-timers was extremely unusual, and it went to show how unique the Vertical Maneuvering Equipment was. Carlo did not seem inclined to make them hew to the prevailing tactics, either, having granted them permission to move at their own discretion, within reason. Meanwhile, Xavi and the other new faces had been spread among the other teams.

A raindrop landed on Kuklo's cheek as he waited for the expedition to begin.

"I guess there's nothing humanity can do about the weather," Cardina mumbled, looking straight ahead. His expression was mildly tense.

I probably look the same way... The reason was clear: they were vividly remembering the nightmare called being chased by a Titan. Though they weren't so terrified as to freeze up, it went to show that exiting the walls was no one's idea of a hobby.

But even more nervous than Kuklo and Cardina were Rosa and the others, who faced their first excursion beyond the walls. While it was in part due to the cold, they looked terribly stiff. As even Kuklo, who had been to the outside world, felt hesitant, faulting them would have been unfair. At the same time, there was no longer any turning back.

Carlo raised his right hand high at the front of the line.

"Forward!" he commanded, and the main gates of Wall Maria roared open even as his voice echoed. Hundreds of frightened birds flapped their wings and took to the air.

The Survey Corps promptly began its advance.

At last... Kuklo grew abruptly more tense, but this was no time to be attending to his feelings, as the town was now at its most defenseless against external foes. They needed to pass through the gates without a second's delay so that the Garrison troops could close them again. Letting Titans in and losing a place to come home to was simply unacceptable.

The first to respond was Team Leader Rosa.

"Forward!" she called out with vigor, spurring her mount to lead the way. There was no doubt in her expression. The responsibility she felt as team leader must have been driving her.

"Now that's a team leader for you. She has some guts." Freed from his stupor, Cardina whipped his horse and quickly began to follow Rosa.

"Right, let's do this!" Kuklo roused himself and charged forward as if to cast off idle thoughts.

The gates grew closer and closer, as did the bleak expanse ahead of them. Dark clouds literally hung over the land, but Kuklo paid them no heed as he passed through Wall Maria.

***

The Survey Corps went on expeditions for many reasons.

"Uncovering the secrets of the Titans" stood as their foremost. Titans only showed interest in humans, and only ate humans, and their harmfulness to humanity was a fact.

Whether or not the Titans were true natural enemies, however, remained unclear. Despite surface resemblances to a relationship between carnivorous predator and prey, Titans didn't actually see humanity as a source of food, as witnessed by their habit of vomiting people out undigested. In other words, humanity did not even know why it needed to be eaten by the Titans.

Where had they come from, and where were they going?

Casting light on Titan behavior was a major mission for the Survey Corps.

That was not their only job, though. Another was to create a map, the current expedition's objective.

While the outside world looked like a sprawling wasteland, it did have some distinct features. There were rocks, trees, and knolls, but most notable of all were the oases. No other places offered themselves as emergency evacuation areas, and knowing the locations of sources of water was essential to increasing the survival rate on expeditions. Of course, no place was secure in the outside world where Titans roamed, but these foliaged watering spots were perfect both for hiding and for shaking off pursuit. Many Titans moved in straight lines, so weaving through trees could save lives.

The map had been completed for a roughly ten-kilometer swath south of Wall Maria. Three oases existed there: one five kilometers south of Shiganshina District, another seven kilometers to the southeast, and one more ten kilometers to the southwest. During the current expedition, they would survey beyond that perimeter.

"Why a map, though?" Kuklo questioned as they passed the nine-kilometer point.

"Didn't I just tell you?" scolded Cardina. "Areas with water are important out here."

"I know, but..." A map was only a map.

"Creating maps is an important duty. Maps of the south are particularly meaningful," Rosa said. "The Titans come from the south side. That means if there's something, that's where. Who knows what that something is, though."

"Maybe there's a town where our outsized friends go about their lives."

"Or some sort of phenomenon that causes Titans to come into existence."

"I see..." Kuklo muttered, satisfied. "So we aren't just looking for oases."

"There's one more reason for these mapping expeditions. Do you know what it is?" quizzed Rosa.

"One more reason?"

"They're playing it safe for us greenhorns' sake," Cardina answered with a wry smile. "We'll get accustomed to the outside world as we map it. Call it the corps' first and last act of kindness."

"So it's like a practice run until next time." Still, they did find themselves beyond the walls, and that fact was enough to keep Kuklo on guard.

The ten-kilometer line came within view. Just then, Team One, which led the advance, came to a sudden stop, bringing them all to a halt.

What happened? Before Kuklo could ask, a red signal flare bloomed in the sky.

"A Titan…"

A red flare, also known as a "Red Star," signaled the discovery of a Titan. Awestruck, Kuklo watched the red smoke spread like a pool of blood.

Next, three yellow signal flares soared into the air in short succession.

"So we have ourselves a three-meter-class Titan. I really would have preferred to avoid any at all," Cardina sighed.

…*It's not Ogre.*

Kuklo couldn't immediately decide whether to welcome or to regret the fact that they wouldn't be facing Ogre. Either way, a monster was now closing in on them.

If they did nothing they were in for a battle, but Commander Carlo's plans apparently didn't call for one. Team One made a U-turn and began heading down a new path, probably toward the southeast oasis. The closest one was at the ten-kilometer point southwest, but the Titan seemed to be coming from that direction.

The Titan was about five hundred meters away. In the dim light, its distant form was hard to make out for Kuklo. As it closed in, however, its figure rapidly grew distinct. The Titan had the features of a geriatric. Its back was hunched, seemingly due to old age, and its body was as scrawny as a withered tree. Yet contrary to its appearance it was athletic. Demonstrating a horse-like speed, it charged toward them. Contact seemed like a matter of time, but if they began fleeing right away, they might outrun it.

Snapping his reins Kuklo urged his mount to turn around, but just then, a green signal flare exploded overhead.

"A Green Star?" Kuklo furrowed his brow. Used to signal an anomaly, it was the exact type that had gone up in the course of Kuklo's unheard-of attempt to smuggle himself along on an expedition. A stowaway certainly qualified as anomalous, but under the circumstances no problem could possibly be bigger than a Titan.

The signal had been fired by the leader of Team Seven, who was about twenty meters ahead. As soon as Kuklo looked his way, his eye opened wide. One of Team Seven's soldiers was charging directly toward the Titan.

That's... Kuklo could tell who it was even from behind. "Xavi..."

Letting out a war cry, brandishing his short sword, Xavi sped forth on his mount. Betraying nothing in the way of strategy, his assault amounted to a suicide attack.

He's going to get killed... Matching power for power was no way to challenge a Titan. While traditional tactics did work against a three-meter-class, it assumed a cohort of trustworthy comrades. Defying a Titan alone was a sure way to die.

"So, what should we do?"

"There's nothing we can do," Rosa told Cardina. She seemed stunned by the unforeseen development, but Xavi's death was a certainty if they did nothing.

"Damn it! I'm going to help him!" spat Kuklo, spurring his horse.

"What did I say about acting on your own?"

Rosa's voice reprimanded him from behind, but Kuklo had made his decision and was on his way, and couldn't stop now.

I promised, too. Sharle would grieve and mourn if Xavi died in battle. A despot of sorts, he'd been a constant source of hardship for Kuklo. Still, Xavi was Sharle's only family, and she wouldn't want to lose him.

Besides, being eaten by a Titan was the worst possible way to go. Regardless of any cause for resentment, Kuklo felt a moral obligation as a human being to help. Of course, the weak and helpless had the right to run away as fast as they could, but Kuklo had been granted the Vertical Maneuvering Equipment, which made him strong. He couldn't allow himself to sit back and watch a Titan eat Xavi.

The rest of Team Ten seemed to agree; Kuklo heard the galloping of horses behind him. The other teams hesitated, perhaps unable to move and adapt on the fly like Team Ten. Rescuing one greenhorn acting on his own accord certainly didn't justify endangering the entire corps. It was only because Team Ten was a living bundle of exceptions that it was able to act.

Reassured and emboldened by his comrades' backing, Kuklo whipped his horse and hurried toward Xavi, who had already engaged the Titan. Doggedly attempting to aim at its weak spot and moving around it, he hadn't challenged a Titan without at least some forethought. He was fighting to win. A Titan, however, was no opponent to be facing alone.

Xavi's short sword sliced at its withered bough of a right arm. The Iron Bamboo sword's sharp edge lopped it off from the elbow down, but the Titan didn't falter. With its left arm it grabbed and plucked Xavi off of his mount and hoisted up his body.

"Aaaahh!!" a shriek, probably from the pain, escaped Xavi as the Titan popped open its long, ear-to-ear mouth.

I won't make it in time... Pulling his controllers from their holsters, Kuklo placed them in his scabbards to extract a pair of single-edged swords. Next, he focused on the Titan's torso. *Can I do it?*

But there was no time to think. Xavi's life was now hanging by a thread.

Kuklo activated his controller's lever, and an anchor shot out from the firing mechanism and burrowed into the Titan's body, true to his aim. Though far less secure than a tree, with no other targets nearby he had to make do. In exchange, he'd approach the Titan via the shortest possible route.

Kuklo stood on his saddle and leapt into the air. Guided by the anchor, he pulled into range. He lopped off the Titan's left arm with one swing of his single-edged blade, then landed on the ground and recovered his anchor. Xavi fell toward the ground together with the Titan's arm.

Xavi was safe for now, but the Titan was by no means dead. While it now had no arms to grab them with, all it needed was its mouth,

and even those arms were beginning to regenerate.

Do I go for the kill?

Before Kuklo could act, the rest of Team Ten arrived. Acting on Rosa's orders, the soldiers began attracting the Titan's attention.

"You'd abandon your dear horse?" Cardina approached with Kuklo's mount in tow.

"Thanks for the help." Kuklo shouldered Xavi's writhing body and placed him on the back of his saddle. Then he got on too.

"Now let's get out of here!" Cardina cried.

Just as he did, a Red Star and multiple Yellow Stars rose through the sky.

These flares were not Team Ten's, but signals from the main force in the distance. The combination of flares told them that a ten-meter-plus-class Titan was heading their way. The incredible racket courtesy of the elderly Titan had kept them from noticing.

Unluckily for Kuklo's team, the ten-meter-plus-class was rushing in from where the rest of the expedition was. The Titan seemed to be four or five hundred meters away. While it would normally go after the larger group of prey, the meal closer at hand was Team Ten. Choosing proximity over volume, the Titan charged toward them without hesitation.

"We can't join up like this," Kuklo warned.

"Grandpa is in our way, too…"

The ground now faintly trembled from the ten-meter-plus-class coming in. The tremors grew stronger and stronger before turning into a full-blown rumble.

And Kuklo remembered seeing this Titan that was roaring in like a tidal wave.

"Ogre…"

The monster running toward them looked like a slender youth. It sported a wide grin, as if it was glad to be joining good buddies for some fun.

"We can't handle two at once. Let's lose them in the oasis." Rosa pointed west then led the way. Since they couldn't regroup with the main force, they would use the oasis at the ten-kilometer point to shake off the Titans. It was indeed the best option available to them at the moment.

Team Ten hurried across the wasteland in single file with Rosa, their team leader, at their head. The dripping rain was turning into a light shower. Heavy rain seemed sure to come.

"You... Why...did you save me?" Kuklo heard Xavi's voice from behind him. "Was it...to laugh at me?"

It was Cardina who replied, "Do you think we'd put ourselves in danger for that?"

"What about you? Why attack a Titan?" Kuklo asked Xavi.

"Results."

"Results?"

"...I am better than you! And to show everyone..."

"You wanted to kill a Titan." But Xavi had failed. Even if he'd been able to defeat a Titan, none would have praised him. Selfish behavior like his courted disaster, and indeed, Team Ten was being chased by Titans as they spoke.

"Why did you save me?"

"I made a promise to Sharle."

"Sharle? I see. So she's alive..." Xavi mumbled in surprise, as though he'd never imagined the possibility. "And that's why you saved me... What a fool you are."

"It wasn't only because Sharle asked. I wanted to myself."

"What?"

"Anyone would want to save a comrade."

Xavi snickered at Kuklo's explanation. "Don't bother with the lip service. I'm your enemy, am I not?"

"Enough with the talk. The oasis is in sight," Rosa interrupted, pointing at a copse about two hundred meters away from them.

There grew trees standing twenty, even thirty meters tall. Snaking through them might lose the Titans. Though fewer in number compared to the forests inside the walls, there were enough trunks to deploy the Vertical Maneuvering Equipment.

The problem was that their speed had taken a nosedive. Traveling through muddy ground required extra stamina, and from the noisy gasps it was clear that their horses were out of breath. Kuklo's mount also carried extra cargo in the form of Xavi, and a snaking path threatened to deplete its last reserves of strength.

The rain had been picking up and was now practically a downpour. Though the cascade muffled its footfalls, Ogre still pursued them. It was right on Team Ten's trail about two hundred meters behind. Meanwhile, there were no signs of the elderly Titan. Perhaps it had given up.

Kuklo carefully probed his surroundings with his sense of hearing, but the only enemy he detected was Ogre, to his rear. Dealing with just one Titan was far easier.

Team Ten entered the woods. Though the rain was somewhat calmer there, it had already found the gaps in Kuklo's cape, and he was, if not drenched, then certainly wet. Combined with the cold air, it was enough to make him shiver. Unless he found warmth, his movements would be dulled soon.

It was not Kuklo, however, but his mount that gave out first. Apparently having reached the limits of its endurance, the horse simply stood and neighed dolefully.

"Damn it!" Kuklo cursed. When he turned around, he was surprised to see that the Titan hadn't encroached on their lead. In fact, it seemed farther away than before.

"Just leave me here... Your horse will probably move then..." A note of self-mockery tinged Xavi's voice.

Kuklo shot down the idea. "I'm not letting you die."

Still, Xavi was right. The horse would probably be able to run with just one rider.

If I took shelter in the trees... The Titan, lacking intelligence, wouldn't think to climb a tree to catch him. In other words, in Ogre's case, Kuklo would be safe if he climbed a tree at least fifteen meters tall. Once Ogre passed by, the main force could come get him. They had replacement horses with them so Kuklo wouldn't have to become extra cargo.

"This rain seems like it's on our side," Cardina said, approaching Kuklo. "It looks to me like the Titan's movements are being hampered by it."

"You're right…" That must have been the reason they were now farther away from Ogre despite their slowing horses.

"It looks like we have an option other than fleeing."

"What do you mean?"

"We kill the Titan," Cardina said simply.

"I see. With its movement hampered…"

"Yes. It's almost like a practice dummy, wouldn't you say?"

"Do you honestly think it'll be that easy?" Xavi jeered.

"It'd be reckless if just the two of them took on a Titan. It'd be no different from you trying to do it alone," Rosa broke in. "But we move as a team. We can do it if we work together."

"I can't believe it… Every single one of you…" Xavi laughed bitterly, then said, "In that case, I'll be your live bait."

"Bait? Do you want to die?!" Kuklo fumed.

"I can't move anyway. Nor do I have a machine like you guys. But I can attract the Titan as bait." They could kill the Titan while it was distracted, Xavi explained.

"You know that's risky," Cardina said.

"Then save me before I get eaten."

"Quit sounding so selfish…" Kuklo muttered.

But their plan was set. Kuklo and the others would use their Vertical Maneuvering Equipment to leap into the trees and spread out among the branches about twenty meters off the ground. Ogre seemed to have a habit of being drawn to whatever prey was closest and would probably go after Xavi on the ground even if it did notice the soldiers in the trees.

Kuklo appended single-edged swords to his controllers and looked to the east. The thick growth made the Titan's position hard to pin down, but he managed to spot it through the foliage. *A hundred meters left…*

Flailing its arms like a swimmer, the Titan weaved through the trees and gradually approached its prey. Meanwhile, Xavi trained a defiant gaze on the Titan. Sitting up straight on his horse, he looked valiant, the very picture of a soldier.

Soon, the Titan was standing in front of Xavi. Having finally caught up to its prey, Ogre seemed to be smiling as wide as it could. Yet, given its ever-present grin, any emotion Kuklo imputed to the Titan only existed in his own imagination.

It reached out to Xavi with its right arm. Unlike the three-meter-class, Ogre had arms as thick as logs, and the power of its grip would be in a different league. Muscles encased Xavi's body like a suit of armor, but he'd never survive being clutched this time.

Rosa and five other soldiers maneuvered first, using their equipment to descend upon Ogre. Rosa swung her single-edged swords at its right wrist, slicing off the hand. No blood flowed from the wound, only steam, and the Titan did not seem to be in any pain.

"Guess it's my turn next!" Cardina threw his body into the air and quickly began maneuvering.

The Titan was trying to grab its prey with its lost right hand but eventually realized the futility of the attempt. It angled its head, then reached out with its left hand.

Cardina was the one who forbade it. In the same manner as Rosa, he sliced off the Titan's remaining hand. It would be unable to grab its prey for the next few minutes.

I can do it… I can kill Ogre… This was Kuklo's chance to sever the accursed bond that tied him to the Titans.

He could not let it pass.

He leapt up off his foothold and immediately activated his equipment.

A bird's-eye view of the world, no different from practice—the fruits of Team Ten's training were on full display. Zipping freely around the Titan, they sliced off one part of its body after another. Chunks of severed meat scattered all about the area, and the steam spouting from the wounds made the air slightly hazy.

If I kill this thing, I can be free! When Cardina and Rosa sliced away both Achilles' heels, the Titan, no longer able to support its giant body, fell to its knees as if to repent its sins. *Now it's just like the training dummy!*

Kuklo circled the Titan, his sight locking on to its medulla oblongata. "There!!" he yelled, activating his controller's lever.

The anchor shot out forcefully. It sank deep into a tree trunk ahead of Kuklo, perfectly on target. Now the wire would carry him toward Ogre.

As he returned the lever to its original position, the Vertical Maneuvering Equipment instantly began to reel the wire in with incredible speed. Bringing the tips of his single-edged swords together in a V shape, Kuklo focused on the Titan's rapidly oncoming nape.

"This—" Kuklo let out a bestial howl, "This is the end!"

With all his might he sliced through flesh. A large clump of meat plopped down from the back of the Titan's neck.

The wound laid bare bright-red muscles and a thick spine, but nothing there was any different from a human's anatomy, no machinery buried there offering up the secret of the Titans. Observing the weak point for longer might have helped, but soon a rush of steam burst from Ogre's nape. Within mere moments, the steam engulfed the Titan.

"The Titan... The Titan's disappearing..."

Landing on a branch, Kuklo watched as the monstrous figure gradually faded away.

EPILOGUE

The members of Team Ten searched every nook and cranny of the spot where the Titan had disappeared. They hoped to find something that might divulge the Titans' secrets, but ultimately came up empty-handed. Their intention had been to recover the severed wrists and chunk of medulla oblongata as samples, but it had all turned to steam and been blown away by the wind. The only thing Kuklo had left in his hands was the sensation of cutting through flesh. Even the conviction that he'd defeated a Titan escaped him.

Looking down at his palms, Kuklo asked no one in particular, "Did Ogre really die?" His hands retained the distinct feeling of cutting into a Titan, but with no body, that feeling was refusing to spread to his heart or mind. Some part of him even wondered if Ogre still lived.

"The same thing happened during the expedition fifteen years ago," Cardina told Kuklo. "They say that Mammon turned to steam and disappeared... Apparently, there were no particular discoveries then, either."

"So as far as we know, that's what a Titan's death looks like. There's no telling if that'll hold true in the future, of course," Rosa said.

"So does that mean I killed a Titan?!"

"Yes, absolutely. All of us here can attest to that," Cardina assured him.

Okay. So I killed it... Kuklo had cut the tie that connected him to the Titans. His body felt the slightest bit lighter.

"It's too bad we couldn't get any closer to the mystery of the Titans, but we did learn that the Vertical Maneuvering Equipment can be used to fight them. That's a big haul," Rosa said with a satisfied look, only to shrug her shoulders right away. "Maybe no one will believe us, though."

The members of Team Ten had wielded the Vertical Maneuvering Equipment to defeat a Titan, but not in front of Carlo or any of the other soldiers. With no corpse, they had no way to prove their deed. Carlo would surely believe them, but the others might laugh it off as the first-timers' tall tale.

"Then we just try again on the next expedition," Kuklo said. Now that they were sure the Vertical Maneuvering Equipment was effective against Titans, fighting another battle wouldn't be difficult. They'd show everyone on a later expedition.

"Hm? I thought defeating Ogre was all you wanted, no?" Cardina probed his teammate.

"Ah!" Kuklo exclaimed, his voice cracking.

I'll have to talk to Sharle about it… Even Sharle might lose her patience with him if he continued to act selfishly. Every decision that he made without her prior input seemed to summon harsh trials. The first time, he snuck along on an expedition and ended up exiled. The second time, he joined the Training Corps to cut his ties with Ogre, and as a result he stood outside the walls as a Survey Corps soldier, worrying Sharle to no end.

Just as Kuklo began to feel concerned, Xavi spoke up. "I'll bear witness. You guys defeated a Titan."

"A witness… Really?"

"I need to repay my debt to you," Xavi coolly reassured Kuklo.

"But it was thanks to your work that the Titan just stood in place. Shouldn't we say that we killed it together?" Rosa offered congenially.

"If I put myself on your side, then my testimony loses credibility. I was about to be eaten by a Titan, that's all." Xavi shook his head. "You really are an idiot, though. Don't you hate me for what I've done?"

"I used to want to kick your ass. But I don't really care now."

"'Don't really care,' huh?" Xavi said with a bitter smile.

"We can settle things once we get back from this expedition. We'll decide who's better."

"I'd rather not embarrass myself any further," Xavi quickly shot down Kuklo's proposal. "Or rather, if I'm to embarrass myself, teach me how to use that thing instead." He pointed at the Vertical Maneuvering Equipment.

"You, the Vertical Maneuvering Equipment?"

"Why not? I think he saw how effective it can be," Cardina promptly agreed.

"The more sympathizers we have, the better," Rosa approved as well.

If what they'd just done led to the official adoption of the Vertical Maneuvering Equipment by the Survey Corps, soldiers would have to train in its use sooner or later. In that case, practicing from now afforded a head start.

Be that as it may, Xavi wouldn't ask to train with them again once he found out how terrifying being ambushed was.

Cardina shrugged. "Putting aside what we'll do after we return, how do we even get back?"

Rosa cast an imploring look heavenward. "I never thought our horses would run off…"

With all of Team Ten resorting to the Vertical Maneuvering Equipment to defeat Ogre, the riderless horses had gone their own ways. As a result, Team Ten was left with no means of transportation.

"Wasn't it obvious what would happen if you used those things?" Xavi asked, appalled.

"No Titans nearby. There's water, and food too. We're fine," Kuklo declared.

Fortunately for them, they were in an oasis. The knowledge and experience they'd acquired through logistics training would help them pull through. Although they'd lost the rations in their saddlebags along with their mounts, they'd be able to fill their stomachs so long as they weren't too picky. The Iceburst Stone gas would even provide them with heat.

"I've said this plenty of times before, but you're the only one okay living like that."

"I did fire a flare, so they should find us…" mumbled Rosa.

In the worst case, they would have to walk to Shiganshina District, but for the time being, they needed to dry their clothes and warm their bodies. Just as Kuklo reached for the gas cylinder on one of his scabbards, he heard a faint explosion in the sky.

"Looks like a flare gun," Rosa said, breathing easy.

"Guess we won't have to sleep outdoors." Cardina stretched out with a sigh.

"I'll go check."

Kuklo looked to the top of a tree and used the lever on his controller. The next instant—

Shaking gravity free, Kuklo soared into the air. In the dark gray sky floated an orb of light that shone like the sun.

THE END

AFTERWORD

Hello, Suzukaze here, relieved that I somehow finished my manuscript. Ah, now I can finally get a good night's sleep…

Sleep is important. No, really.

Anyway, I've been able to deliver another installment of the novelization of *Attack on Titan*. My thanks go out to everyone who picked it up. If you're browsing this afterword at a bookstore, there's a nice employee just waiting for you at the cash register!

Whatever the case, it's only because of all of you that I was able to get to this volume, and for that, I thank you.

I always have trouble writing afterwords, despite having to do one for each of my books. But now that I'm home safe, I guess I'll talk a little about this volume.

I got the idea to write about a "Titan's son" right before finishing the manuscript for *Before the Fall*.

That one was about the Equipment, the predecessor to the invention that this book was going to be about, the Vertical Maneuvering Equipment. The problem was I didn't know who was going to use it. It isn't easy to learn how to use it, and there was no established training regimen for it at the time, either, so I figured the first person to master the Vertical Maneuvering Equipment needed to be someone special. There was the option of having the protagonist of *Before the Fall* reappear, but in the end, I really wanted a Survey Corps soldier to be taking on the Titans…

I might be making it sound like it was a huge struggle to come up with the idea, but it actually just popped into my mind when I was on my way to grabbing a nighttime snack. The Titans don't properly digest the humans they eat, and in that case, I thought maybe someone could survive the experience.

Basically, even though I was trying to go grab a nighttime snack, my head was filled with scenes of Titans vomiting up humans... But thanks to that, this story's main character, Kuklo, was born.

Of course, there was no guarantee that everyone would sign off on the idea. But in case they might, I made a few additions to the manuscript of *Before the Fall* that I was still writing. I bet no one, including my editor, would have guessed had I not admitted it here (lol).

I suppose it all worked out in the end. The back cover illustration really does look like a Titan's son, doesn't it!

All right.

That does it for the prequel. Did you enjoy it? Please let me know your thoughts. You can mail letters to the editorial department, write what you thought online, or send me a tweet (@suzukazeR), and I'll probably see them.

If I do have the chance, I'd love to write again about a different epoch of *Attack on Titan*.

I'm running out of space, so I should wrap up. Thank you, Isayama-sama, for creating the incredible world of *Attack on Titan* and allowing me to have so much fun writing these novels. I'm looking forward to reading more of the manga. A lot, in fact.

Thank you, THORES Shibamoto-sama, for adorning this novel with your wonderful illustrations. I smile like an idiot every time I see copies lined up at the store. The power of good illustrations is immense.

Kodachi-san, Miwa-san, thank you very much for your help on world settings!

Finally, I'd like to thank my esteemed editor, Nabae. I'm sure you grew pale, but I looked even paler than you...

Until next time!

Cherishing the tomatoes on the balcony,
Ryo Suzukaze